We were sitting in a black Escort behind the Customs shed on Immingham Dock. Summer was supposed to be on the way, but with the wind whipping off a steel-grey North Sea it certainly didn't feel like it. There wasn't so much as a hint of sun to lessen the chill – just a blanket of dull cloud hanging there, apparently motionless. The hot and greasy breakfast we'd consumed in a nearby dockers' café was just a fond memory, and one of our two Thermoses was already empty. It looked like being a long day.

Sean's voice came over on the 'net': the cargo ferry would be docking in a few minutes.

'About fucking time,' Sheff muttered, reaching for a cigarette. He dutifully opened his window to let out the smoke, let a blast of cold air in and smiled happily. He was still young enough to be excited by the prospect of imminent action, but I'd been through too many of these moments to count chickens I couldn't see. If the intelligence was good then we were probably in for several hours, and quite possibly days, of boring observation duty. If it was bad, then we'd just have a sense of anticlimax to chew on.

In this particular case it seemed even more of

a toss-up than usual. According to the previous evening's briefing MI6 now had their own liaison man in Moscow, someone who knew which of the high-ranking Russian law enforcement officials were worth trusting. But he couldn't have been on the job long, and I didn't imagine it was an easy one. The Russian mafia, at least in its new incarnation as a global force, was still largely unknown territory.

Still, the lorry in question had driven on to the ferry in Bremerhaven, and with any luck it was carrying what our man in Moscow said it was. It would be the Regiment's first contact with a new enemy, albeit one under someone else's auspices. Sheff and I were currently on secondment to the 14th Intelligence Unit, or 'the Det' as it was generally known. The Det was a secret intelligence-gathering unit which the Army had set up in 1972, mostly because the top brass in Northern Ireland were so pissed off by the service they were getting from MI5 and MI6. It had functioned only in Ulster for the first twenty years of its life, but the impulse to empire-build couldn't be restrained indefinitely, and as the war in the North slowly wound down the new organization had started colonizing the mainland. Sheff and I and half a dozen others were supposedly scattered around Immingham Dock because of a possible link-up between the incoming Russians and our friends in the Provisionals, but there was no actual evidence to connect this shipment with Ireland. We were really just poaching in MI5's wood.

We sat there waiting, unable to see anything from our position behind the Customs shed, but appraised of developments on the net. The ship had docked, the

PAPA ZERO ONE

PAPA ZERO ONE

David Monnery

22

First published in Great Britain 1997
22 Books, Invicta House, Sir Thomas Longley Road,
Rochester, Kent

Copyright © 1997 by 22 Books

The moral right of the author has been asserted

A CIP catalogue record for this book
is available from the British Library

ISBN 1 86238 007 4

10 9 8 7 6 5 4 3 2 1

Typeset by Hewer Text Composition Services, Edinburgh
Printed in Great Britain by
Clays Ltd, St Ives plc

front doors were opening, the lorries were on their way out. The two men aboard the target were both travelling on Russian passports. They were both in their thirties, smiled a lot and generally had the look of men without a care in the world. Their vehicle was a dark green Skoda ten-wheeler, bearing registration plates issued in Belarus.

'We'd better get moving,' I told Sheff. The Customs boys weren't going to linger over the lorry, and hopefully none of them would use the moment to ham it up. The Russians might be confident, but it didn't seem likely that they'd entrust a shipment like this to complete idiots.

Apparently the Customs lads played it to perfection, because when the lorry swung past us on its way to the A180 the two men in the cab were both laughing their heads off. Once it was out of sight Sheff swung the Escort into the traffic and took off in leisurely pursuit. There were two cars already in front of us on a similar mission, and another behind. No one was prepared to contemplate the thought of losing the Russians and their cargo, which, according to the intelligence from Moscow, consisted of enough secondhand Soviet weaponry to make any Third World warlord smack his lips with anticipation. And that was Scunthorpe away to our right, not downtown Monrovia or Beirut.

We had no idea where they were going with all this fire-power. The boys in Balaclavas might be waiting to make a deal in some motorway service station, but the weapons might have been ordered by one of the mainland's organized crime gangs. The Russian Mafia had had dealings with both in the recent past, and its world market share in most illicit commodities seemed to be rising with each passing year. Like anyone else, I'd occasionally read about them in the papers, but it was only at the previous evening's briefing that I'd begun to understand how and why they'd been able to grow so fast. According to our guest expert, the Soviet system had always needed the black market to keep functioning, which meant that the Party bureaucracy and organized crime had been working hand in glove for decades. And when the system collapsed the bureaucrats had used the Party funds they controlled to buy themselves into the black market. Instead of a Western-style free market you had a vast 'official' black market run by the same old gangs, and none of the old limits which communism had opposed. Listening to him, I could understand why there were never any goods from Russia on the TV.

The other thing which I found kind of stunning was that the Russian and Italian Mafias had just held a 'summit' in Prague, at which the former had secured a franchise to launder the latter's drug profits in their domestic banking system. In return, the Italians had committed themselves to protecting the Russians' new narcotics transit corridor between Eurasia and Western Europe. The corridor which the dark green lorry up ahead had happily travelled down. No wonder its drivers looked like they owned the world.

We had them in sight now, having taken over the lead pursuit spot once they turned north towards the M62 on the M18.

'They're a bit fucking conspicuous,' Sheff said. 'They're the only people on the road sticking to the speed limit.'

As expected, the lorry headed westward on the M62. They could have been on their way to Holyhead, but it didn't seem likely – a couple of Russians driving a lorryload of crates on to a Belfast-bound ferry strained any notion of professional credibility. It would probably be Manchester or Liverpool.

We dropped back through the pursuing pack, and for the next half-hour there was nothing to do but stare out at the scenery while we listened to the others confirming that the lorry hadn't suddenly vanished in a puff of smoke. As usual on a motorway, the scenery left something to be desired. Travelling on the damn things was like flying – in both cases it seemed as if the point was to get you where you wanted to go without offering you anything interesting to look at. Even the Pennines weren't immune to the effect – on this bloody great road we might as well have been crossing the Chilterns. Which I found depressing, but then no one ever told me that adapting to the modern world was one of my strong points.

At least the weather was improving. The sky was breaking up, and for once it wasn't raining on Manchester, which proved to be our Russian friends' destination. Once off the M62 they followed an obviously uncertain course into the city, going round a couple of roundabouts twice and generally giving the impression that the map-reader was having trouble with his map. Sheff and I didn't see much of this, of course – we just listened to the sardonic commentaries from whichever of the Det lads were currently in the lead pursuit car.

Eventually the lorry reached its new home, which turned out to be a small, modern-looking warehouse in the south-central district of Moss Side. It stood on a reasonably busy road, flanked on either side by other industrial premises, and facing – as the lads in the lead car gleefully reported – a large and open pub. Maybe lunch was on the cards after all.

'Next to the pub there's a couple of acres of waste ground,' the man on the spot told us all. 'The end near the pub's being used for parking, but the rest looks like it's been turned into a park by the locals. There's swings and a plastic slide for the kids, and a couple of benches for the drunks and child molesters. Ideal spot for our friends from Hereford.'

'Bastards,' Sheff said with a grin.

Sean's voice took over, ordering the lead car into the pub car park and the rest of us to a rendezvous point several streets away. At the RV we left our cars and gathered in a suspicious-looking circle on the pavement, like TV cops just before a raid. We could have easily talked things through on the net but Sean was clearly a man after my own heart, someone who actually enjoyed eyeballing the people he was talking to. We took turns examining the Manchester A-Z which he'd had the forethought to bring – how many other city street plans were packed into his dashboard compartment? I wondered – and two of his regulars were dispatched to check out the unknown sections of the warehouse's perimeter. Ten minutes later they reported in with the news that the building backed on to a disused railway line, and that the only feasible exit – at least so far as crate-loads of weaponry were concerned – was at the front. Which, they added hopefully, they could watch from inside the pub.

'Get back here,' Sean told them, then turned to me. 'You're the only one who looks vaguely old enough to do the down-and-out bit,' he said.

'Thanks,' I said.

He grinned. 'So get yourself a bottle of Strongbow from the off-licence over there,' he went on, pointing across the street, 'and go and sit in the park. We'll arrange the cars to cover all the possible exit routes. And if nothing comes out before dark, then we'll have to start thinking about going in for a look at the merchandise. I don't like the idea of spending days surrounding a legal shipment of caviare.'

I did as suggested and headed for the park, shovelling down a Mars bar *en route*. The lightweight jacket I was wearing looked a bit smart for the character I was playing, but there wasn't much I could do about that, other than hope that the Russians had an inflated notion of what drunks wore in the affluent West. I staggered haplessly through the traffic, encouraging at least two drivers to blare on their horns, and sank heavily on to the nearest seat in the makeshift park. A woman who was pushing her child on the swing ten yards away gave me a satisfyingly disapproving look.

I opened the cider, washed down the last traces of the Mars bar with a hearty swig, and came up with a belch that was none the less convincing for being involuntary. Maybe this was the career I'd always been looking for. I wiped my mouth on my sleeve, and stared blankly across the street. The lead car had watched the Russians drive the lorry into the prefabricated warehouse, but the sliding doors in the windowless walls were now closed and there was no sign of life in the mostly empty yard – just a carelessly parked red Cortina. It didn't look much like a thriving business, but then these days manufacture seemed out of fashion, and you didn't need much in the way of equipment just to sell something on, just a place to hold it. One with windowless walls, if the merchandise in question was a bit on the iffy side. And it didn't get much iffier than Soviet rocket and grenade launchers for enemies of the Crown.

It was about three in the afternoon now, which meant that the dusk was at least five hours away. I gradually settled into that sort of semi-hypnotic state which a lengthy period of observation necessitates, keeping one corner of my mind focused on the warehouse across the road while the rest just floated through idle thoughts and daydreams. Every now and then Sean's voice would sound in my ear, checking that everything was OK, and I'd send back two bursts of squelch by pressing the button in my pocket. I'd only speak to him directly if something happened – it wasn't likely that the Russians were keeping binoculars trained on the local drunk's lips, but you never knew.

The sky was almost clear now, and it was quite a bit warmer than it had been on the other side of the Pennines, but this part of Manchester needed a lot more than sunshine to make it look attractive. The tall blocks of flats which rose up behind the warehouses looked like they'd needed painting about ten years ago, and the road in front of me was as knee-deep in litter as the park was in dog shit. The pub looked its age on the outside, but unfortunately not on the inside, where the usual crap had been installed in the name of modernization. And whichever bright spark had decided that double-decker buses looked good painted bright orange needed early retirement. And probably a new wardrobe.

I sat there watching, letting my mind wander through other times and places I'd done the same. Usually it had been a much hairier business. In Northern Ireland there was always the chance some innocent-looking local would suddenly pull out a gun and blow you away, and on East Falkland there wasn't much cover if you were found by the enemy. The Russians in the warehouse might suddenly take it in their heads to charge across the street with murder in mind, but I didn't think I needed to worry about the woman by the swings or a sudden airstrike. As observations went, this was a doddle.

I took another swig of cider – I needed to be convincing, after all – and thought about Ellen. Tuesday was one of the two days she went into Oxford, and she wouldn't be heading back to Hereford for at least an hour. She might be having dinner with friends and staying over – as she'd told me at the beginning: my life and work weren't the only ones which would occasionally separate us. She had an agenda of her own – in fact these days she probably felt more committed to her work than I did to mine.

I suddenly found I was looking at myself through her eyes: a man sitting on a bench pretending to be a drunk. I looked kind of sad, but kind of lovable too, and maybe a bit silly. The thought ran through my head that it didn't matter how serious the cops and robbers game was – anyone who spent a lifetime playing it was going to have a hard job growing up. It was like being a professional footballer, minus the money. Both the work and your fellow-workers kept you trapped in a glorified boys' own world. And much as I had enjoyed my life's diet of violent action, travel, sexual banter and football talk, these days it was definitely beginning to pall. Maybe it was time to hand in my superhero outfit and do something else.

What, of course, was something else again. I was just turning my mind to another fantasy – West Ham avoiding the drop – when the smaller of the two warehouse doors opened and two new faces emerged, both with a distinctly Slavic turn of cheekbone. Right behind them came the two Russians from the lorry. As I reported these developments on the net, practising skills which offered a possible career in ventriloquism, the four men all piled into the Cortina, which reversed in a shower of gravel, advanced to the gates and turned out into the road. One of the new men got out and walked back to lock the gates, then rejoined the others. The red car accelerated away towards the lights some two hundred yards down the road, where it turned right in the general direction of the city centre.

I relayed all this to Sean, and then heard him ordering two of the Det teams to pick up the Cortina's trail.

'You can sit tight, Fullagar,' he told me. 'Enjoy the evening sun.'

I sighed and pressed down on the button to acknowledge, as a couple of ten-year-olds on the swings lit up what I hoped were only cigarettes.

By the time darkness fell a couple of hours later it had cooled down considerably, and I wasn't having much trouble looking like someone in dire need of a hot meal. Soon after eight the surveillance van pulled into the pub's car park, and Sean invited me to pick my moment and come aboard. Inside the van I found him, Sheff, a Det named Wilkinson and a strong smell of fish and chips. Through the one-way glass the warehouse looked decidedly free of human activity.

The Russians and their two friends – who might or might not have been Russians themselves – were apparently enjoying a Mexican dinner in the city centre. Before going to the restaurant the two lorry drivers had checked into a four-star hotel, paying for their double room in advance with a huge wad of crisp new tenners. The local police were checking on the two friends and the ownership of the warehouse, and had also, according to Sean, been advised to ignore any summons from the building's alarm system. 'Not that you two will trigger it,' he told me and Sheff. 'Not after all that training we've given you.'

'When are we going in?' I asked.

'Probably soon. We're just waiting to see what the Ivans do once they've finished their meal.'

'Fart up a storm probably,' Sheff suggested.

'I could do with something to eat myself,' I said pointedly.

'Why didn't you say so?' Sean said, and pulled a Mars bar out of his pocket.

I accepted it with something less than utter joy. 'And which way are we going in?' I asked.

'Round the back,' Sheff told me. 'From a distance it looks like there's just a six-foot wall to climb. No dogs, no cameras. There's probably not even an alarm system.'

'Sounds too easy,' I said. 'Are we going to tag the stuff?'

Sean had decided not to. 'If it's the Provos it's the first thing they'll look for,' he said, 'and the moment they find the transmitters they'll just close the whole deal down. We'll get jack shit.'

'And if it isn't the Provos?' I asked. I was pretty sure in my own mind that it wouldn't be.

'Then we'll have to make dead sure we don't take our eyes off the ball.'

Half an hour later we heard that the restaurant party had moved on to one of Manchester's sleazier clubs, and that their Det tails had reluctantly been forced to follow them inside. Watching tasselled breasts gyrate wasn't one of my hobbies, but it probably beat slinking along a disused railway cutting in the dark on a near-empty stomach.

Sheff and I clambered up the overgrown slope to the wall behind the warehouse, hoping that no one in the terraced houses on the other side of the cutting was sitting at an open window with the light off. If they dialled 999 the local plod would probably put two and two together, but you could never be sure, and we didn't want a night full of howling sirens.

The wall was topped with three lines of barbed wire, but there was no sign of an alarm system, so getting across presented no problem. We dropped on to a carpet of discarded cans and broken glass behind the warehouse and started working our way round the side which received less light from the road at the front. As usual, the adrenalin was pumping, but there was none of that strange feeling I still got from our breaking-and-entering exploits across the water, where the target was usually someone's house.

Still, the same principles applied that night: get in and out as fast as you can without missing anything and without leaving any traces. The padlocked sliding doors presented the first problem in that respect – if they found their padlock cut in half the Ivans were apt to deduce that they'd had visitors. But fortunately the small door was simply locked, and one of Sheff's skeleton keys soon had us inside.

'Oscar and Juliet are in,' I told Sean.

'We saw you fumbling with the keys,' was the encouraging reply. They were watching with nightscopes.

We could have done with some night-vision goggles ourselves. The sky outside had no moon to provide its own illumination and no clouds to reflect the city's, so there wasn't much light seeping down through the opaque roof. Turning the interior lighting on was always an option, but for all we knew the owners had friends in the terrace of houses.

Slowly our eyes got used to the gloom. The warehouse was about the size of a penalty area, and one end had been filled with lines of cheap metal shelving, which housed a multitude of small boxes. In an opposite corner more shelving had been used to cordon off a small office area, but there were no filing cabinets – just an almost empty desk, a telephone, a computer monitor and a fax machine.

In the centre of the warehouse stood the lorry, back doors hanging open, interior still piled high with wooden crates.

Sheff clambered on to the tailboard and ran his pencil torch across one crate and then another. 'They all look the same,' he murmured.

'There must be a mark of some sort,' I said hopefully.

The seconds ticked away as he kept looking. 'Well, I'm fucked if I can see one,' he said. 'I mean, it may be on a side I can't see – at least not without unloading the whole fucking lorry.'

My heart sank. 'Unloading and reloading the whole shipment would take a couple of hours, and if the Russians returned in the middle of it there was no chance of hiding the fact that they'd been rumbled. Even if they didn't, we still not might find a mark, and then we'd have to start jemmying the crates open, which would be an even bigger give-away.

I passed the whole problem on to Sean, whose first response was short on both syllables and practicality. He was still working on a second when two things happened almost simultaneously. The Det lads in the club, presumably goggle-eyed from tassel-chasing, had just realized that the four men they were watching were no longer the same four. One of the definite Russians had gone AWOL. It was only a matter of minutes apparently, but he wasn't in the Gents. The car they had come in was still being watched by the other Det team, but then the missing man's replacement might have arrived in another.

This information, and Sean's explosion of displeasure, were still echoing in my ear when Sheff appeared in front of me, grinning from ear to ear. I followed his beckoning finger round to the front of the lorry, where two crates were sitting against the wall. To make it even easier for us they had already been jemmied open, and we could see the neatly wrapped rocket-launchers in one, a mixed bag of grenades and Kalashnikov AK47s in the other.

'We've found the stuff,' I told Sean.

'Thank Christ for that. Take a piccy and get the hell out of there.'

I pulled the compact out of my pocket, lined up the shot and pressed the button, taking care to keep my eyes shut through the flash.

Sean's voice suddenly sounded in my ear. 'Shit, they're here. Oscar, Juliet, they're at the gate. Fuck, they've got a remote. They're inside. Get under a bed or something.'

We could see the minivan's headlights through the cracks around the small door, hear the crunch of feet on gravel as someone headed for the padlock on the sliding doors. There was only one possible place to hide: among the shelving at the end furthest from the office space. We scurried in that direction.

The door rolled open with a metallic grinding sound, allowing the van's headlights to flood the interior. The shelving seemed a lot less dense in the light, but Sheff

and I couldn't have crouched any lower if we'd tried.
I eased the Browning High Power from the cross-draw
holster under my jacket and hoped there wouldn't be
any reason to use it.

Then the light abruptly swung away, and it took
a few moments to realize that the driver was turning
the van to back in. Once it was inside, his partner
rolled the door shut and switched on the overhead
lights, which bathed everything in a cold, fluorescent
glow and did nothing to reduce my sense of being
profoundly visible.

Fortunately for us, the two of them had other things
to do than scan their warehouse for skulking SAS
men. After opening the back door of the van they
disappeared in the direction of the two crates, and
we could hear them hammering the lids back down.
Both men reappeared with one crate, and with some
effort loaded it into the back of the van. I tried not
to keep my eyes on them for more than a few seconds
at a time, and hoped that Sheff was remembering to
do the same – people generally sense when they're
being watched.

The two men were talking, but not in any language
I'd ever heard. Our relative fluency in Russian was
the main reason Sheff and I had been picked for this
particular secondment, but this didn't sound anything
like it. One of the Caucasian languages, I guessed,
without really knowing why.

They had both crates aboard now. Our old friend
from the lorry got in behind the van's wheel, and his
friend took one last look round before turning off the
lights and sliding the door open. The van edged into

the outside world, the door slid back, and I told Sean what he'd no doubt already guessed: the Ivans were taking their contraband somewhere else.

It wasn't exactly hot outside, but I could feel sweat running down my back as we clambered back over the wall and dropped into the railway cutting.

By the time we got back to our Escort the chase was a couple of miles away, heading roughly south-west through the inner suburbs, and we'd been on the road only a couple of minutes when the van reached its new home: a line of garages in the middle of a sprawling council estate. Listening on the net we were able to follow the sequence of events – the two men padlocking the garage and walking off in the direction of Levenhulme High Street, where they hailed a cruising taxi and drove off towards the city centre. Twenty minutes later they were rejoining their friends at the club.

The line of garages proved less observation-friendly than the warehouse. The odds were good that at least one of the flats which overlooked the area would be empty, but there wasn't much chance of finding out which before morning, and that meant we wouldn't be able to set up shop until after dark on the following evening. For most of the next twenty-four hours the eight of us would have to cover the area on foot, taking it in turns to look like innocent locals. The good news was that our chances of being exposed by the Russians were probably a lot less than our chances of being mugged. Which might well prove harder on the muggers than us, but wouldn't do much for our cover.

After a few moments' thought Sean reached the same conclusion. 'We'll take the van in and watch in comfort,' he said. 'As long as nobody tries to steal it we should be OK, and we can make ourselves scarce just before first light. I don't think anyone'll be back there tonight anyway.'

Which proved an accurate prediction. The four of us who took turns watching the garages from the surveillance van could have been happily tucked up in the Manchester Hilton for all the difference our presence made. A trio of drunks stopped for a piss behind us, and we watched them try to keep their eyes focused as the streams splashed against the side of the van. It was the only entertainment of a long night, unless you counted trying to sleep in a confined space with two snoring Det men for company.

Soon after five Sean pulled us out, and we were given an hour to find and consume breakfast before resuming surveillance. Levenhulme is not a hotbed of the culinary arts, especially at five in the morning, and we had to practically beg a transport café to open ten minutes early. By six-fifteen, loaded down with cholesterol and sugar, we were back in the Escort, covering one of the only two exits from the estate and breathing in Sheff's secondhand smoke. Who ever said the outdoor life was a healthy life?

The day didn't get any better. The clouds were back, and occasionally a warm, thin drizzle would descend, more like a mist than rain. Like the men in the other three cars, we took turns walking through the estate, and on each occasion the garage containing the arms cache just stared innocently back at us. Sheff and I talked about the Regiment for a while – he was still new enough not to have heard all the famous stories ten times over – and then moved on to other matters of import: football, girlfriends and wives, *The X Files*.

I learned a bit about him that day. His parents had named him Pearson after his grandad, and almost as soon as he could walk he'd swapped it for the first half of his surname. More surprisingly he'd managed to make it stick in the SAS, where having an unusual name was usually akin to painting a target on your forehead. He'd been born only a few miles from where we sat, but the family had soon moved to Northwich in neighbouring Cheshire. He had no brothers or sisters. His dad had worked for the Post Office, but had drowned in a fishing accident when Sheff was only seven. His mum had built up her own hairdressing business, and I could tell from his voice how much she meant to him.

In fact, somewhere inside the slicked-back cynic I had the feeling there was someone who cared about things a lot more than he wanted to let on. But then he was only twenty-seven.

During the day Sean had picked out one of the several empty flats on offer which overlooked the garages and after dark four of us surreptitiously moved in. The flat directly below us was also empty, as was the one to our left, and our new neighbours to the right were either deaf or they had a faulty volume switch on their TV. There seemed to be a crack den three flats along, which probably encouraged everyone on the floor to mind their own business – that particular drug's users are not noted for their community spirit.

Sean had also picked up some information on our Russian driver friends, who turned out not to be Russians after all, but Chechens. Their names were Kazbek Basayev and Aslan Zavgayev, and they worked for one of the *kryshas*, or 'roofs', which 'protected' Moscow businesses from other gangs in exchange for a hefty share of the profits. Both men had apparently been players in the Russian capital's recent 'Casino War', and their particular gang was obviously now diversifying its interests. All of which provided food for thought, but not much else. We were more interested in the identity of their customers.

Whoever they were, they didn't seem in much of a hurry to collect their merchandise. The four of us took turns manning the OP in the bare living room and kipping on a couple of camp beds Sean had installed in the bedroom. This wasn't quite bare – the last tenant had left behind a poster of Samantha Fox which sat there on the wall like a cave painting from some bygone age. The electricity and gas had been disconnected, leaving us to heat up cans and brew tea on a hexamine stove, but the water was still running, so at least we had washing facilities and a toilet that flushed.

Another morning dawned, another day slowly went by, and we began to envy the men in the stake-out cars – at least they got a decent meal every now and then. When a third night went by without any sign of the buyers Sean started getting anxious. The only reason anyone could think of for leaving the stuff that long was a hitch in the deal, but if one had occurred then the Chechens – whose suite at the Hilton rather put our living quarters to shame – weren't letting it spoil their fun. By day they slept and shopped, by night they partied and screwed. They only picked up their hotel room phone to order goodies, and the one at the warehouse wasn't used at all. No doubt they had a sackful of mobiles, but the general consensus was that they didn't look like men with a deal to sort out. They looked like men relaxing after their job was done.

So why the wait? We hadn't actually seen the weapons since they left the warehouse, and ludicrous as it seemed, we couldn't quite shake the fear that they were no longer in the garage.

'Maybe there's a tunnel,' Brian muttered one morning.

'They'd need a vaulting horse to put over the entrance,' Sheff agreed with a straight face.

'Clowns,' Sean muttered, but the longer we watched the stronger the compulsion grew to check that the weapons were still there, and at four the next morning we watched through the nightscopes as two of the Det boys went in. They didn't have much trouble with the padlock, but the scrape of the opening door seemed incredibly loud in the pre-dawn silence, and we could only hope that none of the locals were sitting out on their concrete balconies with insomnia.

'Still here,' the voice came in over the net.

'Thank Christ for that,' Sean murmured.

The two men were on their way out now, looking this way and that like burglars always do in the films. The door made the same noise coming down as it had going up, and they walked swiftly away in the direction of the High Road. I heard Sean breathe another sigh of relief as they disappeared from view.

It was premature. Not much more than a couple of minutes had passed when the stake-out car on the eastern side announced in an excited whisper that a van with three men in it was entering the estate.

We barely had time to share expectant looks when the stake-out car on the western side reported a police car entering from that side.

'Fuck,' Sean growled. He tried to raise the local station but we all knew that it would be too late to make a difference.

The van was in sight now, moving very slowly along the line of garages, like a cat cautiously approaching its prey. The fact that its engine was making no more than a low, purring sound only added to the effect.

The police car suddenly came into view between two of the blocks, and we could almost feel the van driver's hesitation before he slowly picked up speed. He was clearly intending to just drive past the police car and out of the estate.

'Let the bastards go,' Sean prayed at my shoulder, but the uniforms below obviously couldn't hear him. Their car was now blocking the van's path, and they were getting out to investigate.

'Fuck, fuck, fuck!' Sean said. We all knew this would be the end of it. The men in the car would claim to be lost or joyriding or doing a cheap package tour of run-down council estates, and there was no way anyone could prove otherwise. We'd find out who they worked for, and whoever that was would have to start his arms race again from scratch. The Russians would be arrested and the weapons seized, so the op as a whole would be far from a dead loss, but at that moment, watching a week's work of expectations go up in smoke, it certainly felt like one.

2

Secondment over, Sheff and I returned to Hereford, and by the beginning of the next week both of us were helping Training Wing monitor the Selection marches across the Brecon Beacons. Over the weekend the summer had gone back into hiding once more, which suited my mood pretty well. All the way back from Manchester I'd been basking in the anticipation of a weekend with Ellen, only to find a note on the kitchen table announcing that she'd be checking out tourist facilities in St Petersburg for the next couple of weeks. At least I was able to make contact by phone – a privilege usually denied to her when I was on a job – but that didn't take away the feeling of a major let-down.

All of which left me in a pretty jaundiced frame of mind by the time it came to stand out in the rain and watch grown men trying hard not to cry. I watched them all gritting their teeth and rolling their eyes and generally girding up their loins, and found myself wondering what made the SAS such an alluring prospect in 1996. These young men wanted in really badly – you could see it in every grimacing face that went by – but did they want in for the right reasons? Maybe there weren't any; either way, I felt pretty certain that their reasons would be different from those of my generation. We had joined a section of the Army which most people in the outside world thought had been pensioned off after the war, and joined it partly for that reason. In those days the Regiment had seemed mostly made up of loners and eccentrics, and there had been much less of the gung-ho spirit which seemed to pervade it in the nineties.

The Regiment's public image had a lot to do with the change. The photos of individual troopers were still issued with the faces blanked out, but the SAS as a whole seemed to have had more publicity in the last fifteen years than the rest of the services put together. The Iranian Embassy siege and the Falklands had broken down the doors, and the media had been holding them open ever since. The SAS had become the glory boys, the Lone Rangers of the British Army. We didn't need wars to see some action, but when one came along in the Gulf you could be certain we'd be pulling the glamour jobs.

Or so the myth went. In reality a lot had changed in those fifteen years. It was hard to imagine another Falklands, and Hong Kong was all but gone. Gibraltar was a problem that would be solved peacefully. The Belize issue seemed settled, and the end of apartheid had killed off the evil genie in the southern African bottle. The Cold War was over, and after the inept way the politicians had allowed Saddam to survive, I found it hard to imagine the public supporting another war in the Gulf. As far as active soldiering was concerned, that left only Northern Ireland, which was about as glamorous as a weekend in Solihull, and twice as depressing.

That didn't mean the SAS had no future – far from it. But it did seem clear to me that its future would be on the covert side. Our enemies would be terrorists and other criminals, not regular soldiers, and our wars would be fought in the shadows, not in the open. The SAS had always been involved in such activities, but I believed that as the millennium approached these would be its primary *raison d'être*. We would be needing men who excelled in undercover work, not super-fit warriors with itchy trigger fingers.

The current OC knew it very well. When I'd been 'offered' my first secondment to the Det some ten years earlier I'd not been pleased – I had the same instinctive distrust of all the intelligence organizations as everyone else in the Regiment – but refusal had not been one of the options. 'We need complete soldiers,' the OC had told me and a couple of others, 'and you don't become one of those by just prancing round on one side of the fence.' And he'd been right.

Looking back, I guess I'd joined the Regiment at more or less the perfect time, a month before the Embassy siege. I hadn't been part of the team which went in for the hostages, but I did get to see quite a lot of the Falklands War, taking part in the landing on South Georgia, the Pebble Island raid and the diversionary attack on Darwin which preceded the San Carlos landings. No doubt it affects everybody differently, but it seems to me that professional soldiers who never get the chance to test themselves in action always end up feeling that they've missed something really important. I found it all exhilarating, terrifying and sometimes incredibly sad, but even at the age of twenty-three I was glad I'd been through it.

Since then I'd seen a lot of the world. I'd been a member of training teams invited to eleven countries spread through Africa, Latin America and Asia, and I'd visited four more without invitations: a couple in Africa to collect Britons caught up in civil wars, one in Central America to stick spokes in a drug baron's wheels, and one in the Middle East to mount an abortive hostage-rescue operation. And of course I'd done enough time in Northern Ireland to make me a connoisseur of grey skies.

Each place was different, of course, and each taught me something, not just about the world but about myself and what I thought I was doing. When I was badged in 1981 my main professional ambition was to do the job as well as it could possibly be done. Because you never get to that point, ambition never disappears completely, but I think that as far as my generation was concerned – I can't speak for the current crop – in time we started wondering whether a particular job was worth doing at all. Sometimes we really felt like the good guys, other times we were much less happy about things, and a lot of the time we really just didn't know. One extreme example was when I was a member of a team sent to Cambodia to help train members of a resistance group who were loosely allied to the Khmer Rouge. I'd seen the *The Killing Fields* when it came out the year before and I didn't feel good about being on the same planet as those bastards, let alone on the same side, and we

could tell that our bosses felt the same way, even
if they weren't able to say so. After something like
that, you start wondering whether you're doing more
harm than good, and you find yourself saying things
like 'It beats being unemployed.'

And yet within a month of our return from
Cambodia I was part of an operation which saved
fifteen innocent civilians from some of the sickest
psychos in Africa. That sort of result made the whole
business seem almost too good to be true – we were
honing our skills, we were having a hell of a lot of
fun – and all on the side of the angels. Who would do
anything else? we asked ourselves on the way back.

And then we'd find ourselves training an elite squad
for some little sadist to beat his people with and you'd
be back down again. Some men just take it all in their
stride – theirs not to reason why, just do their job,
fuck exotic women and pick up exotic diseases – but
for some reason I wanted to feel good about the jobs
themselves, not just the way I managed to do them,
and life by consequence often had a yo-yo tendency
to it, one which grew even more pronounced when I
met Ellen in 1992. When you meet someone new it's
a bit like looking in a mirror, and when that someone
becomes important to you then you owe it to them to
take a bloody good look.

I hadn't much liked what I'd seen. I wasn't feeling
bad about what I was doing, but I wasn't feeling
particularly good either – it was as if I'd just opted
out of caring and into cynicism. It was a crappy
world, and the Regiment was no more immune to
crap than any other institution. We were soldiers of

the Crown, for Christ's sake, not Robin Hood and his Merry Men. I had only a few more years to go, so why worry about the big questions? I'd be better off figuring out what to do with my post-Army life.

All of which made sense, but I couldn't help thinking that I'd lost something along the way. Five years ago I'd watched other twenty-three- and twenty-four-year-old hopefuls slogging past me with their heavy bergens and mentally wished them all a place in the Regiment. Now, for the first time in fifteen years, I felt ambivalent. There was a life outside the SAS.

Watching the poor bastards 'tab' was almost as tiring as doing it yourself, and by the time the next weekend rolled round I felt as exhausted as most of them looked. There were plenty of booze-ups on offer around Hereford but I wanted to get away from work faces. The prospect of sitting in front of a TV for two days wasn't very appealing; the thought of doing any of the jobs that needed doing around the house even less so. And Ellen wasn't due back for several days. I decided that spending the weekend in London was the best I could manage. Seeing my nieces would more than make up for seeing my brother and sister-in-law, and I might run into some old mates in what was left of the Wapping I grew up in.

My brother sounded as enthusiastic about seeing me as I was about seeing him, but he was much too well mannered to say so, and soon after five on the Friday evening I was heading east towards the M40.

Steve was seven years older than me, our sister

Maureen almost four. I suppose they should have been models for my development, but Steve served as the opposite – his life was like a series of health warnings for mine – and the world Maureen inhabited seemed stranger than science fiction when I was a kid. My dad made much more sense. Harry Fullager was a benevolent patriarch of the old school, a charming old dinosaur who saw home as the place where he rested from the rigours of the outside world. He started work on the docks at the age of fifteen and only stopped when they prised the last capstan away from his still-resisting hands. He was a shop steward and a socialist who saw himself as devoted to his fellow-man, and when he had time to notice his children he was good to them too.

As the last child I had no real complaints. He did the things that dads were supposed to do then: took me to West Ham, took me out on the river, took me to where he worked among the forests of cranes reaching for the sky. And when I got bullied at school – I was small for my age – he took me down to the gym and taught me how to box.

Generally, though, I enjoyed infant and junior schools. I soon realized that I was cleverer than most, and that not flaunting the fact was the way to go. I could always make the other kids laugh and I was good at football – two definite plusses to set against the fact that my dad was a local figure.

I tried following in Steve's trainspotting footsteps, but never got hooked the way he had been. Maybe it was that steam had just about vanished, but the only joy me and my friend Al got was from trespassing in sheds. It was the thrill of the chase, I suppose, and we got pretty good at it. The Bricklayer's Arms shed off the Old Kent Road was considered the toughest nut in London, but we cracked it several times, developing wall-scaling skills that I'd be using for Queen and Country in later life. And we were well organized too. Each of us had a notebook with false names and addresses neatly written inside the front cover, and on those occasions when an irate foreman did manage to grab one or both of us we would pull these out as evidence that we were giving him the true goods.

We generally did the rounds of the sheds on Sundays because that was when they were full. Saturdays we'd go to Upton Park if the Hammers were at home. It was the last years of the Moore–Hurst–Peters era, and though they never won a damn thing they played some lovely football. When they were away we went to Millwall or Charlton, sometimes even Chelsea or Spurs. Millwall was the most fun – when it came to crowd violence The Den was years ahead of its time.

A paper round paid for the games, London Transport and British Rail for our fares. In those days they still cut adult return tickets in half for kids, and you could just flash them at the collector as you walked past. So like thousands of other kids we just bought returns to the next station and travelled rather further. If a ticket collector asked to see the tickets you had two choices: you could either run for it or come clean, by which I mean you could look like you were going to burst into tears as you showed the man the false name and address in your notebook.

A more boring alternative to this scam was just claiming that you'd come from the next station up the line, but it always helped to know what it was. I guess we got too cocky on one occasion, but a ticket collector grabbed us and phoned the next station to ask whether we'd been seen getting on. Imagine our surprise when the answer came through that we had.

I was at secondary school by this time, with all the horrors of homework which that implied. Doing it was terrible – a vicious intrusion into the time reserved for our new TV – but not doing it often carried consequences every bit as appalling. In what time was left for real life the trainspotting urge withered away, and music took its place. The first record I bought was 'Tin Soldier' by the Small Faces – prophetic really, not to mention an early sign of enduring good taste. Which was more than I could say for the second: 'Xanadu' by Dave Dee, Dozy, Beaky, Mick and Tich.

Part of 'Tin Soldier''s appeal was the mystery surrounding its last line. Was he singing 'I want to sit with you' or 'I want to sleep with you'? It certainly sounded like the latter, but you just didn't hear things like that on the BBC in early 1968. We watched Steve Marriott like a hawk on *Top of the Pops* – was that a knowing grin as he mimed the word in question?

Sex, or the prospect of it, was now becoming the dominant force in our lives, and if by some horrible mischance you needed a shit at school it invariably involved begging a cubicle from a bunch of frenetically pumping wankers.

I hated school by this time, and, French apart, my marks fully reflected the intense lack of effort I was putting in. I only got good marks at French because I found it so ridiculously easy. I just had a gift for languages, one which was to turn out very useful in my professional life.

I was still pretty sure I was clever, clever enough in fact to know that there was not much connection between cleverness and academic excellence. And the older I got the more I marvelled that anyone would be stupid enough to make such a connection. I mean, the evidence was right in front of their eyes – here were smart, witty kids leaving school at fifteen to run barrows in the market and here were kids with six O levels who couldn't work out how to open a door. I knew I had a quicker mind than most – I made connections between things which others didn't – and I began to pride myself, no doubt arrogantly, on being uniquely gifted with that most basic of all clevernesses – common sense. It amazed me – it still does, come to that – how many people, smart people too, are so utterly bereft of the stuff.

My family, I slowly came to realize, were all clever in their different ways. I never saw my dad read anything more demanding than his union minutes or the *Daily Mirror*, but he seemed both well liked and well respected by his members, and from what I learned in later years he was pretty damn effective considering the situation he had to work with. The London docks were doomed and everyone knew it – from my early childhood the world I lived in seemed in the process of closing down – but men like him weren't about to just lie down and let 'progress' roll over them. In fact he enjoyed the fight – without it, he'd say later, life wasn't half as much fun. No one who knew him could have doubted his capacity to enjoy being alive, and that, as I've learned over the years, is not a skill which should be underestimated.

My mum always seemed to be clearing up after everyone else, which didn't seem too clever, and she couldn't even find Africa on a map of the world, but looking back I reckon she got every bit as much job satisfaction out of running the home as my dad did out of trying to run the docks. I think her one great skill was deciding what she wanted and getting him to think it was his idea. She had a lot of friends in our street and I remember once listening to about three of them outside our gate doing brilliant impersonations of their husbands. If it's possible to have a patriarchy that's run by a woman then I think our house was one.

My brother was clever in the traditional sense. He always got good marks at school, and he was usually pretty good at anything he turned his hand to. But he had no imagination. Some of my friends had older brothers who were mods or rockers – a bit later there was even one hippie – but Steve's great dream was to be conventionally middle-class. He wanted to understand how things and people worked, but only as an aid to manipulating them. Money and status was what he was after, and by the time I reached double figures he was working in a local bank, dreaming of a manager's office somewhere in the leafy suburbs. I didn't like him much then, and I can't say I do now, but he is my brother, and his kids have so far managed to remain human despite the best efforts of him and his second wife, Joan.

My sister Maureen, like I said, was always a complete mystery to me. For one thing she was a girl, for another she was nearly four years older, and my childhood memories of her are like a series of snapshots – she and her friends giggling together outside Wapping Station, waiting hours to get into the bathroom whenever she had a date, and nerve-racked boys who tried to make conversation with me when they came to pick her up, my dad blowing his top when he found one of them helping her up the stairs at three in the morning. I think she did OK at school but we've never talked about it. She left at sixteen, got a job working in a dress shop in Oxford Street, and moved into a shared flat in West Hampstead. I think she was there about a year, and then she phoned from Dover to say she was catching a ferry to France and then taking the hippie trail to India. Mum and Dad seemed more surprised than anything, but postcards arrived on a more or less regular basis and they got used to the idea. My fourteen-year-old self decided I'd badly misjudged her, and even looked forward to seeing her on her return, but she met an American in Madras and accompanied him back to Arizona, so missing her chance of getting to know me better. The relationship foundered but she stayed in America, and I've only seen her four times since. The last two times were at Mum's and Dad's funerals, in 1991 and 1993 respectively. She's been living with the same bloke now for about ten years, up in the mountains of New Mexico. I have a feeling I'd actually like her if I got to know her, and she has been pushing for us to take a holiday out there in the not too distant future.

These four people made up my nuclear family, and if I say they were all smart it's because I think they all more or less got what they wanted from life. My Uncle Stanley did too, and he probably had more influence on the way my life's turned out than any of them. He was a merchant seaman right up to his death in 1975, so his impact was necessarily spasmodic, but none the less powerful for it. He didn't make much money, but he couldn't spend much at sea and he never married or had children – or at least not as far as I knew – so his flat in Rotherhithe was crammed with interesting things. He loved books and records, so there were hundreds of each spread around his two rooms, and there seemed to be bits and pieces from just about every country in the world either perched on shelves or hanging from the ceiling or just sitting in the middle of the carpet. Only one wall was left empty, and the centre of this was painted white for the slide shows he'd give whenever he came back from an interesting trip. I can remember sitting there in the dark from about the age of five, listening to him talk about the exotic-looking places which appeared on the wall, and I knew that one day I would have to visit the Moluccas and Valparaiso and Zanzibar and all the others. We could see the Thames from his window and he used to tell me that all anyone had to do was simply step aboard while the tide was going out, and the river would take you anywhere you wanted to go.

It was Uncle Stanley who persuaded me that reading

had nothing to do with English Lit as taught at school, and that music – any sort of music, from calypso to opera, Bach to Hendrix – was a way to reach the soul. He'd probably have drawn the line at Dave Dee, Dozy, Beaky, Mick and Tich, but I wouldn't bet on it. That man could find wonder in just about anything, and I've spent most of my adult life wishing I could do the same.

Smart? Who knows. At sixteen I was certain as a sixteen-year-old can be – and that's frighteningly certain – that staying at school and working my socks off in a probably futile quest for A levels and a university place wasn't the way I wanted to go. Even if I succeeded beyond my teachers' wildest dreams I had the feeling I'd just end up in my brother's world. And I was fed up with living at home, fed up with living in an area that was rapidly becoming a yuppie playground. My friends were either depressed, getting into crime or both, and I felt ready to follow Uncle Stanley's prescription and just 'step aboard'. So I signed up with the merchant navy and set out to see it all.

Trouble was, things had been a damn sight more interesting in Uncle Stanley's heyday than they were in the mid-seventies. The variety of vessel types, of cargoes and of routes had all lessened dramatically, and most of the pictures I took were off container and offshore oil terminals. Between ports the main problem was boredom, but at least Uncle Stanley had turned me into an avid reader.

After a couple of years I was fed up with the sight of water, but the urge to travel hadn't been stilled, and when I was back in London between sailings one of my old friends persuaded me to accompany him to the Army Recruitment Office in the Mile End Road. He'd spent the whole year since leaving school looking for a job and not even come close – the Army was all that was left. Even then the Recruiting Officer had trouble getting his signature on the dotted line, and I found myself providing a chorus of encouragement.

'If it's so fucking wonderful why aren't you signing up?' my friend asked.

Maybe it was pictures on the wall – the British Empire still looked so far-flung in those posters – or maybe I just never learned to ignore a dare, but I said, 'OK, you sign, I'll sign.'

He used the pen and handed it to me with a smirk on his face. We were still a couple of years from the Tory doubling of the unemployed, and the Recruiting Officer could hardly believe his luck. The thought flashed through my mind that I should make a run for it, but I didn't. I signed on the dotted line and went home to tell my mum.

She seemed pleased, unlike my dad, who thought but didn't say that I'd gone over to the class enemy. Uncle Stanley had been dead for over a year then, but I didn't think he'd have necessarily disapproved. 'You can do anything well, anything badly,' he'd told me once. 'Except be a torturer,' he'd added after a few moments.

When my mother told my brother he apparently just snorted knowingly, as if to say, 'What else could you expect?'

*   *   *

He was using the last of the light to mow his front lawn when I arrived. Gardening seemed to be his only interest outside work these days, and I had to admit his efforts had paid off – the place was a riot of colour, albeit a neatly ordered one. Joan was sunk in front of the TV with a large G&T – not the first if the affability of her greeting was anything to go by. I was disappointed to know that fifteen-year-old Julie was staying overnight at one of her friends, but Diane, two years younger, was soon inveigling my help with a school project and subjecting me to her new Spice Girls CD. She and Joan both went to bed around half-past ten, leaving me and Steve to sip at large whiskies while we watched one of the kids' *Blackadder* videos. He had even less to say to me than I had to him, but then he probably thought the trappings of success which surrounded him were eloquence enough.

The next day Joan was taking the two girls on a pre-holiday shop – they were off to Madeira for a week – so I decided to take a trip down Memory Lane. A 158 bus struggled through the Saturday-morning traffic to Stratford, where I caught a DLR train to Limehouse. From there I walked down towards Wapping in search of childhood echoes.

They were few and indistinct. I know they say you can never go back, but I didn't think they usually meant it this literally. About the only thing left of the area I'd grown up in was the ground on which it had stood.

I found it all really depressing, reversed my direction of travel and took a joyride on the new DLR extension to Beckton. It wasn't very joyful. I stared out at the new estates and they looked so antiseptic. The river wound along to my right but it no longer seemed the same one I'd seen out of Uncle Stanley's window. It felt as if all the romance had been drained away, but maybe I'd let down my guard and grown up.

Sunday was sunny, and while Steve did a morning's work at his office and Joan cooked lunch the two girls and I went for a long walk in Epping Forest. I got my quarterly update on their hopes, fears and passions, bought them ice creams, and listened to Julie's scathing impressions of boys in general and her first, now defunct, boyfriend in particular. Both girls seemed happy and full of life, and I found myself reluctantly admitting that Steve and Joan had to be doing something right.

Overall, though, it had been a depressing weekend, and I headed back to Hereford early that evening feeling even more rootless than usual. My past had been bulldozed away by the developers and the future looked decidedly unclear. I was feeling sorry for myself, and even Aretha Franklin at maximum volume couldn't lift me very far.

But things looked up the moment I got home. There was a message on the answerphone from Ellen saying she was coming back that day, and I'd no sooner finished listening to it than I heard her car pulling up outside.

After we'd done what even not-so-young lovers tend to do after a separation the two of us retired to the kitchen table in our dressing gowns for American cookies and hot chocolate, and suddenly the world which had seemed so problematic an hour earlier looked just about perfect. But not, it turned out, straightforward.

'How would you feel about me giving up my job?' Ellen asked out of the blue.

'It's up to you,' I said automatically. 'But I thought you were enjoying it,' I added carefully, wondering if I was about to be taken to task for missing signs for months on end.

'I am,' she said. 'I do.' She smiled wryly. 'You remember when we met, and I was so fed up with working at home, how I never met anybody, felt completely cut off, all that stuff.'

'Yeah.' She had been making jewellery for a living for several years, successfully too, but she'd decided she wanted to travel and had set about qualifying herself for a job in the travel industry. The two of us had met on a Russian-language course, and occasionally we still made love with Russian accents.

'Well,' she went on, 'I guess I'm never satisfied, because I feel like I've come full circle – now I'm fed up with always being somewhere else.'

'You want to go back to jewellery?'

'Not full time. A little maybe – I miss working with my hands. But I want to try and write the book too.'

She'd been stockpiling travel anecdotes – many of them hilarious – for several years now. 'Sounds good,' I said.

'And I want to think about having a baby,' she added, as if it was just an afterthought.

'Ah,' I said intelligently.

'Do you want a family?' she asked with the sort of simplicity which leaves nowhere to hide.

'I don't know,' I said, taking refuge in what felt like honesty.

'I'm thirty-four,' she said after a few moments' silence, 'and I think that if we're going to have one we should probably make a start.' She smiled at me, an errant lock of hair falling across one cheek.

'Yeah,' I heard myself say, 'maybe we should.'

'We don't have to start this minute,' she said. 'But maybe we can start getting ourselves ready. Mentally, I mean.'

'Sounds good,' I said.

A few hours later I woke up in a cold sweat, feeling more scared than I'd ever felt in combat. I told myself we should talk some more, give ourselves – by which I meant me – time to get used to the idea. I could spend the next week pondering the impact of fatherhood as I froze my balls off up the Beacons.

Or so I thought. As it turned out, the Regiment already had plans for freezing them off in a far more exotic location.

3

The CO's office seemed as overrun by files and furniture as always, but the Boss himself looked even more tired than usual. He gave the impression of a man headed for retirement, but then he was at least four years older than I was.

Maybe he'd just had one of those nights, I thought, and looked round for the photo of his wife which usually occupied one corner of his desk. It had gone AWOL.

We took turns stirring sugar into our tea.

'A job's come up,' he finally announced, and for once my heart couldn't make up its mind whether to leap or sink. 'Training job,' he went on, 'but not one of the boring ones – most of the training will be on-the-job, so to speak.'

'Where?' I asked.

'Kirghizstan,' he said slowly, as if he wanted to make sure he got the syllables in the right order.

I must have looked suitably amused.

'It's one of the ex-Soviet republics in Central Asia,' he explained. 'The most democratic, I've been told, but I don't suppose that's saying much. Your team will get a full briefing on the local situation from the Foreign Office before you fly out on Wednesday.'

So much for a long look at the pros and cons of parenthood, I thought.

The CO was blissfully unaware of my family planning, or the lack thereof. 'And they may be able to sort out the politics behind all this, which is more than I can do. You know what the CIS is?'

'The old Soviet Union in loose clothes?'

'Something like that. The Russians still run the show, that's for sure. They have a rapidly grow-ing problem with drugs, heroin in particular, and most of the stuff is coming from what's called the Golden Crescent, which stretches from north-east Iran through northern Afghanistan and Tadjikistan into northern Pakistan.'

'The hills are alive with the scent of poppies,' I said flippantly.

'They are, and they're inaccessible hills to boot. Iran's been a no-go area since the Shah's fall, and there are civil wars of varying intensity going on in each of the other three countries. So at the moment there's not much chance of preventing the crops from being grown and harvested.'

'What about the labs?' I asked.

'Same problem. Most of them are in northern Afghanistan, though a few small ones have apparently been springing up in the Pamirs, in Tadjikistan. Both of which countries are off limits, at least for the moment, which brings us to the supply routes. The main one of these is a road which winds across the Pamirs to a middle-sized town called Osh in Kirghizstan. From there some of the stuff goes north to the Kirghiz capital Bishkek, the rest of it west into Uzbekistan. Eventually it all heads north into Russia.'

'So what's worrying the government in Kirghizstan?' I asked cynically.

'No doubt some of the locals have their snouts in the trough,' the CO agreed, 'but drug trafficking's not really the industry of choice when it comes to economic development and building a democracy. And Kirghizstan's President has apparently decided that he wants to put together an elite, and hopefully corruption-free, anti-narcotics unit. They could have asked Moscow for Spetsnaz help, but that would probably have felt a little too much like asking the same old spider back into the parlour. And apparently the President is a fan of ours. He's probably just read one of Andy McNab's books.

'The Foreign Office is eager for two reasons. One, a lot of the heroin is passing straight through Russia and into Western Europe, and two, they see a future for British investment in Central Asia. The countries there are poor, but apparently they've got a lot of potential.'

I resisted the temptation to express my admiration for the Foreign Office, most of whose members, in my experience, knew as much about the world beyond our shores as my mum had. Instead, I asked how long the assignment would be.

'As long as it takes,' the CO said cheerfully. 'Three months, maybe?' You'll have a better idea when you get there and find out exactly what the locals have in mind. I'm assuming it'll be something along the lines of the job you did in Colombia, but it can't be the same, because this time you'll be dealing with the problems of interdiction.'

'Like putting fingers in a dike,' I thought out loud.

'Maybe, but Kirghizstan has no jungles – only a lot of very deep valleys and very high mountains. There aren't many routes the traffickers can use, and while these may be pretty remote, there's not much in the way of cover.'

'Makes sense,' I agreed. 'How many in the team?'

'Four. I've got two of the others pencilled in – Dave Llewellyn and Brian Crawford. They've both got some Russian, and Crawford picked up some Farsi in Oman. Any objections?'

I shook my head. Neither Llewellyn nor Crawford were friends, but I'd worked with both of them in the past, and knew something about their backgrounds. They shared a tendency to plough a lone furrow, but not much else. The first thing you noticed about 'Lulu' Llewellyn was his size – at six foot four and fifteen stone, with beard and longish curly hair, he looked a bit like what you would expect to find waiting at the top of a beanstalk. He came from a slate-mining family in Blaenau Ffestiniog, but both his parents were now dead. He had either two or three sisters – I couldn't remember which – both or all of whom were married. Lulu was single and probably a bit afraid of women. About ninety-nine per cent of his emotional energy went into animals, and the cottage he'd bought near Hereford with some windfall or other was apparently more full of furry creatures than the average ark. He wanted to be a vet when the SAS cast him loose, and he already had some of the qualifications. His one serious vice – as I'd found out up-country in Belize – was a weakness for show tunes. And if you don't think that's a serious vice then you've never heard the stillness of a jungle dawn broken by an out-of-tune rendition of 76 *Trombones*.

If Lulu was one of the Regiment's characters, then so was Brian Crawford, or 'Gonzo' as he was universally known. Walking into the canteen on his very first day at Stirling Lines, he'd been rechristened on the spot, and the nickname had never looked remotely like falling into disuse. His resemblance to the Muppet of that name was hard to pin down – he didn't have a ridiculous nose or anything like that – but you couldn't miss it. He was always coming up with mad ideas, but unlike the real Gonzo's, his usually worked. He was also a bit of a mystery: an eccentric, unorthodox, far from handsome loner, who also happened to be married to one of the loveliest women in Hereford. He always seemed interested in everything, he took holidays in places like Lapland and Venezuela and Albania where no one else went, but I never got the feeling there was any moral sense at work. He was a bit like my Uncle Stanley, and the opposite of my dad: much too interested in the way the world was to wonder about how it should be.

A fine pair, I thought.

'So how about a fourth?' the CO asked, as if he was trying to fill a bridge table. 'There are a couple of Russian-speakers in G Squadron, but they're on the Team at the moment, and I don't like . . .'

'Sheffield's got Russian,' I said.

'He hasn't got any experience as an instructor.'

'No, but this looks like a good way to get some.'

The CO grunted. 'I suppose it is. OK, you fill everyone in, and I'll get the names to the Foreign Office to arrange the visas. You'll be staying in Albany Street tomorrow night, get your briefing in the morning and then get out to Heathrow for the evening flight to Tashkent. I think it leaves at around eight, but we'll get that checked. I'll see you all here before you leave tomorrow afternoon.'

I went off in search of the others. Lulu was in the crew room cleaning his kit, and didn't seem at all surprised to discover that he'd soon be off on a job. He asked where we were going, but I didn't tell him. This particular job, unlike many the Regiment signed on for, didn't seem to have 'Top Secret' or 'Need To Know' notices plastered all over it, but I still wanted to wait until we were all together before spilling the destination.

Gonzo was also on base, teaching a signalling catch-up course – the technology changed so fast we seemed to need one every few weeks – but Sheff had to be brought back from the checkpoint he was manning out in the wilds, so we didn't actually get together until mid-afternoon. Then I mentioned the magic word Kirghizstan, fully expecting a row of blank looks and demands for an explanation. I should have known better. Gonzo immediately started rabbiting on about some unpronounceable lake – it was the deepest mountain lake in the world, he said. And it was five times the size of Lake Geneva, he added, which was undeniably a useful comparison for anyone who knew how big Lake Geneva was.

Not to be outdone, Lulu started mouthing off about some giant sheep named after Marco Polo which lived in the Central Asian mountains. They had spiral horns which could grow as long as two metres, he claimed. Which was probably five times as big as any you could see on the slopes above Lake Geneva.

A whole generation with its minds destroyed by Blue Peter, I thought sourly.

'Anybody got any idea what the women are like?' Sheff asked.

I went home intending to break the news to Ellen, but she was just getting out of the bath when I got there and something else came up. We'd already arranged to eat out at one of the country pubs we liked and I eventually filled her in as we sat waiting for the food to arrive.

'How long?' she asked, and anyone who didn't know her would have thought she wasn't even breaking stride.

'A couple of months, maybe,' I said none too truthfully. 'It could be a bit longer,' I admitted, seeing the look on her face. 'There's no real way of knowing until we get out there.'

She sighed, and I sighed with her.

'I know you've got to go,' she said at last. 'I was just looking forward to some time together.'

'So was I,' I said, and realized almost with a shock that I meant it a hundred per cent. This job might – probably would – turn out to be interesting, but for the first time in my life I was in a relationship which was more involving than work. 'If it helps, this might well be the last,' I told her.

She gave me an 'oh yeah?' smile.

'I've been thinking about going for a permanent spot in the Training Wing,' I said. 'Spend my last couple of years passing on all the wisdom I've accumulated.'

'Whether they want it or not,' she murmured, and that moment the thought of spending three months away from her was about as inviting as a night with one of Lulu's giant sheep.

Having sorted our personal kits, the four of us got together the next morning to talk weaponry. This didn't take long, since the Kirghiz government had already made it clear that the training programme would be built around their existing supply of ex-Soviet weaponry and communication gear. Still, it seemed advisable to take along enough personal combat equipment to make us feel comfortable. Browning High Powers and Heckler & Kock MP5 machine-guns seemed a minimal requirement, and Lulu wouldn't be parted from his M72 light anti-tank weapon.

We saw the CO for the promised goodbye kiss, and then climbed into the back of a van for the trip to London. It was nearly dark by the time we were shown to our luxury suite in the Albany Street barracks – it was here that Maggie had come to congratulate the Iranian Embassy lads – and the other three seemed happy to just watch TV in the rec room. I went for a walk along the Regent's Park Canal, just strolling on until the Lisson Grove tunnel forced me to turn back. I knew that once we got on the plane I'd be focused on the job in hand, but that night I felt anything but. Ellen was looming a lot larger in my mind than Kirghizstan and its problems.

Next morning we met the man from the Foreign Office in one of the visitor rooms. He was younger than I'd expected, younger than me in fact, and he seemed mercifully free from the usual diplomatic affectations. He spread a large map out on the floor between us and started off with a description of the geography which could hardly be faulted for verbosity. 'Mountains and deserts,' he said. 'The mountains are very high and the deserts are very dry. People live on the edges of these, in foothills, valleys, oases. The biggest valley by far is this one' – he pointed with his Bic – 'it's called the Fergana valley, and as you can see, three countries have a piece of it – Uzbekistan, Tadjikistan and Kirghizstan.

'A thousand years ago this was a really important area. It straddled the land routes between China and Europe – the various Silk Roads – and cities like Samarkand and Bukhara were some of the wealthiest in the world. But for the last five hundred years it's been a backwater, just a batch of squabbling local khanates until the Russians finally took them over in the late nineteenth century. They were ruled from Moscow until 1991.'

He looked round at our faces, presumably to check that we weren't falling asleep, and went on. 'The Soviet era was more of a mixed blessing than most people realize. The Russians looked down on the locals, of course, in much the same way as we looked down on Africans and Indians, and they ran the local economy very much with Moscow's interests in mind, creating a series of ecological disaster areas in the process. But they also brought in standards of education and health care which, though not stellar by our standards, were certainly impressive when compared to what was going on over the border in Iran and Afghanistan. And though they didn't get rid of the various ethnic grievances they did keep the lid on them.

'A lot of the Russians have left in the last five years, and more will probably follow, but there are still a lot who want to stay, provided the locals make it possible for them to do so. If they're not treated like second-class citizens, if their language is respected and if they don't suddenly find themselves having to obey Islamic law, then I think a lot will stay. Most of them were born there after all – they have no real roots in Russia or Ukraine.

'OK, Kirghizstan, where you're going. It's the most mountainous of the states, about ten times the size of Wales with less than twice the population. The Kirghiz people were traditionally nomadic herdsmen, and animal husbandry is still the main occupation in the upland areas. The two main areas of population' – the Bic reached out again – 'are here in the Chu valley and in the Kirghiz bits of the Fergana valley. These days the government likes to call the country "the Switzerland of Central Asia" but they've got a long way to go before that sounds convincing . . .'

'You need an advanced culture to produce Toblerone,' Sheff suggested.

The man from the Foreign Office managed not to giggle. 'Right,' he said. 'But the Kirghiz have managed to hold what was considered a fair election, which is more than any of their neighbours could say. They're supposed to have a lot of minerals in the ground, and the tourist potential is not at all bad. The main problem is that they have no hotels to speak of. The whole republic was closed to foreigners in the Soviet era, partly because of the strategic minerals, partly because Lake Issyk-Kul was used by the Soviet Navy for weapons experiments.'

He did another round of our faces. 'I'll just say a couple of words about the other two countries. Uzbekistan has by far the biggest population of the Central Asian states: way over twenty million. The old communists are still in charge, and they've banned the main Fundamentalist opposition party, but there's still a significant minority, most of it in the Fergana valley, who are hankering for an Islamic state.'

'Aren't the Kirghiz Muslims?' Gonzo asked.

'Yes, but I suppose you'd have to say they're not very devoted by Central Asian standards. Or not aggressively so anyway.'

'Thank Christ for that,' Sheff said. 'I don't want to be mistaken for Salman Rushdie.'

'Fat chance,' I said. 'He's good-looking.'

'Mmmm. Moving on to Tadjikistan. This is a completely different kettle of fish. It's poorer, more evenly split between Islamicists and people who support the old communists, and it shares a highly porous border with Afghanistan. There were several months of bloody civil war in 1992, and though there was no doubt that the communist government won it, the victory was far from complete, and the government's writ still doesn't run in the eastern, most mountainous third of the country. There are periodic outbreaks of fighting in the other two-thirds, and frequent border skirmishes. Not surprisingly, the government is very dependent on Russian help, and the Red Army's still much in evidence, particularly on the Afghan border. It's a CIS force in both name and composition – there are Kirghiz units attached to it, for example – but there's no doubt that the Russians call the shots.'

'So just how independent are these countries?' Sheff asked. 'This CIS – is it just the Soviet Union with a new name.'

'No, it's a lot weaker, and politically these countries are independent in most of the ways that matter. But they are intertwined, both with each other and with Russia. A few months ago Russia, Belarus, Kazakhstan and Kirghizstan signed what they called an integration agreement, promising to set up a common market, customs union, joint energy and transport system – all that sort of thing. They even discussed re-establishing a single currency in the future.'

'So it's something like the EEC?' Gonzo suggested.

'Something. But imagine getting all the West European countries to agree to that lot if they'd only declared independence from Germany six years ago.'

'So what about the drug problem?' I asked. Our briefer was more concise than some I'd endured, but I always found these spiels more interesting in retrospect, once I'd visited the places in question.

He went through the general background stuff I'd

got from the CO – the Golden Crescent, the difficulty of getting to the poppies before they were harvested and refined into heroin – and we all got down on our knees, heads almost butting, to trace the various routes north into Kirghizstan which the traffickers supposedly followed.

Lulu traced a large finger along the line of mountains which formed the southern boundary of the Fergana valley. 'There must be a hundred little passes across this lot,' he said.

'There are,' the Foreign Office man agreed, 'and there's no way the Kirghiz Army can man them all.'

'But so what?' Sheff asked. 'If all the stuff goes through this Osh place, then why freeze your balls off in the mountains? Why don't they just play the spider, and wait in the middle of the web.'

'They probably do,' I said. 'Only instead of confiscating the stuff they're getting a cut for letting it go by.'

'That's about the size of it,' the Foreign Office man admitted.

'And of course the government's five hundred miles away in Bishkek,' Gonzo observed cynically. 'They're not getting any cut at all.'

We were chauffeured across the city to Heathrow late that afternoon. I stared out of the window, watching the city's dwellers struggling to cope with the congealing evening rush hour, feeling full of the benign affection I saved for my fellow compatriots on days of departure. On our return from the world's nether regions as I knew only too well from past experience, the same people and scenes would have the opposite effect, and just make me angry.

At Heathrow the security people were waiting for us, and we were soon being ushered through the usual maze of corridors, bypassing not only the various passport and luggage checks but also the duty-free shops. Sheff prevailed on one of the security men to go and buy him 200 cigarettes – that was my passive smoking for the next week organized – and we settled down to wait for our personal flight call in the small lounge, wondering who other than travelling SAS teams ever got to enjoy its spartan comforts. Film stars and football managers, we guessed, but one of the security guys told us it was mostly used as a holding cell for prisoners who were being extradited.

I said more goodbyes to Ellen on the phone, and found myself getting depressed again at the prospect of a long separation. There was the possibility of light in the middle of the tunnel, though: she was trying to fix up a work trip to Samarkand and Bukhara for a few weeks' time, in the hope that I could take a few days off from training the Kirghiz and join her.

Back in our holding cell, Sheff was stretched out on one of the sofas, 199 cigarettes resting on his stomach, the other creating a cloud of smoke above his head, which was deep inside an *X Files* paperback. I was pleased to see it was one I hadn't read.

Lulu was ensconced in one of the armchairs, eyes closed and lips slightly open as he rapturously listened to something on his Walkman. Fearing the worst, I walked over to examine the cassette case on the chair's arm. It was *South Pacific*. I looked down the list of tunes and wondered if Kirghizstan was ready for 'Some Enchanted Evening', let alone 'There Is Nothing Like a Dame'.

In what was left of the room Gonzo was doing Tai Chi exercises, and at that particular moment he looked like he was trying to simultaneously hail a taxi and shake dog shit off his boots, all in slow motion.

I think I probably sighed as I sat down.

About an hour later we were summoned to a private boarding of the plane, but any idea of stealing enough seats for a decent sleep was scuppered by the news that the flight was full. The MoD had inexplicably neglected to send us first class – these days cost cutting was so endemic that I was surprised we hadn't been tied to the wings – so we sat squashed together like sardines in the main cabin of the still otherwise empty Airbus, listening to Gonzo's account of the post-Soviet airlines' abysmal safety record. 'But Uzbekistan Airways are OK,' he finally conceded, as the rest of us pondered last-minute codicils to our wills. 'They've got an arrangement with Lufthansa for flight crew training and aircraft maintenance.'

'Yeah, but who's taking us from Tashkent to Bishkek?' Lulu wanted to know.

'We'll go overland,' I decided, hoping that was practicable.

The other passengers began filing aboard. There were a few who fitted my notion of what Uzbeks looked like, but most were citizens of the subcontinent beyond – the plane's final destination was Delhi. They were also overwhelmingly male and clearly pleased to be travelling to the land of their ancestors, if not their birth.

We took off on time, and were soon flying east through clear skies above the North European plain, the lights of first Germany and then Poland visible far below. The near-festive atmosphere on the plane made sleep seem unlikely but I did eventually drift off somewhere over western Russia, hoping that the local air traffic controllers were more awake than I was.

4

I awoke to a samosa-scented dawn and the news that we were about half an hour from touch-down in Tashkent. The others had all managed a few hours' sleep – if there's one thing life in the SAS teaches you it's the ability to grab your kip when you can.

Looking out of the window I could see no clouds below us, only an almost featureless, dun-coloured desert. After a few minutes this briefly gave way to a ribbon of cultivation straddling a wide, brown river – the ancient Jaxartes, according to Gonzo – and then there was more desert, almost up to the point where the outer suburbs of Tashkent came into view. Central Asia's largest city seemed greener than I'd expected from the air, but the early summer was probably its best time. The snow would have melted in the mountains, and the summer sun hadn't yet had time to dry out what the water had allowed to flourish. I suddenly found myself feeling a bit less reluctant about the job – visiting somewhere new had always been one of the things I enjoyed most in life.

The machine-gun-toting guards in the arrivals hall put a temporary damper on these expectations, but we hardly had time to worry about the airport's reputation for general corruption when our reception committee from Her Majesty's Embassy in Uzbekistan arrived. His name was James Seagram. He didn't apologize for being late, merely flashed us a public-school grin, brushed back his blond hair with a sweep of the hand and introduced us to the grinning local with the Saddam Hussein moustache who was standing behind him. This individual then guided us swiftly past the bottlenecks already building around some of our less fortunate fellow-travellers – one Brit gave me a particularly reproachful look – and out into the forecourt, where our canvas bags full of weaponry were already being loaded into the back of a huge black limousine.

The sky above was a piercing blue, and even at eight in the morning the heat was impressive. We all shook hands with Saddam, then climbed into the spacious rear of the limousine, which looked like a definite hangover from Soviet days. 'The Embassy bought it from the KGB,' James said, as if guessing my train of thought. He rapped on the partition window, whereupon the driver slowly and reluctantly folded up his newspaper, engaged the gears and pulled out into the whirling scrum of taxis. The air-conditioning wheezed rather than blew, and after a while we followed the driver's example, opening the windows to admit the dusty breeze.

'You're staying one night at the Hotel Uzbekistan,' James told us with an encouraging smile, though why we should be encouraged by this news wasn't clear. 'And you're booked on the morning flight to Bishkek.'

'We need to travel overland,' I said authoritatively. 'I'm not . . .'

'I assumed the arrangements had already been made,' I lied. 'There's no reason why we shouldn't, is there?'

'No, I suppose not, but it may take some arranging. First, we'd have to find a vehicle. And then there'll be all the various permits and visas. Outside the cities you can hardly drive a mile without running into a checkpoint, and with what you're carrying . . .'

'We can ship the weaponry by air,' I suggested. 'I don't suppose we'll be using it before we get there,' I added with a straight face. I knew I was making his life more difficult but, air-safety considerations apart, I did want an unofficial look at the sorts of roads and border crossings which the drug traffickers were negotiating. In these days of pressurized jets no one ever learned much about the ground from a plane trip.

'I'll see what I can do,' James agreed, and I went back to looking out the window. There were few buildings of more than two storeys – most of the city had apparently been destroyed by an earthquake in 1966 – and the main impression was European rather than Asian. As we neared the city centre a few high-rise hotels loomed into view, along with some notably Russian-looking stone buildings, but we'd still had only one distant glimpse of a mosque when the limousine pulled up in front of the Hotel Uzbekistan.

This looked like modern hotels look everywhere, and somewhat to my surprise the air-conditioning was working. James checked us in at reception and handed over two keys and a wad of local money to feed ourselves with. 'I'll hang on to the arsenal,' he said, 'and I'll get back to you later today about travel arrangements. If there's any problem ring the Embassy,' he added, plucking a business card from his jacket pocket. I half-expected to see 'Our Man in Tashkent' embossed on the stiff paper, but there was only the Embassy's address and phone number.

We eyed the apparently functioning lifts with suspicion – if they couldn't maintain planes, then how about these? – but no one had the energy for climbing eleven floors' worth of stairs, so we dared and won. Sheff and I took one room, Gonzo and Lulu the other. They weren't exactly spacious, and the hot water in the shower was a long time coming, but the rooms were nice enough. From the small balconies we could see out across the city, or at least as far as the heat haze would allow. The mountains to the east were just about visible, but soon they'd disappear behind a curtain of dust and smog.

'So that's where we're going,' Sheff said, blowing smoke over my shoulder.

'That's where. The heart of Asia,' I added poetically.

'Middle of nowhere,' Sheff muttered appreciatively. 'You remember that film with Sean Connery and Michael Caine – *The Man Who Would Be King*, or something like that. They're Brit soldiers from the old days who find this kingdom no one's ever heard of and decide to take it over. It was somewhere round here,' he added, peering rather more optimistically at the fading line of mountains.

'I bet it ended in tears,' I said.

'It did that,' Sheff agreed.

After a couple of hours' kip we collected Gonzo from next door – Lulu pronounced himself uninterested – and went out for a look at the town. Gonzo had already bought an old Soviet guidebook from the small gift shop in the lobby, and after admiring the photos of Politburo leaders we followed the enclosed map west towards the old dividing line between the Russian and native townships. The buildings of the former were the standard stone in pastel colours, those of the latter mostly conspicuous by their absence. One huge mosque was beautifully decorated with patterns of ceramic tiling, but generally speaking both the pre-Russian past and the post-Soviet future seemed thin on the ground.

The locals didn't stare at us as much as I'd expected, so either they assumed we were Russian or they were used to tourists.

We went for a ride on the two-line Metro – so modern it put London Transport to shame – and ended up admiring one station which had been designed like a sci-fi comic in tribute to the Soviet space programme. Back at the hotel we continued our research into Russia's impact on the area by sampling the infinite varieties of vodka on sale in the third-floor bar. The sun had sunk behind several yard-arms – or several suns had sunk behind the same one – when James discovered our hiding-place.

He ordered a double shot of the pepper vodka and

told us with a decidedly smug smile that everything was arranged. Our car would be delivered the following morning, along with letters from the Ministry of Foreign Affairs and NSS – the new initials for the old KGB – which should smooth our way through all the various checkpoints between Tashkent and the Kirghiz border. Working on the assumption that the six-hundred-mile trip would take around twenty hours, and that we would be leaving at about seven in the morning, we should reach the border soon after noon, and Kirghiz officialdom had been alerted to expect us around then. We could spend the night at a hotel in Tashkumir, Karakul or Toktogul, depending on how far we wanted to drive on the first day. Our armoury was taking the plane, and would be picked up by someone from the American Embassy – it seemed that, European solidarity notwithstanding, we were still on better terms with them than the Germans. The UK didn't even have a consulate in Bishkek, though according to James one was in the works.

'Great,' was my reply to all this, and James looked suitably rewarded. I expected the usual questions – 'Were you at the Iranian Embassy? Was there a team on the Argentinian mainland during the Falklands War? Were the rumours about the one in Bosnia true? – but none came. Our Man in Tashkent obviously had a date, because after one look at his watch he sluiced down his vodka and hurried off, leaving the four of us free to debate the more important questions of our time. Did the millennium end on 31 December 1999, we wondered, or on 31 December 2000? How could anyone survive having Madonna for a mother? Why was *Neighbours* still on?

At seven the next morning we were gathered in the lobby, looking somewhat the worse for wear, when James arrived with our transport, a black Lada saloon whose rough exterior hopefully hid an efficient engine. James looked a little red-eyed himself, and seemed more anxious about waving us off into the great unknown than he had on the previous evening.

But wave us off he did, and soon Sheff was aiming the Lada eastward out of Tashkent and towards the grey wall of mountains. I was navigating in the front, while Gonzo and Lulu jostled each other for space in the back. The car felt full, not to say heavy, with its Regimental load, and my head was carrying the dull ache vodka leaves behind, but I could still feel that lifting of the heart which always accompanied me on journeys into the unknown. Arrowing across the irrigated cotton fields of Uzbekistan, I was Uncle Stanley stepping aboard on his beloved river, on my way to anywhere and everywhere, exploring. I sometimes think it's a gene that comes in all strengths from practically non-existent to overpowering, and there's not much doubt in my mind which end of the spectrum I'm on. As a kid in London I'd always take a new path or road to somewhere when one offered itself, just to see what was there. Sometimes it would be a dead end and I'd end up walking twice as far, but that didn't matter. I'd explored, I'd been somewhere new, I'd expanded my world.

Our road would cross a spur of the mountains into

the vast Fergana valley, and then run east all the way to Osh in Kirghizstan, at the valley's head. If you imagined a huge upside-down A lying on its side, Osh would be at its apex, and the two sides would represent the two principal drug routes to Russia, the one on the left running north-west to Tashkent, the one on the right north-east to Bishkek. We were now travelling down the one on the left, but not with the intention of driving all the way to Osh. Instead we would save several hours of driving by taking the A's crossbar, a road which snaked up out of the Fergana valley to join the Bishkek road.

That was the plan anyway, all by the grace of local officialdom and our noble Lada. In the process I was hoping we'd see a lot of natural beauty and learn a bit about the job in hand. Thinking that, I eyed the vehicles passing in the opposite direction and wondered which were carrying fresh supplies of heroin for the hungry youth of Europe. One car or lorry in a hundred, or more than half of them? Was drug-running round here a way of life or was it still just a criminal endeavour?

The first place we came to was possibly the ugliest I'd ever seen. Angren, a coalmining town set in a flat basin surrounded by mountains, was a mess of power stations, rusting pipes, sulphurous smoke, broken windows and concrete blocks of flats set beside a bloody great hole in the ground. If William Blake had seen it he'd probably have renamed it 'Jerusalem', but all the gods hereabouts seemed to be old ones – you could still see the communist murals flaking on the crumbling walls.

'What a fucking dump,' Sheff murmured somewhat unnecessarily.

After Angren the road started climbing in earnest – eager to get out of the pit behind – and soon it was clinging to the side of a spiralling valley, a river far below, giant slopes of unstable-looking scree on all sides. I was just thinking that it was a bit like Tolkien's approach to Mordor when some giant rocky crags loomed into view, cementing the impression. And then suddenly we were driving through patches of clouds, glimpsing snow-covered heights above us and feeling distinctly chilly in our T-shirts.

It didn't last. Ten more minutes and we were descending a wooded valley, crossing and recrossing a tumbling stream, shooting through villages which clung to the steep slopes. Men sat around on mattresses watching the traffic go by, while women could occasionally be glimpsed either peering from doorways or working in the precipitous patches of cultivation. The trees – silver poplar and apricot were the only ones I recognized – came in a variety of sunlit colours, and Angren felt a long way behind us.

We quickly encountered our second and third police posts – the first had been on the other side of the mountains – but so far our letters were working like a charm, converting looks of pure avarice into the kind of obsequiousness which only royalty takes for granted. We hadn't even needed to grease any palms with one of the ten-rouble notes which James had handed over for that purpose.

Buoyed by this success, we stopped at a *chaikhana* in one of the villages and enquired after breakfast.

They were apparently out of Egg McMuffins, but glasses of sweet green tea were followed by omelettes and freshly baked bread which tasted three times as tasty. We sat outside in the sun, consuming this feast and gazing at the valley around us, feeling good. The *chaikhana*'s owner joined us for a moan about how his country was going to the dogs, or at least that's what we thought he was saying. His Russian was worse than ours, and Gonzo had trouble translating his Tadjik, but there was no doubt he was pissed off about something, and there was still a poster of some communist bigwig on the wall inside.

It was almost ten in the morning by the time we left, but it was hard to feel any great urgency. I took over the driving, and we drove down towards what looked like a vast plain but which we knew was in fact a vast valley. The Fergana valley is a huge, flat-bottomed, pear-shaped bowl about two hundred miles long and up to eighty miles wide, flanked, except for its narrow western exit, by mountain ranges nearly ten thousand feet high. The Syr Darya – Gonzo's ancient Jaxartes – flows through its centre, and the whole bottom is criss-crossed by both irrigation channels and streams which flow down from the surrounding mountains. There are enough cotton fields to keep Marks and Sparks in business for ever, but many orchards remain as a reminder of the pre-Soviet world.

As we reached the plain, Gonzo and Lulu, for reasons best known to themselves, broke into a loud and harmony-free rendition of Abba's 'Dancing Queen'. Not only *Blue Peter*, I thought, but seventies music too.

About fifteen minutes later we reached the spot where a smaller road – the A's crossbar – struck off to the left, but before taking it we couldn't resist driving the extra mile down to the river. It was about three hundred yards wide, sluggish and a deep yellow-brown in colour. The road crossed on a long pontoon bridge, which cranked alarmingly when the lorry that had been behind us set out manfully for the farther shore.

We drove back to our turn-off, which soon settled into a bumpy course running parallel with the river. There were frequent villages, all with their quota of staring children, but no checkpoints, which seemed less surprising with each bone-jolting mile. The cotton fields were bordered by lines of felled mulberry trees which storks seemed fond of using for nests. To our left the mountains rose to snowcapped heights, and far to the right the other side of the valley was wreathed in haze. Despite the roughness of the ride it all felt quite idyllic, and Hereford seemed a hell of a long way away.

We left the river behind, climbing into the foothills and passing through a couple of small towns before we hit our next police post on the outskirts of Namangan. Our accreditation worked its usual trick, turning gun-waving hostility into grins and shouts of 'Gazza!' and 'Maggie Thatcher!', and I drove on into the city, thinking it was kind of scary that my two most famous compatriots were a man-child without a brain and a woman without a heart.

Namangan had been our intended spot for lunch, but the streets seemed as empty of restaurants as they were full of hostile stares. The city also seemed a bit of a dump, and if it had a centre we missed it, because the next thing I knew I was driving out the other side. Luck was with us, though, for about ten miles short of the Kirghiz border, wedged between the road and a river under two towering willows, a *chaikhana* presented itself. The owner, a friendly Tadjik, seemed pleased to discover that we weren't Russian, and the meat pancakes which emerged from his kitchen had what's usually called an interesting taste. We consumed two helpings and sat there with tall glasses of green tea, thinking that this was one of those days when we really earned our meagre Army pay.

The border itself was a pushover. The men on the Uzbek side could just find the energy to lift the barrier and those at the Kirghiz post two hundred yards up the road seemed so overjoyed to see us that we had trouble getting back on the road. To add insult to injury, Gonzo and Lulu dipped into the Abba songbook for a version of 'Super Trouper' which would have brought tears to their eyes if I hadn't needed to keep both hands on the wheel.

A few miles beyond the border we turned north on to the road from Osh to Bishkek – the other side of our A – and the climb out of the Fergana valley began in earnest. The road shared the valley with a river – the Syr Darya, but here it was called the Naryn – and a single railway track which looked distinctly abandoned. The line ended in the elongated mining town of Tashkumir, the first of James's suggested stopovers, but there were still several hours of light left and the place looked too depressing for words.

We continued on up the valley, which rapidly turned into a gorge, with river and pylons far below, the road clinging to ledges hacked from the sheer walls of sandstone. It was impressive, though after the first hour the thrill began to wear off.

Karakul was the next possible stopover, but this not only looked marginally more depressing than Tashkumir, it also boasted a handwritten sign which said, in English: 'Welcome to fucking Karakul'. We stopped the car and looked at this for a while, before Gonzo got out and took a photograph.

The sun had abandoned the bottom of the valley by this time, but we decided to press on anyway. It was getting dark when we saw the lights of Toktogul winking across a vast reservoir, and after what seemed like hours we finally reached the town's only hotel. It was dirt cheap, and it didn't take long to find out why: the toilets were filthy, there was no hot water and the buffet downstairs was close to inedible. After forcing down some food we went out for a stroll, but the plummeting temperature and an inordinate number of angry dogs soon drove us back to the hotel. In the lobby several snazzily dressed young Tadjiks were looking at *Baywatch* on a flickering TV, and I wondered if this was a common lay-over spot for the drug run from Osh to Bishkek.

There was no sign of them next morning, and we didn't pass them on the road that day. The drive to Bishkek didn't look much more than two hundred miles on the map, but the hotel proprietor told Gonzo the buses were scheduled to take nine hours for the trip, so we were forewarned. And some journey it was. We climbed up a beautiful valley to a snow-clad pass over ten thousand feet high, drove down a long high valley with occasional clusters of nomad tents, lunched at a truckstop café that stood by a junction in the middle of nowhere, climbed up and over an ever-higher pass and descended a dramatic canyon to the plain far below, where our road joined another which skirted the foothills from Dzhambul to Bishkek. We drove into the Kirghiz capital in mid-afternoon, having learned at least one thing from our epic drive. As Gregory Peck was forever repeating in the film of the same name, this was a big country.

The city itself seemed like a miniature version of Tashkent, with smaller factories, smaller blocks of flats. There were more trees, though, lots more, and the wooden cottages with their carved eaves seemed more reminiscent of Europe than Asia. So did the people on the streets, most of whom looked distinctly Slavic.

'The Kirghiz make up only about a third of the population,' Gonzo read from his guidebook, just as a passing young blonde almost caused Sheff to rick his neck.

The Ala-Too Hotel, into which Our Man in Tashkent had booked us, seemed as laid-back as the town at first sight – we didn't yet know about the disco next door – and our rooms offered a welcome contrast with those of the night before. Both had the balconies which overlooked the street and railway station opposite, offering a vista of the snowcapped mountains rising to the south.

We'd been enjoying the view for about forty minutes

– Sheff was on his third cigarette – when Kadir knocked apologetically on our door. He was wearing what looked suspiciously like a Red Army uniform, but then I don't suppose most of the post-Soviet states had had either the money or the inclination to refit their military forces to reflect their new-found independence. Unlike most of the people we had seen since arriving in Bishkek, he was certainly a Kirghiz, albeit one with a grasp of the Russian language that was much better than ours. Kadir was about five foot six, with distinctly Mongoloid facial features, a rough-hewn crewcut and a barrel chest. He was older than he looked – thirty-five, as we later found out.

Were our rooms satisfactory? Did we need anything? Tomorrow morning at nine o'clock he would take me to meet the Minister, and later we would all be driven to the barracks on the edge of the city which would be our new home.

I asked him about our weapons, and he said they were waiting for us at the American Embassy. We could pick them up *en route* to the barracks the next day.

Gonzo asked him about restaurants and he recommended one in another hotel, which made me wonder, but not ask, what the fuck we were doing in this one.

'This is a nicer hotel,' he told me, as if he'd actually heard the question. 'And it is a pleasant walk to the Dostuk, though after . . .' He stopped and laughed, displaying one gold tooth in a row of shining ones. 'I was going to say that after dark the streets can be dangerous,' he said, 'but

I think you men can probably take care of your-selves, yes?'

'Probably,' I said drily, feeling somewhat disappointed. The city had looked so peaceful as we drove in. But then these days the feeling of safety I could just about remember from my childhood only seemed to exist in the barbed-wire enclaves of the rich. I'd probably been born at the wrong time – I remembered Uncle Stanley saying that it was the fifties and early sixties which were the aberrations, not the violence-prone times which preceded and followed them.

Kadir was edging his way backwards out of the room, a smile of welcome still shining on his face. 'Nine o'clock,' he said again, just in case I'd forgotten, and disappeared through the door with the suddenness of a conjuror's rabbit.

'So, time to walk the mean streets?' Sheff asked, an unlighted cigarette dangling from the corner of his mouth.

We were all hungry, and the walk up the main boulevard was as nice as Kadir had claimed, at least until the moment we emerged from the near-forest of oaks which bordered and bifurcated the thoroughfare into a vast stone square surrounded by ugly-looking buildings. In the centre a large plinth stood suspiciously empty: Lenin, I guessed, had been removed but not yet replaced.

We eventually found the Dostuk Hotel and its ground-floor restaurant – the Arizona! – which served expensive burgers and beer. No doubt this was what Kadir thought we would like, but it was definitely the worst meal we ate in Kirghizstan. The German beer was some compensation, but not enough, and I made myself unpopular by limiting us to a couple of cans each. I wanted us to make a good impression on the next day, and I didn't think I could stand any more Abba tunes on the way back to the hotel.

5

I was in the lobby at ten to nine the next morning, waiting for Kadir to collect me. There were a few Western tourists in evidence, most of them men, and what seemed a fair cross-section of Kirghiz society, from apoplectic Russian grandmothers to insolent Uzbek teenagers wearing Snoop Doggy Dogg T-shirts. Kadir came through the doors at exactly one minute to nine, greeted me with a happy grin and led me outside to his jeep.

We set off up the wide boulevard along which the four of us had walked the night before, and which was now full of traffic. Kadir hadn't said exactly what the point of our visit was, and perhaps there was no real need for me to know before we got there, but this whole job was beginning to seem almost alarmingly casual. Usually on training stints like this everything would be fixed up well in advance – we'd spend weeks brushing up on the language and enduring endless in-depth briefings on the destination country before we even got on a plane, and when we finally arrived we'd have a clear idea of what was expected of us and who expected it. And here we were in sunny Kirghizstan after only the most cursory briefings and with precious little idea of exactly what was going to be required. There didn't seem much urgency from the Kirghiz point of view, so I could only assume that the MoD's budgetary difficulties were even worse than I'd supposed, and hiring out the SAS by the hour was the only way they could make ends meet. Either that, or someone somewhere had a political agenda which I couldn't even begin to guess at.

We circumnavigated the square with the empty plinth, took a left turn down an important-looking street and almost immediately came to a halt outside one of those buildings which reek of government. Inside the front doors two uniformed soldiers stood guard over a marble-floored lobby containing a single polished wooden seat. As Kadir explained our presence I noticed a faded rectangular patch on the wall where a painting had recently hung. Lenin again, I thought, and wondered if all the portraits and statues and badges and books had been destroyed, or just hidden away by true believers to await a second coming.

'This way,' Kadir said, and I followed him into a decidedly antique-looking lift. 'This is the Interior Ministry,' he volunteered as we scraped skyward.

On the second floor we emerged into a sunlit corridor, at the end of which open doors beckoned. The room seemed almost as bare as the lobby downstairs, but that was partly because of its size. There was an ornate-looking desk on one side and worn leather sofas arranged as three sides of a square on the other. Through the window was a sea of roofs and treetops.

We were gestured to a sofa, and our two hosts, neither of whom was in uniform, took opposite ends of the one facing it. The older of the two had grey hair, blue eyes and a pronounced Slavic physiognomy; the younger was a stout Kirghiz with Kadir's haircut and a shifty look in his dark eyes. Their names were Lisinov and Orozbakov.

It soon became apparent that Orozbakov was nominally in charge, but who possessed the real authority was less clear. What did become apparent as the discussion unwound was that Lisinov had more interest in – or perhaps more enthusiasm for – our presence than his Kirghiz colleague. Which, to my mind at least, raised some interesting questions.

My first priority, though, was to find out exactly what we were being paid for.

'I understand you travelled by road from Tashkent, through the Fergana?' Lisinov asked.

'Yes. We wanted to get an idea of the country.'

'It's beautiful, isn't it?' the Russian said with a possessive smile. He wasn't an outsider, I realized – he'd been born here, and before independence he would have been the senior man.

'It is,' I agreed. 'And hard to police, I should think.' Orozbakov grunted in reluctant agreement, and I pushed the point. 'And the situations in Russia and Tadjikistan will make things even more difficult,' I went on, feeling very diplomatic. 'Drug trafficking is hard enough to stop when the countries around you are at peace.'

Orozbakov looked marginally less hostile than Lisinov, which gave me some hope. I could understand his being pissed off at being pressured into bringing in a gang of foreigners so soon after independence, but I didn't want to find out that he had his snout in the narco-trough and was just protecting his own interests. If the guy in charge doesn't want you to succeed then you might as well forget it.

'This is a CIS problem,' Lisinov was saying, 'not just a problem for Kirghizstan, and we have asked for your assistance with that in mind.'

'Perhaps you could give me an idea of exactly what you do have in mind,' I suggested.

'Certainly,' Lisinov said. 'Our aim is to create an elite force, and we want you to create the nucleus of that force. The main remit of the force will be to combat the drug traffickers, but other goods are also smuggled out of our country. What we really want,' – here he turned to Orozbakov for confirmation – 'is a unit strong enough in its own identity to resist the corruption which comes with narcotics.'

'Untouchables,' I murmured, remembering the film. 'It's an admirable aim,' I agreed, 'but there's more to that sort of force than skills. A lot will depend on how well paid they are, for example. Even the most upright soldier tends to weaken when he's offered ten times his annual salary just for looking the other way.'

'We understand that,' Lisinov agreed, 'and we don't expect you to replicate the SAS here.' He smiled. 'What we need is for you to take the men we offer – we have thirty-six of them, if that seems a reasonable number . . .'

I nodded.

'To take these men,' he went on, 'assess their current

abilities and then build up their skills to what seems an appropriate level.' He looked questioningly at me.

'Weapon-handling, patrolling, observation duties, close target reconnaissance,' I suggested, hoping my Russian was good enough to handle the technical stuff.

'Exactly. And I understand that in South America your people dealt with finding and destroying the laboratories in which the drugs are refined?'

'I understood the labs were in Afghanistan and Tadjikistan,' I said.

'They are. For the moment, at least. But it's possible that this unit will eventually find itself on CIS duty in Tadjikistan – our governments will be cooperating very closely in this business.'

'Ah,' I said, wondering if the Foreign Office knew the forces we'd been sent to train might one day be placed under Russian command. Or maybe Lisinov had visions of hiring out his elite unit in the same way the FO hired out the SAS. A few years down the line we could all play musical countries.

'I think the next step should be for you to meet the men and start the assessment process,' the Russian said. 'In a few days you should have a better idea of what's required, and then we can meet again. If anything comes up in the meantime, Lieutenant Karalayev' – he nodded in Kadir's direction – 'will be serving as your liaison with this office. Anything you need, ask him first.'

The interview was obviously over. After shaking hands with both men, Kadir and I went back to the jeep. Lisinov hadn't gone into detail but I thought I knew exactly what it was he wanted, and why. For the Russians who remained in Kirghizstan the idea of a 'Switzerland in Central Asia' would be more than attractive – it would be almost a condition of their survival. They were the minority now, and they needed law and order, not a society reduced to anarchy by the predations of the drug trade. An elite force of incorruptibles could mean the difference between a Switzerland and a Panama.

The Orozbakovs – those who weren't already slurping at the trough – would have a more ambivalent attitude. They'd share the Russians' desire for law and order but there'd also be an inclination to turn a blind eye, particularly if the economy wasn't producing the good life in any other way. Drugs could bring a lot of money into Kirghizstan, and at a fairly minimal cost, always assuming that the locals didn't get into consumption. If they didn't, and it was just the youth of far-off Europe who were smoking and shooting up the stuff, then maybe this was one for the Third World, a small payback for all the riches which had flowed in the other direction. I'd heard that argument from ordinary, sane Latin Americans a few years before, and I had to admit it was a tough one to counter.

That said, it was our job to train these guys to piss on the drug traffickers' parade, and I can't say I was going to lose any sleep about doing it. But if the guys we were given to train felt at all ambivalent about what they were being trained to do, that would certainly make our job twice as difficult.

Kadir and I got back to the hotel. Sheff and Gonzo were in the lobby, the former chatting up the blonde in the gift shop, the latter checking out excursions to Lake Issyk-Kul – five times the size of Lake Geneva! – at the Intourist desk. Lulu had apparently walked across the road to investigate the railway station.

I dispatched Sheff to find him and half an hour later we were all packed and ready to check out. This we did with some reluctance, knowing from bitter experience how sumptuous the usual military accommodations are, and Kadir's description of our new home did nothing to cheer us up. We loaded up the Lada with ourselves and our bergens and followed Kadir's jeep across town to the US Embassy, where a local minion – the resident Yank was out playing golf – handed over our canvas bags of goodies with the air of someone delivering laundry. A quick check reassured us that nothing had been nicked in transit.

From there we headed back south, crossing the railway lines after waiting for a long goods train to pass, and threaded our way through the leafy sub-urbs, catching tantalizing glimpses of the mountains ahead. A low-flying plane suddenly crossed the road a hundred yards in front of us, suggesting either an imminent crash or an airport in the vicinity, and the lack of a subsequent explosion confirmed the latter. A couple of minutes later Kadir's jeep turned off the road into what was clearly a military camp. Like everything else in Bishkek it seemed half-hidden by trees, but as we waited for the lads at the gate to let us in I could just about make out a row of barracks in the distance.

The trees thinned out a bit as we reached the centre of the camp – enough to leave room for a small parade ground – and as we parked outside an obvious admin block the mountains to the south were suddenly visible in all their snowcapped glory.

'How far away from China are we?' Sheff asked for no apparent reason.

'About a hundred and sixty miles,' Gonzo told him.

'Then there should be some decent Chinese restaurants in town,' Sheff decided.

Kadir, who had followed this interchange with a growing look of incomprehension, shook his head – presumably to clear it – and asked me to accompany him into the admin block. Once inside we were made to wait for several minutes before being ushered into the presence of the camp CO, an ageing Russian colonel who obviously wasn't too thrilled to have us on his base. I practised my diplomatic skills a bit more, and even managed to coax a smile out of the old bastard. It had apparently already been decided which area of the base we would be using for our training routines, and this didn't seem like the time to explain that different routines might need different environments. Kadir could arrange all that later, I thought, and could see from his face that the prospect had occurred to him too.

The next step was to examine our own quarters, which turned out to be a reasonable-sized hut close to the southern perimeter of the base. Inside, the plumbing looked worse than it was – the shower actually coughed up hot water – and we had an outside chemical toilet all to ourselves. Six bunk-beds stood up against three of the walls, and a table with four chairs stood in the centre of the wooden floor. The wind was whistling through cracks in the walls, but I had to admit I'd seen a lot worse. We had running water, a roof and a private shithouse. It was early summer. And they hadn't put us in with the locals, which would have made it hard to keep the kind of distance we would need in the training process.

The others weren't moaning yet. Sheff was stretched out on an upper bunk with his paperback, Gonzo was pulling strange and wonderful things out of his bergen and Lulu was fiddling with the antenna of his short-wave radio, presumably in search of the World Service. I only had a Walkman with me, and God only knew how many weeks it would take Ellen's tapes of the Sunday-morning *Archers* to reach me. I idly wondered if Gonzo knew how far we were from Ambridge.

Kadir was still standing by the door, watching us with the sort of expression people have when they're trying to memorize something. I suppose we were strange animals to him, but then Gonzo and Lulu were strange animals anywhere.

'Lunch at one,' he said, looking at his watch. 'I'll come and take you over to the canteen.'

'Great,' I agreed, and he sidled out of the door, disappearing into that limbo where liaison officers go when they're not liaising.

Over the next ten days we gradually got to know the thirty-six men entrusted to our tender care, at least to the point of being able to distinguish one from the other. Surnames weren't much of a help

– Mroznichenko and Obolbekov don't exactly trip off an English tongue – but the array of first names, often suitably shortened, meant we could soon tell our Kazats from our Bakays and Ishens. Still, it soon became apparent that we had inherited a thoroughly mixed crew, in more ways than one.

Racially, the Kirghiz certainly predominated, though whether it was deliberate policy or happenstance we never found out. There were four Russian lads, who tended to stick together; we put one in each of our nine-man squads and they soon seemed to fit it. There were also a couple of Uzbeks, who at the outset seemed determined to out-macho everyone else, but soon discovered the error of their ways. The Kirghiz, though undoubtedly macho by Western standards, would have seemed like women's dreams in Colombia.

Our job was also complicated by the existing hierarchy. Three of the thirty-six were officer rank – one captain and two lieutenants – and another eight were NCOs. There didn't seem to be any obvious class distinctions at work, but the officers clearly felt they had more in common with each other than with the men below them, and they had the usual instinctive dislike of being treated in the same way. Fortunately for us the resentment this provoked was held in check by their overriding desire to see the unit succeed. Whether this desire stemmed from a crusading anti-corruption spirit or a simple calculation of where the future perks would lie was hard to tell. A bit of both, I thought in my more generous moments.

Keenness and suitability did not, of course, necessarily go hand in hand. From the first full day I spent with my nine-man squad I knew two of the NCOs – Ishen Saliyev and Kazat Aitmatov – were almost perfect material for the unit we were trying to build. They were both hardy Kirghiz, fit and alert, keen to learn but self-contained. They had the ability to focus on the task in hand, and though at the beginning they had little idea of how to handle their weapons or read a map, they were open to learning. By contrast, their fellow-Kirghiz Bakay was already too full of himself to let anything else in. He talked a lot but he didn't listen, and I already knew that sharing an OP with him was going to be a real character-building experience for some poor bastard.

In an ideal world I would have had him binned on the first afternoon, but we weren't running a selection course – this was the hand we'd been dealt and as far as I knew this was the hand we were going to have to play. By the same token, at the end of the first week I'd have handed out a few promotions and demotions, giving authority to those who'd shown they deserved it. But those powers were also denied us, and when the time came we'd have to devise ways of keeping the upper ranks happy while the real jobs went to those supposedly their inferiors.

But at least we'd not been stiffed with a bunch of complete no-hopers. The vast majority of these lads were pleased to be where they were, fit and far from stupid, and reasonably happy to sit, metaphorically of course, at the feet of their new military gurus. As a much-travelled guru myself I'd seen a lot worse in the way of potential disciples. It was going to take time, but all things being equal we had the makings of a half-decent unit. And one, moreover, that I was beginning to think Kirghizstan deserved. The place and the people were definitely growing on me – no mean feat considering that for the first time I could remember I'd rather have been at home.

During that first ten days most of the training was done on-base. There was a firing range hidden among the trees in one corner, and we spent a lot of the first week teaching our lads the finer points of gunnery. Few of them had ever had reason to fire their AK74s in anger, and none of them had found out the hard way that squeezing the trigger until the magazine was empty was an excellent way of leaving themselves defenceless. We got them in an ammo-conservation frame of mind, and went back to basics – shooting lying down, kneeling and standing with a particular target in mind. It's amazing how many people instinctively think of the machine-gun as a potential shield, as if a continuous burst somehow functions as a wall around the firer. It doesn't, and the ammo runs out in a matter of seconds.

On our first evening on-base the four of us had decided that our remit, and that of the unit we were training, was vague enough to suggest a training regime geared to just about any local eventuality, from anti-smuggling operations through hostage rescue to the search for, and destruction of, drug laboratories. The men would need combat skills for both rural and urban environments, and for both open and covert operations. So while two of the squads were out on the range with the AK74s the other two were in the surprisingly well-appointed base gym, learning about close-quarter fighting. It was hard to know how well the lessons learned in Belfast's alleys and pubs would translate to Osh's alleys and *chaikhanas*, but one thing was immediately clear: our lads didn't need telling twice that the Queensberry rules had been suspended. In fact, a cynic might have thought they'd never actually reached this part of the world, and that gouging, biting and testicular assault were as Kirghiz as mutton pie.

During the second week, when Kadir had cobbled together the necessary materials, we set one group of lads to work making and painting target figures, and once these were finished we created a rough simulation of the Stirling Lines 'Killing House' in one of several empty barrack blocks. Some of the targets would represent friends, some enemies, and the troops would be expected to tell one from the other and act accordingly. Not surprisingly, quite a few allies bit the dust in the first few run-throughs, but the men soon learned. After a couple of days of this the targets were transported to an area of forest a few miles to the south, and the men were sent through the target area both singly and in groups to test their reactive skills. Again, the learning curve was satisfyingly steep.

The men were beginning to enjoy themselves, and for several obvious reasons. It was all new and different, a break in the usual routine; each man was boosting his individual self-esteem, and, with few exceptions, was acquiring a collective pride to go with it. And, of course, like most men everywhere, they enjoyed playing cowboys and Indians, or whatever the Kirghiz equivalent was. Mongols and Kirghiz, I suppose.

It wasn't all fun, either for them or us. The map-reading sessions were intensely frustrating for all concerned until our linguistic connections improved, and two meetings with Lisinov did nothing to dispel the impression that the whole exercise was vaguely conceived and alarmingly open-ended. Would the four of us end up like colonial emissaries from the days of Empire, sent off to some remote corner of the world and then forgotten for decades? I liked Kirghizstan, but not more than three months' worth.

Trying to pin Lisinov down was a fruitless task. He always seemed to come up with what I asked for – either in person or through Kadir – in the way of equipment, logistical support or accommodation, and always seemed pleased with the reported progress, but he wouldn't sanction any binnings or replacements and insisted on postponing any talk of promotions. I sent Hereford a lengthy report by e-mail and was told to stop moaning and get on with it.

The hours we spent off work were more problematic than those on the job. We were on friendly enough terms with most of the men, but doing a lot of socializing with them would break down barriers that we would still be needing in the training situation for a while yet. The invitations were pouring in for us to visit various homes during future days off, but we tactfully turned those down too – we couldn't accept all of them, and we didn't want to pick favourites.

We did accept an invitation from Kadir, though, and spent a pleasant evening at his apartment in Bishkek. His wife smiled a lot and cooked us a traditional local stew, his two sons stared at us – and especially at Gonzo – for the whole evening, and Kadir himself proudly displayed his membership cards to the great world outside: a shelf of eighties pop cassettes, a small Japanese TV and, in pride of place, a Teasmade which he said he'd bought in a Kabul bazaar, and which had probably been looted from the British Embassy. I resisted the temptation to demand it back in the Queen's name and asked him whether he'd served in the war in Afghanistan. It turned out he had, for more than two years in the early eighties. A sad shake of the head accompanied this response, which I took to mean that he'd rather not talk about it, or at least not in the bosom of his family.

That was one of four evenings we ventured into the town – on the other three we went unchaperoned, and behaved about as well as could be expected. There were several good restaurants and bars, the German beer flowed freely and we got moderately pissed on two occasions, rather outrageously pissed on the other, though the only damage done was to the locals' sleep patterns and aesthetic sensibilities. And they could always tell their grandchildren that they'd heard 'The Surrey with the Fringe on Top' sung in Welsh. Several times.

The rest of the evenings were spent in our luxury hut on-base. We soon finished our own books, cursed our way through the appalling crap the others had brought with them and then sent Kadir out to scour the town. After his first try he returned with two Enid Blytons which had been published in the forties and a Russian translation of Frederick Forsyth's *The Day of the Jackal*. The second was rather more successful, yielding an omnibus of Soviet science fiction, two John Grishams and a novel about the breaking of the Enigma code in the Second World War.

Sometimes we tried listening to Lulu's radio, but the reception was never good – because of the nearby mountains, probably – and when we did manage to make out something through the snap, crackle and hiss it was usually bad news, like an England batting performance or the Tories stumbling on something new to sell off. No *Archers* tape had arrived from England so I had no idea what was happening in Borsetshire.

We all had our Walkmans, of course, and had chosen to believe Kadir's promise that Bishkek was awash with replacement batteries. I revelled in Otis and the Jam, Sheff twitched to his hip-hop and rap, Lulu listened, mostly in silence, to his appalling show tunes and Gonzo, needless to say, flipped from Bach to Thelonious Monk to Abba and nicked everyone else's cassettes when we weren't looking.

Other than that we ate and slept and, in Sheff's case, went outside every ten minutes for a cigarette. The food in the base canteen wasn't as bad as we'd expected, and we'd bought enough tins of tuna and baked beans and packets of savoury noodles – Stroganoff was the favourite – to give ourselves a treat every few days. We washed it all down with tea, coffee and hot chocolate brewed on our hexamine stoves, and generally opened the windows once a day to prevent a methane chain reaction. The bunks weren't too uncomfortable, and provided you got to sleep before Lulu started snoring there was plenty of time to dream about home.

And I did. I missed Ellen. We talked on the phone every few days, but somehow that emphasized the distance as much as it shrunk it. There was no point moaning about it – I hadn't exactly been press-ganged – but I wasn't about to pretend to myself that I was just taking this separation in my stride. The job was going better than I'd expected, I liked the place and the other lads were a laugh – most of the time, anyway – but I missed her anyway.

On the surface at least, the other three were coping with distant exile better than I was. Beside spending more time with headphones clamped over his head than the rest of us put together, Lulu had somehow managed to adopt a dog, which slept in the bunk under his and followed him everywhere. He named it Mutt, which seemed appropriate enough – its breed was either unknown to us or too muddled for identification. Lulu also spent a lot of time just sitting staring into space, looking for all the world like Buddha's evil twin, but no deep philosophical pronouncements emerged. Sometimes there was a look in his eye which seemed to portend something profound, but it was only a fart gestating.

Don't get me wrong, though – he wasn't unsociable, and he got on with the locals as well as any of us. There was something so damn straightforward about him, and he never seemed to get angry with anybody.

Gonzo was popular with the locals too. He was so interested in everything about them and their lives and their country and they responded to that. He'd been struggling with a Kirghiz phrase book since we'd left England and after a couple of weeks he started trying out a few words on them, which impressed them even more. The rest of us only picked up the usual few words: yes/no, please/thank you, hello/goodbye, good/bad. We particularly liked the Kirghiz word for good, which was *jakshy*, and thought it sounded even better in its emphatic form – *fucking jakshy*.

If Gonzo missed his wife and kids it was really hard to tell. He was always full of them, wrote great long letters to them both individually and collectively, but he never expressed any discontent at the separation. I eventually decided that he was one of those lucky people who manage to live in the here and now, and don't, like most of us, waste half their lives wishing they were somewhere else.

Sheff had no one to miss – if you didn't count Western womankind, that is – but he was having a harder time settling than the other two. He got on with the locals OK, but he wasn't a natural teacher. He was used to communicating in jokes, something which is a lot harder to do in someone else's language, and at first he found having to explain his witty asides really frustrating. At the same time, he was clearly fascinated by the way Gonzo established such an easy rapport with the men, and I put their two squads together whenever I could. This was what I liked about Sheff, and the main reason I'd wanted him along – almost despite himself, he found the world a really fascinating place. He was reluctant to show it – something I understood from my own childhood – but he really wanted to learn and grow.

The schedule we'd arranged with Lisinov involved everyone having each second weekend off, and by lunchtime on our second Friday on-base we were ready for a break. Those of our men who lived within travelling distance were allowed home a few hours early, and the rest had more time than they'd expected to prepare for a riotous night on the town. The four of us, along with our faithful liaison officer, headed east, still basking in that sudden popularity which teachers always gain from an early dismissal.

We were heading up towards Lake Issyk-Kul and the Tien Shan mountains, partly as sightseers and partly in preparation for the weeks ahead. The lake was about a hundred and ten miles away, the town of Karakul more than twice that, but we'd only gone about forty when Kadir's jeep turned off on to a side road, apparently at the gesticulating Gonzo's insistence. The other three of us followed in the Lada, idly wondering where we were being led. We were out of school, and it seemed much too nice a day to get upset by a change of plan.

Five or six miles down the road we found ourselves admiring a sixty-foot minaret. It was, Gonzo explained, all that was left of a city which the Mongols had spared.

'I'd hate to see the ones they didn't,' Sheff muttered, looking round.

'They renamed it Golbalik,' Gonzo went on, doing

the tour guide bit to perfection. 'It means "good city".'

'They must have patted it on the head with a sledgehammer,' Sheff said.

It wasn't much of a monument, but the setting was stunning. The minaret stood in the mouth of a valley, the soaring mountains at its back, the foothills and plain at its feet stretching out towards Siberia and the Arctic. I could just about imagine the bloke up top calling the faithful to prayer six hundred years ago, enjoying the view as he did so. Except, of course, for the morning on which he saw the Mongols pouring over the horizon. He wouldn't have known what a good mood they were in.

We restarted our journey, having replaced Gonzo with Lulu as Kadir's companion in the jeep. This arrangement did more to block the view ahead, but unless we ran into a flock of sick animals it was likely to speed things up.

Once back on the main road we did make better time, climbing out of the Chu valley through a dramatic gorge, breasting a bare and rocky pass, and curving down a narrow valley to the shores of Issyk-Kul. The name meant 'Warm Sea' according to the ever-helpful Gonzo – despite lying at over four and a half thousand feet, the lake never froze. Eighty rivers ran in, none ran out, and it played host to the world's smallest navy.

It was a gorgeous sight, a vast sheet of shifting blues surrounded by snowcapped mountains, beneath an azure sky hung with a few lost-looking clouds. And as we drove east along the road which hugged the northern shore the fiery white summits of the Tien Shan range sparkled in the mirror-like surface of the lake.

It was late afternoon by now, and we were soon driving in shadow, the sunlight receding up the slopes to our left. We passed through several small communities, one of which boasted an enormous complex of concrete buildings. It looked like a prison, but Kadir later told us that it was a famous sanatorium.

Darkness had fallen by the time we reached Karakul, the main town in the basin and our destination for the night. After two weeks in a hut we were looking forward to two nights in a hotel, but Kadir was eager to visit the local Army base before those in charge disappeared for the weekend, and we foolishly agreed. The base, which occupied a large area on the south-west corner of the town, had been built by the Tsars, used by the Red Army, and was now host to part of the CIS border force, most of which seemed to be composed of Russians. The Siberian in charge had already been warned to expect us, and seemed only too pleased to offer our unit accommodation over the next couple of weeks, but for the moment he and his staff of officers were more interested in giving us a sample of Russian hospitality.

We all knew what to expect, but there was no diplomatic way to avoid it. I remember the first couple of hours and the first ten or so shots quite vividly, along with a lot of deafening singing, but after that everything got very fuzzy very fast and I wasn't surprised to wake up in a bunk-bed with a particularly bright sun lancing through the window.

I sat there massaging my temples for a while, hoping we'd made friends rather than enemies.

According to Kadir, who appeared a few minutes later, we'd behaved in exemplary fashion. The Siberian CO, who was apparently an Abba fan from way back, had particularly enjoyed discussing the philosophy behind 'The Winner Takes It All' with Gonzo. Apparently he hadn't realized that the song was a prophetic hymn to the end of the Cold War.

Neither had I, but then what did I know?

We said our goodbyes, booked into a hotel and took a bleary look round the town. Its centre was full of the usual Soviet concrete, but elsewhere there were lots of old Russian gingerbread cottages and wooden colonnaded shop fronts which suggested the Wild West. Or, I suppose, the Wild East.

Businesswise, we talked to several of the local tour people. Gonzo was fascinated by the honey-tasting trips which one firm organized, but unless honey smuggling was becoming rampant in the area we didn't see how we could justify it. More to the point, we got an idea of the various treks on offer, and then sat down with a good map of the area to discuss possibilities. Once we'd come up with a rough plan of action Kadir was sent off to fill our want list, which included things like a helicopter, ground transport and accommodation at an army camp higher up in the mountains. It was time our lads started putting their fitness and map-reading skills to the sort of tests they couldn't get on-base. We were a long way from the Brecon Beacons, but the Tien Shan mountains looked like they'd just about pass muster as a substitute.

6

We drove back to Bishkek on Sunday afternoon and settled down to wait for Lisinov to fill our latest shopping list, half-expecting either a long delay or outright refusal. But someone obviously wanted this unit to prosper, and half a lorryload of hard routine gear arrived on the Monday afternoon. The men fingered their new Gore-tex sleeping bags as if they couldn't believe material that thin could possibly keep them warm, and eyed the cold rations with understandable distaste.

On Tuesday morning we set out in two lorries for the CIS camp in Karakul. A Mil Mi-8 'Hip' helicopter could have ferried us up there in a quarter of the time, but we didn't fancy being totally dependent on the Russians for road transport once we got there. Our trusty Lada was left to gather rust in Bishkek.

We arrived before nightfall this time, and the evening was spent settling in and warding off Russian requests for a rerun of Friday night's get-together. Life obviously got boring for border troops, I thought unsympathetically, little realizing that soon I'd be finding out just how boring at first hand.

Our lads were anything but bored the next morning

when we announced that half of them were setting off on four-day hikes. Two groups, accompanied but not led by Sheff and Lulu, would cover one of the favoured local trekking trails in opposite directions. It wasn't a particularly difficult trail, climbing one valley into the mountains and descending by another after crossing a twelve-thousand-foot pass, but the men would be on hard routine – there would be no fires, no hot food, no shelter from the wind but what they dug or constructed for themselves. They'd have the chance to bond as a unit. Or kill each other.

The other two squads were set a different task. On the previous Sunday morning we had driven up to Inylcheck in the Tien Shan, and soon after turning off the road from Karakul to Kazakhstan, in a lovely alpine valley, we'd come across a checkpoint manned by a surly bunch of CIS border troops. According to Kadir, this had once been the spot beyond which unauthorized climbing and hunting expeditions could not pass, but these days Kirghizstan's hunger for foreign currency meant that all such trips were authorized, and the reasons for this checkpoint's continued existence were a mystery.

It had its use for us, though, as an object for observation. The two squads were delivered to within six miles of the site with instructions to set up OPs on different sides of the valley, to keep the checkpoint under observation for forty-eight hours, maintain a detailed log of anything and everything which they thought relevant, then make their way back to a prearranged pick-up point – all without being observed. Without telling our lads, we actually alerted the border troops to their presence, but apparently they did a pretty good job of staying out of sight. The logs weren't bad either, though one squad was a lot more thorough than the other when it came to recording the vehicles which passed through the checkpoint and the various routines the guards followed. We pointed out all their mistakes at the debriefing, and lavished praise where it was due, but the main point of the exercise had been to give them a taste of the boredom and discomfort which long periods in an OP often require. Shitting in plastic bags isn't everyone's idea of a good time, and some people have trouble keeping still for five seconds, let alone five days. We couldn't weed out the 'hypers', but we could at least confirm who they were, and give them a chance to learn a bit of the old Buddhist calm. Later on, jumping from foot to foot was likely to get them killed.

Saturday was spent on-base in Karakul, going over the lessons which had and hadn't been learned, and on Sunday morning the four squads switched places. Gonzo and I had our chance to see the mountains, while Sheff and Lulu watched the watchers above the checkpoint. Since we'd arrived in Kirghizstan the temperature had seemed to rise almost daily, and now the days were really beautiful, the sun shining out of that deep blue sky which high altitudes bring. At night it was still bitterly cold, but the stars were more numerous than I'd ever seen, and at dusk a new moon hung over the silhouetted western peaks like something out of a photo magazine.

On Thursday and Friday we tried a variation of the OP exercise. In the abandoned cottage which Kadir had found in a nearby valley, he, Sheff, Gonzo and two of the lads set up a dummy heroin-refining lab. The props were mostly sheets of plywood with things like 'refining equipment' chalked on them in fairly small letters, and each of the workers wore a small cardboard badge explaining his role. Gonzo, needless to say, was the head chemist.

The four squads were then amalgamated into two, and each was given a map reference for the place and twenty-four hours to observe, mount a CTR (close target recce), and come up with an operational plan for the seizure of the lab and its workers. The location wasn't ideal – there was much more cover than seemed the norm in Kirghizstan – but it gave them an idea of what might be required, and apart from allowing the head chemist to escape they handled it pretty well.

By Friday evening both they and us were pretty shagged out. Most of the men came from families who had been city dwellers for a couple of generations, and they weren't much more used to the thin air of the high pastures than we were. The four of us were fitter to start with, but treks at twelve thousand feet are still bloody hard work, and we were looking forward to a nice peaceful weekend in Karakul before starting up again on Monday morning. As we set off for the first beer we were still blissfully unaware of the fact that Lulu was about to start another world war with the Germans.

On our first day in Bishkek, I'd come back from my meeting with Lisinov and Orozbakov to find a group of mostly Western men examining the pelt of a snow leopard. It was apparently on sale for $10,000, which seemed precious little for one of the most endangered species on earth, but I heard an American voice complaining that this was three times the usual market price. Later I saw brochures at several places in Bishkek and Karakul extolling the variety of rare animals available for killing in Kirghizstan, ranging from obscure species of duck through ibex and brown bears to the giant Marco Polo sheep.

I asked Kadir what he thought about it all, and got a helpless shrug. The hunters paid upwards of $5,000 for a licence, and more than that for their helicopter shuttles to the high pastures and their Kirghiz guides. A lot of the money was funnelled back into ecological surveys and breeding programmes, he claimed, sounding almost as unconvinced as I was. And his country needed the money, he added. Which was no doubt true.

In Bishkek, as I found out over the next two weeks, it was hard to avoid the hunters, who tended to congregate in hotel lobbies and the more expensive restaurants. They were all men, most of them aged between their mid-thirties and mid-fifties, and they came from all the rich nations. They reminded me of my favourite Bob Dylan line: 'When money doesn't talk, it swears.'

I guess I've always thought that shooting essentially defenceless animals for trophies was kind of pathetic, but this bunch had taken it to a completely new level, shooting endangered species just for the thrill of killing something rare and different.

All of which is offered by way of a background to the events of that Saturday night in Karakul. Our destination was a restaurant-bar we'd discovered two weekends before, which had a nice outside terrace overlooking a street and the park beyond. There was an open space between the restaurant and the hotel next door, and as we walked past Sheff noticed a van with a strange cargo. The faded red cross on its side suggested the vehicle had previously done time as an ambulance, but it had now been relegated to ferrying the dead, and not even the human dead at that. Visible through the gaping rear doors, curled up to safeguard the amazing spiral horns, lay the body of a Marco Polo sheep.

There's a scene in the film *Starman* in which Jeff Bridges, an alien in human form who's trying to get back home, comes across a dead deer on the back of a hunter's truck, touches it gently and brings it back to life. Watching Lulu reach out to caress the creature's head I half-expected it to start breathing again, but, despite all indications to the contrary, Lulu had been born in a human body, and the animal remained depressingly dead.

It was then that the Germans appeared. There were four of them, which in retrospect seemed a thoroughly appropriate number.

Now I know there are nice Germans out there – I've met a few myself – but there's a particular type of moneyed aristocratic German that seems to just love hunting in the world's more inaccessible places, and for this select group of men the phrase 'arrogant bunch of bastards' was the perfect fit.

'Get away from my kill!' was the first greeting thrown our way, and it kind of set the tone for the whole exchange. The Germans strode towards us, and I swear if they'd been carrying leather gloves they'd have been slapping their thighs with them.

Lulu still seemed oblivious to everything but the dead sheep, and when the first German tried to shove him aside he looked up with a start, like someone waking from a dream. And then his face hardened around the dreamy eyes, and the two men eyeballed each other for what seemed an eternity but was probably only about five seconds. It was like a picture of worlds colliding, on the one side utter certainty, on the other complete incomprehension.

The next thing I knew Lulu had smashed the German in the nose, splashing all of us with blood, and Sheff had done much the same to the one behind him. I suppose what followed could be called a fight, but I think even a Marco Polo could have taken on this lot without their monogrammed hunting rifles.

It was stupid, of course, and the whole business would have fairly far-reaching effects as far as I was concerned, but looking back I still find it hard to feel any real regret. More often than not there's a little bit of justice on both sides of a dispute, but every now and then there's a group of people who just deserve all they get, and this was one of those.

We celebrated the victory for righteousness with several local beers – German brews seemed inappropriate – and when the local police arrived we obligingly accompanied them to the local nick. Various phone calls were made, and eventually a tight-lipped Kadir arrived with the news that the whole unit was being transferred to Osh. In the south of the country, he told us, we would have a better chance of breaking Kirghizstan's most lucrative trade: drugs. And less opportunity of wrecking their number-two earner: dead animals.

We all piled into the lorries on the following morning for the return journey to Bishkek. Our lads had already heard what had happened, but I went through the incident for them anyway, adding that I hoped our actions wouldn't prejudice the future of the unit. I expected at least a few reproachful glances, but nobody seemed in the least put out by the turn of events, and the mood on the drive back seemed, to me at least, surprisingly upbeat. Only Lulu seemed really sorry about what had happened, and when he started on his third apology the rest of us had to tell him to put a sock in it.

We arrived back in Bishkek in mid-afternoon to find a summons from Lisinov waiting at the base. Kadir dropped me off outside the Ministry, claimed he had our travel arrangements to see to, and promptly disappeared in a cloud of exhaust. I sat in the lobby for about half an hour, feeling like a kid outside a headmaster's study, before Orozbakov and Lisinov deigned to see me. The former just gave me smug looks, as if all his forebodings about us had been realized, while the latter tried hard not to say how disappointed he was by our behaviour. Of course he understood that we'd been provoked, but I had to understand how important these people were to the country's economy, and that in the interests of forestalling further trouble he had been forced to remove us from the area. He hoped that our training programme was well enough advanced for the change of scenery not to matter, and that the unit's relocation to a place nearer the heart of the problem would actually prove beneficial.

I agreed with everything he said, partly because I knew we didn't have a leg to stand on, and partly because he was right.

We then got down to talking about the unit, which I told him seemed to be gelling pretty well, and where it would fit into the current police and military set-up in Osh. The local commander's name was Genghis – no relation, apparently – Borkeyev, and for the time being we would answer directly to him.

There was something in Lisinov's tone – a hint of distaste perhaps – as he mentioned Borkeyev, which made me wonder. I couldn't exactly ask, 'Do you think the guy's a crook?', so I just asked him whether Orozbakov and himself were still our real bosses.

He took the point immediately. 'You can always contact this office if you have problems,' he said. 'With Borkeyev' were the two unspoken words at the end of the sentence.

I left the Ministry feeling more positive than I'd expected, but a subsequent fifteen-minute chat with the CO in Hereford left me rather the worse for wear. The four of us – and me in particular as the man in charge – were definitely in the Regimental doghouse. MoD and Foreign Office minions had been practising their sarcasm on the CO, and we hadn't left him with anything to fight back with. SAS training teams were not supposed to get in public brawls; on the contrary, they were supposed to be damn-near invisible. If we were unlucky, and the ongoing attempts to suppress news of the incident ended in failure, then there would be rabid anti-German headlines in the tabloids, Questions in the House and heaven only knew what else. Our little contretemps in Karakul would make it harder to sell the Regiment to the Treasury as the jewel in the crown of the British Armed Forces, and harder to sell our services to the rest of the world.

I listened to all this, tried to absolve the others of all responsibility – I had only two more years to serve – and pledged to be a better boy in future. When I got the chance to string a whole sentence together I told him the job was actually going well, and that with any luck Kirghizstan would soon have the beginnings of a unit to be proud of.

I could hear the sigh. 'Just don't fuck up again,' he said wearily.

Next morning we took possession of a whole carriage in the yard outside Bishkek station, and were eventually shunted on to the back of the afternoon train to Tashkent, which was scheduled to arrive in the Uzbek capital at eight the following morning. From there another train would take another sixteen hours to pull us through the Fergana valley to Osh. It seemed a hell of a long way round, but Kadir's explanation for our not flying – that there was a chronic shortage of aviation fuel – seemed ludicrous enough to be true. I could certainly understand why Lisinov didn't want to let us loose on the mountain roads – we might run into some hunters and do our Animal Liberation Front impersonation again – but what I couldn't fathom was his not having our carriage windows boarded up. What would happen if we disliked something we saw *en route*?

Maybe he'd realized that most of the trip to Tashkent was in darkness. The four of us had a long talk in English about what we thought we'd achieved, and which shortcomings we should be concentrating on next, and then joined the rest of the unit in a fruitless search for the Land of Nod. The state of the track was bloody dire, and the occasional decent stretch did nothing more than lull us into a false sense of security, offering the prospect of sleep only to jerk it away at the last moment. Several times during the night I was convinced we'd actually come off the rails, but the train just rattled onward. Dawn seemed a long time coming.

We had an hour-long lay-over in Tashkent, which gave the lads time to go scavenging for food and James from the Embassy time to give me my third earwigging in twenty-four hours. The only thing which seemed to mitigate our crime against the British Empire was his sudden discovery of an even greater one: our wilful abandonment of the Lada. The news that it was sitting unattended in the base we'd left behind brought on a paroxysm of anxiety, and he immediately disappeared in search of a phone to call the American Embassy in Bishkek.

We were attached to another train, which pulled

us southward for nearly another hundred miles, to the junction with the Fergana valley line. Another wait, another train, and we spent the rest of the day and half the following night meandering eastwards up the valley. There were frequent stops for inspection by Uzbek police, two lengthy frontier stops as the line passed in and out of Tadjikistan, stops to let people on and off, stops for no apparent reason whatsoever. All those people who complain about British Rail have obviously never travelled on trains anywhere outside Western Europe. In Uzbekistan the 125 would have to be renamed the 12.5.

Our carriage finally reached Osh courtesy of a goods train at about three in the morning, which is not usually the time to see a town at its best. Borkeyev had someone waiting for us, though: a liaison officer to liaise with our liaison officer. They talked for a while, then announced that I was expected in Borkeyev's office at eight sharp. That decided, we settled down to wait for the lorries which were supposed to be taking us to our new home.

They arrived three hours late – clearly the drivers hadn't fancied night work – and transported us about half a mile down the road to a dusty-looking base area with the usual rows of barracks and limp flag. This time we were in with the unit, which didn't worry us half as much as it seemed to worry Kadir. By the time we'd all grabbed our piece of territory and sorted out our kit I just about had time for a shave and a lukewarm shower before setting off for my appointment.

*　　*　　*

Like Bishkek, Osh had its backdrop of snowcapped mountains, but Kirghizstan's second city had a very different feel to it. Maybe it was the predominantly Uzbek population, and cultural subtleties which I was only half-aware of, or maybe it was just that it seemed a lot hotter, drier and dustier. Bishkek had seemed to straddle some sort of line between Russia and Central Asia, but Osh left no room for doubts on which side it sat. This was Islamic Asia, and it was Soviet concrete architecture, not the minarets, which seemed out of place.

Genghis Borkeyev's office, to which my two liaison officers delivered me – the new one's name was Sagim – was in an old Soviet admin building just south of the city centre. He seemed to be Osh's equivalent of a chief constable, but even Kadir didn't seem sure of what post he officially held. I assumed he was ex-KGB, and probably some sort of local Godfather. I only hoped he needed Lisinov as much as Lisinov seemed to need him.

His office was full of modern knick-knacks: cellular phone, fax machine, one of those ornaments full of silver ball bearings which click away into infinity. There was a large map behind his desk and two almost identical paintings of whirling horsemen on the opposite wall. Through the two windows there was a view of roofs stretching away towards the mountains.

My first impression of Borkeyev himself – one that refused to go away on subsequent meetings – was that he looked like a Chinese Mussolini. The Kirghiz facial features weren't exactly reminiscent of Milan High Street but the bald head, barrel chest and thrusting jaw – the whole stance of the man, in fact – suggested that Il Duce had been reincarnated in Osh.

We shook hands formally, and my smile wasn't returned. On the contrary, I was getting the sort of suspicious once-over usually reserved for just-discovered animal droppings. Just where the suspicion came from I didn't know, but I could hazard a few guesses. He might have heard about our problems in Karakul, he might not like the idea of intruders on his patch, he might not like foreigners full stop. He might see us as Lisinov's fifth column, or he might have his snout in the local trough. Then again he might just be a miserable bastard.

He certainly wasn't talkative, so I took up the running. I said I assumed he knew about the unit and what duties it was intended to perform, explained how far along we were in our training programme, and asked what, if anything, he would be expecting in the way of operational duties while the programme continued.

He looked out of the window and asked if I had any suggestions.

'Well, first I'd like to take a couple of days to familiarize ourselves and the unit with the town and the area,' I said, 'and then I think it would be a good idea to put a couple of checkpoints under observation.'

That got his attention. 'You want to spy on my men?' he asked, trying but not quite managing to sound outraged.

'The stuff's getting through,' I said flatly, 'which means that someone's not doing their job. And the sooner we find out who the sooner your good men will be free of suspicion,' I added with a straight face.

He thought about that for a while and then nodded, as if he'd just managed to convince himself. 'And after that?' he asked. 'Will your unit man the checkpoints?'

'That's not the intention,' I said, getting up and walking towards the map. It was the most detailed I'd yet seen of the area. 'These tracks across the mountains,' I asked, 'are they usable by vehicles?'

'In the summer, sometimes. In the winter there is too much snow, in the summer there are often rockfalls,' he explained. 'And we don't have the resources to cover them all.'

'Do all the drugs from the south come through Osh?' I asked.

He shrugged. 'We think so.'

'Then why not concentrate your resources closer to the city?'

'If we did that they would simply offload the merchandise further out and bring it in on foot or by bicycle or in any number of ways. The valley is too heavily populated, and we can't search everyone or cover every path. If we're going to intercept shipments then it must be in the mountains.'

'What happens when the drugs reach Osh?' I asked. 'Are they transshipped immediately or stored? Or do the original carriers just keep driving?'

Another shrug. 'Some go north, some go west,' he said unhelpfully.

'I think we need to discover a major shipment *en*

route, let it pass, then see where in the city it ends up,' I said bluntly.

He nodded slowly. 'That sounds like a good plan,' he said, sounding about as sincere as a logging company boss extolling the beauty of trees. 'Our country cannot afford to become a haven for criminals,' he added, as if it was a line he'd just remembered. 'But it is this office that is ultimately responsible for bringing these people to justice, and I must insist on being kept informed of any operations involving your unit.'

'That goes without saying,' I said.

'Major Sagim will be permanently attached to your unit while it remains in Osh,' he continued, as if I hadn't.

We obviously weren't going to suffer from any lack of liaison.

For the next few days we did what I'd told Borkeyev we'd do, and familiarized ourselves with the area. A couple of the men in our unit were from the city itself, another from the nearby town of Ozgen, and with these three as guides we crammed ourselves, officers, NCOs and liaison twins into the three jeeps on offer and set out to explore. The rest of the unit, meanwhile, were dispatched on foot to wander the town and bring back whatever intelligence they might find.

The population of Osh was only about 250,000, but the place had an air of bustling self-importance which many a larger town lacked. It had apparently been around since the fifth century BC, which was longer than either Bruce Forsyth or Cilla Black. There were no great monuments, though, and according to

Gonzo the only site of interest was the hill of bare rock which loomed over the town, and which we could see from our base. It was called Solomon's Throne for reasons that no one seemed sure of, and visited by pilgrims who believed that Muhammad had once prayed there.

The modern centre of the town comprised two parallel roads running north-south between the rock and the river, and squeezed between river and road stretched a mile-long bazaar which sold everything from embroidered hats to plastic buckets, freshly forged horseshoes to Madonna cassettes. Like most markets east of the Mediterranean, it was nearly noisy enough to wake the dead.

In other words, Osh seemed like a normal Islamic town, full of young men in groups, mangy dogs and food-stall aromas beckoning you down the slippery slope to dysentery. One of our lads had told us about the hundreds killed in race riots here in 1990, and how the Uzbek community was still simmering with rage at a hopelessly corrupt Kirghiz administration, but it didn't feel like a town awash with tension. Nor, in daylight at least, did it seem like a drug traffickers' paradise – much less the new capital of the world heroin trade.

I got a slightly different picture that evening when, with the indefatigable Sagim almost stapled to my side, I drove to the Hotel Osh in search of an international telephone line. This took about half an hour to arrange, and in the meantime I was treated to several varieties of rudeness from the staff, some of the loudest and worst music I'd ever heard, and the sight of several groups of men in surprisingly sharp suits who looked like they'd just come back from auditions for *French Connection 3*.

It was a depressing sight, but Ellen soon cheered me up with the news that she'd be arriving in Samarkand in two and a half weeks' time for a four-day stay. If I could get those days off and find transport from wherever I was . . .

Of course I could, I told her, wondering how the hell I was going to get from Osh to anywhere in less than a week.

We spent most of the next day on the road, exploring the local countryside. To simplify somewhat, Osh is the focal point of an X-shaped crossroads, with four major arteries heading out to the four corners of the compass. The one to the north-west soon enters Uzbekistan's portion of the Fergana valley and eventually ends up in Tashkent; the one to the north-east circles the end of the valley and then joins the road to Bishkek which we had taken ourselves a long month before. The drugs from Osh which were destined for Russia and the rest of Europe took one of these two routes.

The road to the south-west follows the foothills of the Pamir Alay mountains, which separate the Fergana valley from Tadjikistan. The one to the south-east crosses a spur of the same mountain chain to the town of Sara-Chay, where it trifurcates, two roads continuing through the mountains into Tadjikistan, a third crossing into western China.

These, with the exception of the last-named, were

the roads which carried the traffic in refined drugs from Tadjikistan and Afghanistan, and it was these which we traversed on our second and third full days in Osh. The south-western road was much less used, but there were frequent turn-offs to the left, leading up heavily forested valleys towards the bare mountains beyond. According to our local men there were more passes than could be counted, but even the best of them were impassable for vehicles. The stuff could be coming over on packhorses, to be later loaded aboard lorries or van, but it would be an exhausting process. And from everything we'd heard it didn't seem likely that the local traffickers were having to raise anything like that sort of sweat.

On the other hand, we passed only one checkpoint on that road, and a pretty sleepy one at that.

Still, the other road, the Osh to Khorog section of the old Soviet M41, seemed by all accounts – police reports, journalistic reports, hearsay – the favoured route. We drove about two-thirds of the way to the border with Tadjikistan, marvelling at the beauty of the scenery and counting checkpoints. There were eight on the road, and apparently another three at the border itself – one manned by the Kirghiz border guards, one by Tadjiks and one by CIS troops. We were told that all three border posts conducted reasonably thorough searches of most vehicles, and a bare rock pass at over eighteen thousand feet wasn't the sort of place you could easily bypass.

The topography was obviously not particularly smuggler-friendly, which meant that the local authorities probably were.

7

Next day we resumed the training programme proper. Nine men from two of the squads, along with two of us instructors, were to establish and man OPs overlooking the lone checkpoint on the road running south-west from Osh and two of the checkpoints on the Osh–Khorog highway, those roughly twelve and thirty miles from the city. These last two carried out regular vehicle searches, rather than just identification checks.

The other eight men from these two squads would be on twenty-four-hour stand-by in Osh itself, ready to investigate any vehicle which those in the OPs had reason to believe was carrying drugs. The other two squads would be in class, trying to improve their map skills, catching up on all the ingenuity which humankind had devoted to the concealment of drugs in seven continents, and training their eyes and nose to spot the presence of the various substances.

The team I was accompanying was nominally led by Ishen Saliyev, whom I'd managed to get promoted to lieutenant before the incident of the Dead Sheep. We had drawn the straw for the further OP on the Osh–Khorog road. The checkpoint we would be watching was situated on a bend amid the green foothills of the Pamir Alay, and from what we'd seen on our drive scattered clumps of bushes and trees offered an excellent chance of getting close enough for our purposes. A small and ancient-looking Soviet helicopter lifted us into a valley some ten miles from the checkpoint in mid-morning, and we had no trouble covering the intervening distance before dusk. Ishen and the other two lads moved across country like they'd been born to it, and they probably had, but I preferred attributing their skills to good training. We were carrying weapons, but not because I anticipated us needing them – I just wanted them to get used to carrying a full load. We would also be on hard routine once we got established in the OP, whether or not there was a convenient spot for after-hours shitting on the other side of the hill. Again, I wanted them to get used to the idea of living in cramped conditions for days on end.

They picked the best sight for the OP without any help from me: just behind the lip of a slight fold in the slope some twenty yards above the road, and about two hundred yards from the crumbling concrete pillbox which served as a shelter for the men who manned the checkpoint's weighted gate. They also dug out the star-shaped scrape with an admirable economy of sound, even though it wasn't really necessary – the men below seemed to like their music as loud as the mafiosi in the Hotel Osh.

And then the boring bit began, sleeping in shifts and shitting into plastic bags, eating cold food and dreaming of a brew-up. At least the weather was kind, the days a perfect blend of sunshine and cool breeze, the nights several degrees above frostbite level. On the first night I lay on my back counting the stars, wishing I had Ellen beside me, but rather doubting whether she'd like the smell of sweat and farts which filled our star-shaped home.

There wasn't much traffic on the road at night, and the Kirghiz soldiers sitting round their fire by the gate below didn't have to jump up very often. After dawn the flow of vehicles picked up dramatically, as if everyone had been parked by the side of the road waiting for light before they started driving, and for a while we reached the dizzy peak of six an hour. There were more lorries than cars, but every vehicle travelling north was given a better-than-cursory once-over, meaning that the guards went so far as to rummage around in sacks of produce, but not so far as to start dismantling vehicles in a search for false compartments.

There did seem to be a lot of lorries for a road from the middle of nowhere, and I realized with some shame that I'd made no attempt to find out about legitimate patterns of traffic in the area. What was in all these lorries?

'Sheep,' Ishen told me. 'Meat. Wool.'

The men below showed no signs that they knew they were being watched. There were six of them, and like us they worked and slept in two shifts. According to Ishen one man was a sergeant, the others privates, and they were all ethnic Kirghiz. They seemed happy enough, whether just sitting round talking with each other, joking with the drivers they stopped, or just staring idly into space. And they had hot food, which was more than we could say for ourselves.

In the middle of our second full day a lorry from the army camp outside Osh arrived with a replacement team for the men below, this one led by an officer, which Ishen thought seemed strange. But there was no discernible difference in the routine of stop-and-search, and when we were relieved by Gonzo and three other members of the same squad that night I had more or less decided that this particular checkpoint, though probably ineffective, was clean.

Back in Bishkek I found that those manning our other two OPs had come to similar conclusions. Which meant one or more of several things: we'd just been unlucky, drug traffic was unusually slow for reasons we knew nothing about, or everyone was being good until the new boys went away.

Or came on board. I also discovered that at various times over the past three days four members of the two squads which had remained in Osh had been approached by men with vague proposals of rewards for services rendered. At least, there were four who reported the fact – others might have kept quiet, either because they imagined even an offer would look bad or because they were entertaining an acceptance. The would-be bribers, according to those who did talk, had not identified themselves as fellow-officials, or indeed anything other than 'friends'.

It occurred to me for the first time – I don't know why it took so long – that I could probably get quite rich quite quickly myself. Trouble was, trying to live with myself if I did would probably cost the earth in psychiatric bills, so I reluctantly resigned myself to doing without all the fashion accessories which seem to go with living the life of a drug lord. Personally, I like jeans or worn cords, and I don't think Pablo Escobar would have been seen dead in either.

Of course, if everyone was being good until the new boys went away, you had to wonder how they knew who we were and what we were doing here. It was possible that one or more of the men in the unit had been blabbing a bit in the town, but we'd made it pretty clear that they shouldn't, and somehow I doubted that they were the source. It seemed much more likely to me that someone in Borkeyev's office was responsible, and there wasn't a lot we could do about that, not with Sagim dogging our every move like a demented traffic warden. We would either have to persuade Lisinov to take us out from under Borkeyev's wing or get very cunning.

First, though, I thought I should address all those members of the unit who were in Osh, which was about seventy-five per cent of them. I wanted to bring the attempted bribes out into the open, make it clear to the men that they could expect more, and that any contact with the 'other side' was at least potentially useful. After doing that, I told them that the better they got at their job the more money they'd be offered, and that they should see this as a sign of both the traffickers' desperation and their own excellence. It was all a bit corny, but they seemed to like it. In an ideal world I would have finished up with a morale-boosting showing of *The Untouchables*, but Hollywood videos seemed to be about the only things which weren't on sale in the town bazaar.

Perhaps someone else realized that the squeaky-clean traffic reaching Osh was a bit suspicious, or maybe the Central Asian drug trade could only be put on hold for so long on account of a few Brits and their disciples, but soon after ten o'clock the following morning Gonzo's OP was on the radio link-up. A car containing two men, travelling from the south, had just driven off from the checkpoint. The car was an old black Zhiguli with the registration number 96-45-44, the two men both smartly dressed Uzbeks in their mid-twenties. The car had not been searched, but money had definitely changed hands between the Uzbeks and the officer in charge. At this moment the latter was sharing it out, no doubt unfairly, with his fellow-soldiers.

It might have been a donation to the Osh Police-men's Ball, but it didn't seem likely, and Sheff and I waited with something close to bated breath for the Zhiguli to reach our other monitored checkpoint some twelve miles down the road.

Here, according to the team Lulu was with, a strange little play was acted out. The two men got out of the car, which was then given a search by two privates which brought new meaning to the word 'cursory'. The officer in charge of his checkpoint, contrary to his usual practice, did not emerge from the concrete hut, a fact which seemed to confuse the two men as much as it did our men in the OP. The two Uzbeks kept looking towards the office, and one of them eventually started moving towards it, only to be stopped by one of the privates. He turned and gave his partner a shrug, whereupon the partner said something which made them both laugh. Still grinning, they climbed back into the Zhiguli and accelerated away down the road.

They were now about half an hour away from the checkpoint on the edge of town, and it was time for the stand-by teams to get busy. Borkeyev had reluctantly loaned us three unmarked Ladas, one of which was already waiting about six miles outside town to pick up the trail of the incoming Zhiguli. Ishen, myself and two other members of the squad now headed for the other two, which we planned to position on the town side of the last checkpoint. We were all in plain clothes, and I was wearing a rather fetching embroidered hat in the hope that it would fool a fleeting glance in a rear-view mirror. With three cars playing leapfrog I thought we'd have a pretty good chance of tracking the traffickers to their lair in the town. It would be like tailing an arms shipment in late-eighties Derry, only without the drizzle.

Ishen and I reached our prearranged position just up a side-road two hundred yards from the check-point. We couldn't see the barrier or the low concrete structure beside it, but the Zhiguli would have to pass through our line of sight to enter the town.

I checked in with the other two cars, and found that our target was now about five miles out. Ishen and I watched a man lead a string of horses along the main road, the last horse shying as a packed minibus hurtled by in the opposite direction. The sun was reaching its zenith now, and I had the distinct feeling I could have fried an egg on the bonnet of our Lada.

I could also feel the adrenalin beginning to flow.

As I checked my watch for the umpteenth time Kazat's voice came through loud and clear on the radio: 'They're approaching the checkpoint. We're three cars behind them.'

In the seat next to me Ishen let out an explosive sigh.

A few seconds rolled by. 'The soldiers are talking to them . . . they're getting out of the car . . . they're walking inside the building.'

More seconds. An exclamation of surprise. A hesitant voice: 'Gunfire – I think that was gunfire.'

'Shit,' I muttered, engaging the clutch and propelling the Lada round the corner and on to the main road in a shower of dust. Up ahead I could see the Zhiguli stranded behind the barrier, two soldiers standing nearby, their heads turned towards the concrete building on the left. They both looked stunned, and as Ishen and I leapt out of our car they made no attempt to intervene.

Kazat arrived at almost the same moment. 'Check the car,' I shouted over my shoulder as I yanked the Browning from the holster underneath my shirt. 'Police!' I yelled as I reached the side of the open door.

Someone inside said something in Uzbek, and whatever it was it encouraged Ishen to advance across the threshold. I followed him in, gun in hand. Inside it was remarkably cool, and almost dark after the brilliance outside, but there was no mistaking the man sitting against the wall, legs splayed and head bowed, several overlapping entry wounds on his chest. There were thick streaks of blood on the wall above him, where he had slithered down.

His partner was stretched out on the concrete floor, one leg bent, one arm outstretched, as if he was climbing. Half his head was blown away, and flies were already buzzing round the torn flesh and brains.

Neither man had a gun in his hand, and there was no sign of one on the floor.

Ishen, meanwhile, was talking to the two live men in the room, neither of whom was wearing a uniform. They looked like Kirghiz to me, but the cold indifference in their expressions didn't bode well.

'Security police,' Ishen explained to me in Russian. 'They say they've done our job for us.'

One of them must have noticed the look of incomprehension on my face. 'These men,' he said in Russian, 'drug traffickers.'

'Why were they killed?' I asked as politely as I could manage.

'They resisted arrest,' the man said.

I locked eyes with him for a moment, but he just stared placidly back at me, so eventually I just nodded and walked back outside.

Kazat was waiting for me. 'There's a kilo of heroin in the glove compartment,' he said.

'Now there's a hiding place,' I murmured.

Ishen came out, followed by the two security policemen, who had apparently just remembered the object of the exercise. One walked across to the car, went straight to the glove compartment and removed the plastic bags. 'Evidence,' he said, and his partner almost managed to stifle a smile.

Yeah, I thought. But evidence of what?

By the time, about three hours later, that Ishen and I were finally granted an audience with the busy Borkeyev, I had my anger back under control. This was probably just as well: getting in a stand-up shouting match with the man would get me absolutely nowhere. If the man was guilty, and I was already half-convinced he was, then we needed solid evidence to prove it.

He was certainly unfazed by the failure of our operation. 'Just a communication mix-up,' he said airily. 'The important thing is that the criminals were caught, and the drugs seized.' He supposed that their deaths had been 'unfortunate', but was inclined to see the bright side of this too. 'At least these people have been shown that we mean business,' he concluded smugly.

He was less pleased with the emphasis I put on the fact that the security police had obviously been waiting for the two men. 'They may have been listening in,' he suggested. 'Old KGB habits,' he added, almost sorrowfully. The officer at the checkpoint who had been seen accepting the bribe would, of course, be questioned, but he didn't think it likely the man would know anything. I found myself almost hoping for the poor bastard's sake that he didn't. If he did, his chances of being shot while 'resisting arrest' seemed a lot better than ever.

Interview over, Ishen and I drove slowly back to the base. Halfway home we passed a *chaikhana* and it occurred to me that a two-sided conversation over a cup of tea might be a good way of finding out what Ishen, and by implication most of the others, were thinking about the way things were going.

'So what do you think happened?' I asked the young Kirghiz once the glasses of tea had arrived.

He thought for a moment, and returned my question with another: 'Why did the men at the second checkpoint not search the car? They weren't paid not to.'

'If they'd found the drugs then they'd either have had to arrest the men or be seen taking a bribe,' I suggested.

'But if they knew they were under observation then why didn't the officer at the first checkpoint?'

I'd been wondering about that myself. 'Perhaps they wanted him caught. A settling of scores, maybe. Or they just needed a scapegoat, and he was the one chosen.'

Ishen shook his head, sighed and suddenly looked for all the world like a worried little boy. 'Why were they killed?' he said quietly.

It wasn't really a question but I answered it anyway. 'So they couldn't lead us anywhere.'

'So why were they allowed to get that far?'

'I don't know. Maybe just to show us who's really running the show.'

'Borkeyev,' he murmured, and behind the little-boy mask I thought I could see the angry determination I was looking for. Suddenly he smiled and looked up at me. 'Sheff told some of the men about that film you wanted them to see,' he said. 'And now we have a nickname for the unit: the Untouchables.'

I grinned. It was the best news I'd heard all day.

* * *

It also made me feel a lot better about sending the whole unit off on the five-day leave I'd arranged with Lisinov so soon after the fiasco of our first operation. But after what Ishen told me I had fewer visions of them sitting round at home telling their families and friends what a waste of time it all was, and rather more of their boasting about the unit they were in, how different it was, how much a part of a better future for their country.

Needless to say, the days I'd chosen were those that Ellen was going to be in Samarkand – the compensations of rank, I think they call it. Most of the men were grabbing overnight buses to whichever corner of Kirghizstan they lived in, and Lulu had accepted an invitation from one of the Osh lads to spend a few days with his grandparents in the mountains to the south. Gonzo and Sheff were coming with me, Gonzo because he couldn't wait to see Samarkand, Sheff because he couldn't think of anything else to do. Or at least that's what he said, but I think the mere name worked its spell on him too.

Not that he knew much about it. 'So what's so special about this place?' he asked as we began the descent into its airport. The journey had been far easier to arrange than I'd expected: a dawn drive to Fergana in the Uzbek part of the valley, a ninety-minute flight to Tashkent and another to Samarkand itself.

'It was Tamerlane's capital,' Gonzo began.

'And who was he when he was at home?'

'He hardly ever was. He was a fourteenth-century warlord who claimed he was descended from Genghis

Khan, and though he probably wasn't, he was almost as successful. He started out in this area and ended up conquering India, Russia, Persia and half of Turkey. He was on his way to conquer China when he died. One of the all-time military geniuses. And a chess master.'

'I heard he wasn't too big on the Geneva Convention,' I said.

'He did have a bit of a dark side,' Gonzo admitted. 'When he conquered a city everything was razed to the ground, so that you could see the mound of skulls from a long way off.'

'A real boon to the building industry,' Sheff murmured as our plane dropped towards what I hoped was the runway, offering glimpses of the city through the windows.

There were next to no formalities at the airport, a taxi almost leapt to greet us the moment I raised an arm, and we were drawing up outside the Hotel Samarkand not much more than twenty minutes later.

Ellen had already checked in. 'See you in three days,' I told the other two, and heard Sheff mutter 'lucky bugger' as I stepped into the waiting lift.

There was no answer to my knock on room 621's door, but when I tried the handle it opened. She was sitting out on the balcony, the city spread beneath her, but I can't say I really noticed the latter – in the words of the song, I only had eyes for her. She was wearing a simple white cotton dress and the sort of loving smile which everyone should see aimed their way at least once in a lifetime.

'Welcome to the fabled city of Samarkand,' she said.

By the time we'd finished making love on the bed inside the sun was setting on the other side of the hotel, its last rays brushing the distant hills to the east. As we lay there I suddenly realized that she hadn't taken the usual precautions, and without thinking about it my mind went straight to why.

'You're pregnant?' I said, making it sound more of a question than it felt.

'Yes,' she said, raising her eyes up to look into mine.

A few months earlier, and I would have expected to be feeling every emotion in the book at that moment, and probably a few that weren't, but so much had changed in that time. Now, knowing that we were going to have a child just felt fantastic.

'How do you feel about it?' she asked.

'Wonderful,' I said, keeping it brief for once.

She looked into my eyes long and hard, as if she wanted to be absolutely sure that I meant what I was saying, and then her face just broke out in this incredible smile. Lips, eyes, even her nose seemed to be smiling.

And I smiled back, and there we were – two more people in the world's most commonplace situation, and its most magical.

After that Samarkand really didn't have much of a chance. We did all the sights – Ulug-Bek's giant telescope, the Shah-i-Zinda mausoleums, the Registan, Tamerlane's tomb – and Ellen took copious notes on all the various services available to tourists. I was particularly interested to see the crypt below the tomb, on account of several SAS colleagues having been involved in a hostage situation there a few years earlier, but it was closed. Ellen spoke to one of the keepers and came back to report, with a completely straight face, that they were still trying to scrub off the words 'Who Dares Wins' which someone had scratched on the old sweetie's tombstone.

All the famous buildings were stunning in one way or another, but all I really wanted to do was run around like a happy headless chicken shouting out that I was going to be a father. Occasionally we ran into Gonzo or Sheff, both of whom seemed to be having a great time, Gonzo revelling in the history and Sheff in a tour guide named Irina whom he'd met in the hotel bar. Ellen and I spent most of our non-sightseeing time in our room, making love like we'd just discovered how good it was.

Four nights and three days wasn't enough, but then it's hard to imagine what would have been.

8

Our return trip to Osh took a lot longer than the journey out, thanks to a four-hour wait for the connection at Tashkent. The three of us drank unbelievably bad coffee in the airport restaurant, took stock of where we thought we'd got to with the job in hand, and wondered out loud about what we should do next.

We all agreed the unit was shaping up well – better, in fact, than we'd expected – but that the chances of it being allowed to fulfil its original purpose in Osh were less than bright. Strictly speaking, of course, the uses to which the unit was put were none of our business, and one option open to us was simply to complete the training programme and leave it at that. We would have created a unit that was capable of doing the job required, and it would be up to the Lisinovs to see that it actually got done.

Trouble was, that felt a bit too much like washing our hands of the whole business. It didn't feel right for starters, and there were a couple of good reasons to go with the feeling. Capability, as football managers are always saying, is about confidence, and it seemed to us that the unit needed a result, needed to get a win under its collective belt to really come of age. And secondly, as the briefers back home had made abundantly clear, this particular stream of drugs flowed all the way across Asia and Europe to lap at the shores of dear old Blighty. Like it or not, it was our business.

So, having found the necessary excuses for doing what we wanted to do anyway, we talked about how we were going to do it. The logical step was to mount the same op as before, only without telling anyone outside the unit that we were doing so. Or at least, no one in Osh. At first it seemed like a good idea to get Lisinov's blessing in advance, but there were practical difficulties in that: we couldn't think of any means of communicating with Bishkek which wouldn't give us away. All telephone calls from Osh would no doubt be monitored, and a personal trip to the capital would put Borkeyev on his guard, just when we wanted to lull him into a false sense of security. We could have tried to call Lisinov there and then, but I wasn't even prepared to trust the Tashkent phones. Uzbeks were up to their ears in the drug trade, and it seemed likely to me that the old KGB's Central Asian network was still pretty much in place.

Lisinov would just have to be pleasantly surprised by how much initiative his blue-eyed boys in Osh were showing.

But fooling the locals wasn't going to be easy. If Borkeyev had any sort of brain he would be expecting at least the possibility of something like this, and Sagim would presumably be counting us out and counting us in with more than his usual devotion to duty. Somehow we would have to find another way of accounting for the men who would be deployed in the OPs, and we were still discussing various possibilities for this when our flight to Fergana was finally called.

This was so bumpy that we had to abandon all conversation, and for what seemed hours I just sat there gripping the metal arms of my seat, hoping that the plane wasn't really shaking itself to pieces, and feeling it couldn't be right – one moment a potential father, the next splashed all over a Central Asian mountainside.

The plane eventually touched down, and we could tell from the stricken looks of the local passengers that we hadn't been alone in finding the flight a touch on the hairy side. After that, the two-and-a-half-hour drive back to Osh was a real joyride. I sat in the back thinking about future trips to Upton Park with my son, as I watched the shadows of evening fall across the deeply indented mountains to the south.

We reached the Osh base around eight, found Lulu already in residence, and took him out for a walk beneath a starry sky. This was nice enough in itself, and had the advantage of putting us beyond the range of any listening devices which had been installed in our absence. I explained to Lulu where we'd got to in our cogitations, and he came up with a suitable smokescreen. In the mountain region to the south-west where he'd spent the last few days everyone knew of several small heroin labs which had been set up by farmers to boost their income. The raw opium came over the Pamir Alay on mules, and generally speaking it was a small-scale business, a sort of drug equivalent of the old moonshine stills that were set up during Prohibition in the US. We were after Kirghizstan's Al Capones, not the local Beverly Hillbillies, but these labs could be useful just the same. We could send a couple of teams up into the mountains ostensibly to root out them out, but actually redirect them across country to take up OP duty above the checkpoints on the Osh–Khorog highway.

It was Sheff who gave voice to the question we were all avoiding. 'Who do we tell?' he asked.

It was a difficult one. Letting the unit in on our plans would probably be as good for morale as deceiving them would be bad. But could we count on all thirty-six men keeping quiet? With the best will in the world I found it hard to believe that not a single man had been persuaded to pass on information to his own country's security police. I said as much.

'Running ops on a "need to know" basis doesn't have to imply lack of trust,' Gonzo argued, and he had a point.

'OK,' I said. 'Ishen and Kazat should lead the OP teams, and they should be in the know. They can brief their men once they're in the mountains. The other squads can be let in on what's going on as the need arises.'

Two days later the unofficially billed Operation Bollock Squeeze was ready to go. Borkeyev had rubber-stamped our plan to clear a few labs from the southern valleys of the Pamir Alay, and had even, it has to be said, rubbed his hands at the prospect. Maybe he didn't like the competition or maybe, against all my instincts, he wasn't as bent as we thought he was. That morning Sheff, Ishen, Kazat and three other men were driven as far as the road would take a vehicle up a valley which supposedly, in its more inaccessible upper reaches, played host to a functioning lab. A time five days hence having been set for their collection, the vehicle then returned to Osh. The six men, meanwhile, struck out on the first leg of the forty-mile trek which would bring them to their real destinations above the M41.

In Osh the rest of the unit continued with the training programme. We gave them refresher courses in weapons-handling and close combat skills, continued the uphill struggle to instil map-reading skills, and practised observation from cars in the town. This last was partly to keep the enemy nervous – we didn't think it would be convincing if we just lay on our backs with our paws in the air – but also partly to get everyone used to our presence in the town. When the calls came in on the specially arranged frequency we didn't want to give the game away by suddenly acting differently.

We had three days to wait, during which time it had been decided not to risk contact between ourselves and the teams headed for the road. They were observing radio silence, we told Sagim, and there was no way of knowing exactly where they were.

The two teams eventually reported in at the pre-arranged times of two and three in the morning. They had both established new OPs on the other side of the road from our previous efforts, a precaution that proved necessary in at least one case – later that day they observed the officer in charge of the further checkpoint climbing up the opposite side of the valley to inspect the old OP, though whether out of interest or to check that it was empty we never found out.

Most of that day, as reports came in from the OPs at regular intervals, I kept Kadir and Sagim busy on a couple of hastily contrived tasks, talking to the local air force about helicopter availability and possible jump-training, and the local army about an inter-unit football match. The reports themselves made interesting listening: the devotion to duty on display during our previous period of observation seemed to have lapsed rather alarmingly. A few vehicles were being searched, but according to one of the men with Sheff they were all driven by Tadjiks, and the searchers were probably more interested in fundamentalist propaganda than drugs. Many lorries were not searched, and several were not even stopped, the guards simply waving them through with a smile. These merited an asterisk on the list of vehicle types and registration numbers which both OPs were keeping.

In Osh we were receiving periodic updates of this list. Since we had no real way of knowing which of the vehicles heading our way were most worthy of attention, and since we were at pains not to attract any attention to ourselves, it had been decided that, rather than following particular cars or lorries, we would simply try and narrow the search. Our three Ladas, ostensibly on observation training duty, were positioned near three of the town's most strategic intersections, and by cross-referencing sightings it was possible to better pinpoint the area of town that most of the target vehicles were heading for. Next day we stationed the three Ladas accordingly, and focused the search still further. Later that evening, as they cruised round the city looking for familiar registrations, one struck lucky. An eighteen-wheeler which had been waved through the first checkpoint almost thirty-six hours earlier was emerging from what looked like a sizeable car repair shop. In the yard were another two lorries, which further observation confirmed were on our wanted list.

Thinking about this, I knew that we might just as easily have stumbled on a genuine firm – one whose drivers were well enough known to warrant a wave-through at local checkpoints – as a drug-trafficking operation. This was what Det work in Ulster had been like: a lot of possibilities to shuffle through before you homed in on one of the Provo arms shipments you were looking for.

That said, this certainly smelled right, and I was more than hopeful that a closer look would prove conclusive. I summoned the unit's two local boys and told them we were going to search out a site for an OP overlooking the property in question. This wouldn't be like setting one up in the mountains, I told them – for present purposes we had to think of Osh as enemy-occupied territory, and we would be carrying weapons.

They nodded, looking nervous but willing.

An hour later we drove into the town. It was only about ten o'clock but the bustle of the day had vanished, leaving a dark maze of ominously empty-looking streets and alleys. I parked the Lada on a piece of waste ground about a quarter of a mile from the target, and the three of us zigzagged our way down several alleys towards it, the black mound of Solomon's Throne looming above the roofs ahead. It occurred to me that the hill itself would have provided a perfect observation site, but for the fact that it was solid rock and bare. The sprawling Muslim cemetery on the lower slopes might conceivably have offered a concealed vantage-point, but I doubted whether our predominantly Muslim lads would relish the idea, and I certainly didn't fancy being lynched by the local fundies.

We reached the obviously new fence which surrounded the property, and slowly began circumnavigating it in search of a likely spot. There were lights on in the larger of the two buildings inside the fence, and one of the two lorries that had been seen earlier was still parked in the large yard. For a moment I thought I heard music coming from inside, but either I imagined it or the breeze shifted because the sound vanished, leaving only the hum of a distant vehicle and the barking of a far-away dog.

Most of the surrounding buildings were one-storey and clearly occupied, and we had nearly completed our circuit when we found an uncompleted and obviously empty two-storey building almost facing the main entrance. It stood close to the foot of Solomon's Throne, but was still high enough to offer a good view of the repair shop from the second storey. This was just a shell, but for some reason one window had been boarded up, and enough building materials had been left lying around to offer concealment. The watchers would be looking into the sun, and would have to be careful with reflections, but otherwise the set-up seemed close to perfect.

An hour before dawn Gonzo and the two men who'd accompanied me moved in with everything they would need for a forty-eight-hour watch. Three more suspicious-looking lorries were waved through the checkpoints on the M41, and two of them ended up in the yard we had under observation. Gonzo took photos of the lorries and all the other visitors, both wheeled and legged, who put in an appearance during the day. Shortly before nightfall he snapped two men whose relayed descriptions seemed more than familiar: they were the two security policemen with a penchant for murder.

I spent the next couple of hours wondering whether to mount a CTR later that night or just bust the place. A CTR would obviate the chance of us getting major egg on our faces, but it would also be a risky business. I wasn't convinced our men were good enough yet for getting in and out undetected, and a fuck-up would let all the local Mr Bigs off the hook. Better to go for broke, seize whatever people, drugs and records were on offer, and nail all the bastards we could.

By the same token the sooner we went in the better. Our presence on the streets would be less remarkable at eight in the evening than three in the morning, and unless the traffickers slept on the premises we would have a better chance of bagging a reasonable haul of prisoners. The only obvious problem was

Sagim, who would still be awake. Rather than complicating matters unnecessarily – by devising some super-devious ruse to get him out of the way – I just told him we were conducting an exercise that evening, and that he was invited along. He accepted without much enthusiasm, little realizing that a task he was beginning to find intensely boring was about to get rather too interesting for comfort.

The number of men I could use was limited by the available transport, and in any case, according to Gonzo there were only five members of the opposition currently inside the repair shop. Lulu's B Squad was the one currently on stand-by, so I went with them. Their OC was Alijon Kassimbekov, a lieutenant whom I'd initially thought too lackadaisical for the job, but who'd come on well under Lulu's tutelage. The squad contained another six Kirghiz – including Bakay, the man I'd have binned at the start, but who'd also come on in leaps and bounds – one Russian and one Uzbek. They received the news of a live ammo exercise with more nerves than I'd expected, mainly, I realized with a sinking feeling, because they had already guessed that it wasn't just an exercise. Sagim seemed infected by the same twitchiness, and I told Lulu to watch him like a hawk.

I outlined what we were about to do, not specifying where we were going to do it, and then handed over to Alijon, who came up with the same plan of action I had. Just before eight we took to our transport, three men in the one lorry we had at our disposal, the other six members of the squad, Sagim, Lulu and myself sharing our three Ladas. Before we left I did the rounds of the vehicles with the cheery news that this was not an exercise but the real thing.

Ten minutes later we were climbing out into a street some two blocks south of the repair shop. On the walkie-talkie Alijon first confirmed that the lorry was in position just over half a mile to the west and then checked in with the OP. There were still at least five men inside the target building.

A couple of men walked past our little gathering, not bothering to hide their curiosity, and Alijon sensibly waited until they were out of sight before setting us in motion. We jogged down one dark alley, crossed a street that was little better lit, and entered another alley, causing one skeletal-looking cat to leap a wall and an invisible dog to start barking. The sound of eighteen booted feet slapping on baked earth was almost musical, and I had the absurd thought that Paul Simon could use it as an intro-cum-background to one of his songs.

We reached the alley which ran along behind the target. The back of the repair shop was just a windowless breeze-block wall, but the two small windows high on the side which faced the other building glowed with light. We all stood there in the gloom, listening to the snip-snip of the heavy-duty wire-cutters, feeling the adrenalin beginning to flow. It was hard making out faces, and maybe I was imagining it, but the look on Sagim's seemed particularly unhappy. Either he knew exactly where we were or just guessed that it wasn't a place his boss wanted us to be.

The hole cut, we passed through it one by one, and worked our way in single file down the gap between the two buildings. No recognizable sounds were coming from the repair shop, but there was a smell in the air, a heavy sweet smell, which made me sigh with relief. Whatever happened in the next few minutes, we hadn't picked the wrong place to hit.

And so far everyone seemed to be doing their best to make their trainers proud. The noise level was excellent, no weapons had been discharged by accident, and the men, though obviously nervous, gave the impression of having something to prove, both to themselves and us. As we stood there, checking the yard ahead for movement, I remember thinking that not many Englishmen get to feel proud of their work while involved in breaking and entering a Kirghiz car repair shop.

Alijon whispered 'now' into the walkie-talkie and we waited, listening for the rumble of the approaching lorry to drown out the myriad small sounds of the evening. It only took a few seconds, and there it was, growing louder and louder until it seemed as if the whole town must be able to hear it. The headlights swept into view on the road at the front, and then the lorry's horn sounded, two short toots in quick succession, just like other drivers had signalled their arrival earlier in the day.

A few seconds later we heard the small door open. There were footsteps, and then we could see the man walking towards the gate.

Alijon gave the hand signal, and we followed him round the corner to where the light poured out through the open door. He ducked through it without hesitation, and didn't make the classic mistake of stopping

to get his bearings, thus creating a bottleneck behind
him. Once inside he moved quickly to the right, and
I, immediately behind him, moved to the left. Both
of our minds raced to take in the scene which greeted
our eyes, fingers ready on the AK74 triggers.

Two-thirds of the interior was just parking space,
enough for three eighteen-wheelers, I'd have thought,
though getting them in and out would have taken
some skill. There was only one there now, and inside
the open rear doors which were turned towards us
a kneeling man was staring towards us, a lighted
blowtorch in his hands, shock in his eyes. Off to
our right was a familiar Zhiguli saloon, and a few
feet away from it another man had been caught in
arrested motion, a suspicious-looking plastic bag in
either hand. He was one of the two security policemen
from the checkpoint.

Beyond the open area, the other third of the building
had been divided off into two or more other areas, and
it was in the doorway to the one on the right, only a
few yards from the Zhiguli, that the second security
policeman appeared for a split second, just as Alijon
was giving the customary warning shout to the two
men fully in view.

They just stared back, but the man in the doorway
abruptly pulled back out of sight, opening fire with
what sounded like an automatic seconds later. The
shots hit the wall above our heads and everyone
promptly went to ground, which gave the security
policeman with the plastic bags a chance to dive
behind the nearby Zhiguli.

The man in the lorry raised the hissing blowtorch,

probably in token of surrender, but a burst from one of the squad's AK74s brought him down, just as another took out all the windows in the Zhiguli. The man behind the car fired blind over the bonnet, hurting no one but discouraging any advance.

There had been no more fire from inside the doorway, but I could hear someone shouting somewhere in the back of the building, and then there was the sound of glass smashing. The bastard was obviously leaving his partner to hold the fort alone, and, just as I was wondering how to get after him, his partner seemed to realize as much. Surrender would have been the wise option, but he took the other, making a dash for the doorway. Our time on the shooting range in Bishkek had obviously paid off, because he didn't even get halfway.

Alijon started towards the open doorway, motioning one of his men to accompany him and two others to investigate the closed door of what I guessed was the laboratory. I stood where I was for a few seconds, thinking. Assuming that the escapee wasn't counting on finding the hole we'd cut in the fence, his only easy way out of the yard was the gates.

I ducked back out of the door and looked left. Sure enough, a figure was moving cautiously along the inside of the fence, all his attention on the lorry which was blocking the gates and the men waiting beside it. One of these – the man who had responded to the hooting horn – was kneeling with his hands behind his head; the other two were standing, weapons ready, staring in the direction of the repair shop. Unfortunately they'd neglected to turn off the lorry's headlights, which meant they'd have trouble seeing anything outside the cone of illumination, like the man by the fence. I was just about to shout a warning when more headlight beams swept across the houses opposite and two cars came squealing to a halt behind our lorry.

Half a dozen men poured out, and it wasn't hard to make out the figure of Borkeyev among them. He strode in through the gates as if he owned the place, which, of course, he may well have done. Glancing to the left, I saw the man by the fence walk towards him, hands in the air.

Our men by the lorry, obviously unsure what to do, had stayed with their prisoner. Deciding that we ought to have a delegate at the conference which was just about to convene in the centre of the yard, I moved quickly forward, but by the time I got there several words had already been shared, and Borkeyev was no doubt up to speed on what had happened over the last few minutes.

He turned to me, and the smile on his lips was a damn sight less convincing than the fury in his eyes. I looked pointedly from the mobile phone in his hand to the one still being held aloft by his underling, and then locked eyes with him. I wanted him to show his hand, and for a moment I thought he was angry enough to do so, but he managed to bring his temper under control. He gave his underling a quick 'don't worry, we'll sort this out later' glance and asked me in Russian what we'd found in the repair shop. 'At least one major shipment,' I told him. 'And probably a lot more – we haven't explored the whole building yet.'

'I assume it's secure,' he said, starting towards it.

There had been no gunfire for several minutes, which meant that Alijon and his men should have seen all there was to see. Which was just as well, because I would have needed to put a gun to Borkeyev's head to slow him down.

We were about ten yards from the door when Alijon came out. 'Lieutenant Kassimbekov is in command of the operation,' I said.

'Is he?' Borkeyev said, and brushed past the lieutenant.

'Well?' I asked Alijon, as we stepped in after him.

'There's a lab in the back room,' he said. 'We found the chemist hiding under a table. And there's a lot of opium bricks. More than fifty kilos, I'd say. Not much of it's been refined, though – just a few kilos. And there doesn't seem to be any paperwork anywhere.'

I walked across to the lorry, and up the ramp which had been placed behind it. The blowtorch was still breathing fire, but its wielder would never breathe again. He was lying on his back, one foot dangling in the space between the original metal floor and the one which his opposite numbers in Afghanistan or Tadjikistan had welded on top of it. A few strips of opium were still visible, lying snugly in their narrow niche.

Fifty kilos would be worth about $25,000 here in Osh, and at least ten times that once it reached the streets of Moscow, Berlin or London in user-friendly form. It should have been a big loss for someone, but I had the distinct feeling that the only people who'd suffered that evening were the two that had died. I'd known from the word go that we wouldn't be able to confiscate the drugs, but I had hoped for enough time to destroy them in a convenient fire.

Still, we'd done the job we were supposed to do, and as far as I was concerned the unit had come through with flying colours. We had a corpse and a prisoner to prove security police involvement, and if that didn't convince Lisinov and his superiors that a purge was overdue in Osh, then it was hard to think what would. Next morning I would be on the phone to Bishkek, and I wouldn't be worrying about who was listening in.

I made the call bright and early, and Lisinov listened to my report of what had transpired over the last few days, occasionally asking for clarification, but otherwise without interruption. I half-expected the line to go dead at any moment, but maybe Borkeyev was too interested in what Lisinov had to say to cut us off.

'I must congratulate you,' was the first thing he said, which wasn't a bad start. 'Your men and the unit,' he added. But then there was one of those pauses which always come before something one caller doesn't want to say and the other doesn't want to hear. 'Look,' he said at last, 'I would like you to believe in my sincerity, to take me at my word. We are withdrawing your unit from Osh, but not for the reasons that you are probably thinking.'

I said nothing.

'As you know,' he went on after a moment, 'Kirghizstan regularly supplies troops to the CIS force which is stationed on the border between Tadjikistan and Afghanistan. And yesterday – long before anyone in Bishkek was aware of the situation in Osh – it was decided that the unit you've been training could only benefit from the experience a three-month deployment would provide. It was also hoped, subject to your government's approval, of course, that you and your colleagues would accompany the unit for at least the first month.'

I didn't know whether to believe him or not. 'Whatever your reasons are,' I said, 'Borkeyev's going to think he's won.'

'Anyone who counts on our not being serious about fighting the drug traffickers will be making a big mistake,' Lisinov said. 'The old guard had seventy years to dig themselves in, and it'll take us a few more to dig the last of them out, but we will. Believe me, we will. We have no other way forward.'

I had to believe him, or at least believe that he believed what he was saying. After all, if everyone was in it then there'd have been no reason to ask a bunch of Brits to create knights in shining armour.

I put down the phone, wondering how the men were going to take the news.

They didn't like either part of it very much. Leaving Osh without a real result pissed them off, which certainly pleased their instructors. Deployment on the Tadjik–Afghan border wasn't any more popular, but from what I could gather, doing time in a war zone didn't worry them half as much as being under Russian command.

My British colleagues weren't leaping for joy either:

now that the excitement of the last few days had fizzled out they'd begun to notice that Central Asia was wearing a bit thin. Gonzo admitted to missing his kids, Sheff was yearning for something with custard, and Lulu was beginning to pine for his menagerie.

'What do you think the boss will say?' Gonzo asked.

'No idea,' I said, but I was also hoping for a ticket home. Border patrols weren't exactly a Regimental speciality, and my wife was pregnant.

In lieu of any other means of communication – we'd originally been told by the Kirghiz government not to bring any radio equipment of our own – I headed down to the Hotel Osh for another battle with Central Asia's telephone system. The others came with me, and we all went fully armed, not knowing how many bosom buddies of the men we'd killed would be frequenting the hotel's pool room. And there did seem to be a convention of local hoodlums underway, giving the whole place an air of *Key Largo* revisited. Eventually Allah and British Telecom conspired to connect me to Hereford, and a mental picture of the old man sitting in his office only made the whole situation seem even more surreal.

He was unsympathetic, as I suppose I knew he would be. The Foreign Office wanted us to accommodate the Kirghiz government by completing the training programme. Her Majesty's Government in general wanted the drug trade halted in its tracks. The Regiment wanted the experience we would gather from such a unique part of the world and such an unusual arrangement – to wit, working under our old enemies the Russians. 'A month,' the CO half-promised, and if I'd had any sense I would have asked him to confirm that in writing.

9

Moving us south was easier decreed than done, so we were to spend several more days twiddling our thumbs in Osh. There was no train to take us where we wanted to go, and aviation fuel was still in short supply. This last, according to Gonzo, was good news – the flight into Khorog, the small town close to the Afghan border which was our destination, had been the only one in Soviet times which entitled Aeroflot pilots to danger money.

Our only other potential means of transport, short of us all walking the four hundred and fifty miles of the Pamir Highway, was a couple of lorries, but these seemed surprisingly hard to prise out of the local Kirghiz authorities. While we were waiting for Bishkek to solve this impasse more briefing material was sent by fax from the Foreign Office to Tashkent, whereby our old friend James spent another few hundred pounds of taxpayers' money delivering it to Osh by hand. In the couple of hours he was with us he offered tales of even greater largesse – the FO was apparently funding a soap opera called, believe it or not, *Crossroads* for Kazakhstan's TV network. It featured the intertwined lives of one

Kazakh and one Russian family, and was, according to James, supposed to counter the current mood of disillusion with capitalism, which was threatening to cause problems for British investors. In the soap inflation was the number-one evil, corrupt officials were always caught, and women had to be careful they didn't end up as single mothers. The free market was portrayed as a stern but fair master, sometimes harsh but always efficient.

All of which James seemed to find quite normal, though he did seem slightly amused by the fact that the producers had refused to incorporate a Foreign Office list of twenty reasons to be cheerful about private enterprise. I listened to him, surprised that I wasn't surprised. It was one of those moments when I knew for a fact that the man who wrote *Catch-22* knew exactly how the world worked.

Reading the briefing I wondered what sort of soap opera the FO had planned for Tadjikistan. Independence had come in 1991, but even before that there'd been serious communal riots, and the removal of Moscow's controlling hand seemed to have exacerbated the polarization of the contending forces. The old communists rechristened themselves the Socialist Party, won a reasonably fair election and celebrated by calling themselves the Communist Party again. The Islamic opposition parties mounted big demos, armed clashes broke out, and the whole thing had escalated into several months of civil war, which ended with the communists in control of most of the populated parts of the country. They had then tried to gild the lily by letting loose death squads on what remained of the opposition, and these remnants, not surprisingly, had headed for the unpopulated hills of the south-east, where they'd linked up with like-minded fellow-Tadjiks across the Afghan border and set in motion a still-recurring cycle of cross-border incursions and retaliations. Somewhere in the middle of this mess a lot of drugs were being harvested, refined and moved.

After much consideration, Gonzo and I decided that the Tadjik soap opera should revolve around a lovable family of drug-running Tadjik fundamentalists who were getting rich on free enterprise. There would have to be alternating episodes for the male and female sides of the family, and we'd need some pretty spectacular all-body garments to bring out the women's sex appeal, but it could be done. We decided to call it *The Al-Arqas* – an everyday story of narco-folk.

Eventually two lorries arrived, putting an end to our flights of fantasy. For reasons best known to the Kirghiz authorities they had been driven all the way from Bishkek, but despite the rigours of the drive seemed in good enough shape to get us across one of the world's highest roads. We'd been ready to go for several days, and soon after dawn on the next morning we went, waving our farewells to Kadir, who was returning to Bishkek, and the crossroads of the Central Asian drug trade.

At least we were heading towards the source of the stuff, I told myself. With any luck we'd still get the chance to do some real damage before we went home.

But first we had to get there. Even without any major breakdowns the journey was going to take two full days, and the state of the road – 'badly surfaced' was how Gonzo's guidebook described it – did not augur well. A couple of nights in luxurious motels would have suited us fine, but the only available accommodation between us and Khorog seemed to be selected yurts and the old Soviet barracks near the Kirghiz–Tadjik border, where we had reservations. I wasn't expecting TVs, king-size beds or a three-course meal, but at that altitude I was definitely hoping for heat.

We'd done two-thirds of the first day's journey soon after our arrival in Osh, but this time round I wasn't so fixated on smuggler-relevant information, and managed to notice a bit more. There seemed to be sheep everywhere as we climbed the valley behind Osh, and their skulls even decorated the occasional roadside grave. For a couple of hours we had occasional sightings of herders on horseback and clusters of yurts, but then clouds began to fill the valleys and the first patches of snow appeared. Soon we were drifting in and out of the clouds, driving between steep cuttings in the blood-red earth, emerging into sudden panoramas of snow-covered peaks. There seemed to be no wheeled traffic heading in the opposite direction, but at one point a shepherd and his flock suddenly loomed out of the mist, and our driver was forced to slam on the brakes.

Soon we were on our way down again, the clouds parting to disclose a valley big enough to lose a small country in. Groups of wild horses watched us corkscrew down towards the bottom, where a braided river full of red silt looked for all the world like rivulets of blood. This was the kind of landscape which made humans feel humble, made them reach for belief in something bigger than themselves, and gazing at this vast valley I found it much easier to understand the local fundies than I would have done in a briefing room.

Our road hit bottom at a crossroads in the small town of Sary Tash. The place looked suitably humbled by its location, but a depressed-looking *chaikhana* provided hot tea for everyone and a chance to stretch our legs. Then we were heading upwards again, past the remains of several lorries which had taken curves too fast, once more leaving the green valleys and meadows for the red earth and snow. We were waved through the Kirghiz checkpoint after about twenty seconds, we crossed the unmanned border in a desolate pass, and we were then subjected to an hour's wait at the Tadjik border post while its commandant checked with the Russians a few miles further on.

The latter's post was built by the side of a crater lake – the highest in Central Asia, according to Gonzo – and the clutch of concrete buildings which housed its occupants looked about as forlorn as human habitations get. We were shown to the one earmarked for our stay, and gazed around the gloomy interior – it was getting dark now – with less than complete enthusiasm. There were four walls, one ceiling, one floor, and . . . nothing else. Our host handed me a fistful of candles and told me the CO would like to see us when we were settled in.

'At least we won't have to worry about the sheets not being clean,' Sheff said.

'I'll take the stain in the corner,' Gonzo chipped in.

It was quite a squeeze getting all forty of us in, so our chances of sharing each other's body heat were pretty good, and maybe, I thought, at that very minute they were setting up a banquet in one of the other huts. I should have known better. They were Russians, they were lining up bottles, and after an hour or so we wouldn't be caring how cold or hungry we were. My only clear memory of that evening was the story the Russian CO told us – presumably early on – about a local forester in the early years of the century who'd kept a pet bear in his cellar. Every guest who came this man's way was given a lethal concoction of tarantula schnapps, which he made from putting hungry spiders in a glass with a few dried apricots and then mixing the poison-injected pieces of fruit with fermented grapes. Once the schnapps had paralysed the guest drinker he was fed to the bear, who had been converted to man-eating by a starvation diet.

All this came out when the forester, captured by the Bolsheviks in the civil war, confessed to disposing of 411 men in this manner. Not sure whether to believe him, the commissar in charge dispatched a Red Army unit to the man's home with instructions to search the cellar. There they found a very angry-looking bear camped out on a thick carpet of human bones. The forester was condemned to death, but before sentence could be carried out locals kidnapped him from the jail, tied him to two camels and stuffed pepper up the animal's backsides. They charged out into the desert, dragging the man behind them, and when he was found several days later the vultures had just about finished with his skeleton.

Another cheery tale from the past, I remember thinking, before the vodka reduced us to raising toasts on behalf of Boris Yeltsin, Gazza and all the James Bonds, even George Lazenby. Still, there were no more complaints about the accommodation, and when dawn reared its ugly head over the mountains to the east there was more than enough lamb fat soup for everyone who could face it.

We were on the road in half an hour, climbing to yet another pass, the highest of the journey at over fifteen thousand feet. I insisted on a five-minute stop to inspect the vast circle of snowy peaks, clambered up a few yards of rockface for a better view, and rapidly found myself out of breath. You could almost feel the thinness of the air, and you could certainly see it in the startling blue of the sky.

The road wound down again, and for a while it ran almost alongside the barbed-wire fence which marked the Chinese border. There was nothing to see on the other side but more mountains, and I couldn't help thinking that there was something more than a little ridiculous about this shiny barrier in the middle of nowhere. It was pathetic really: just one more example of the human compulsion to claim every last piece of land that was going, whether anyone really needed it or not.

Another hour and we were driving into Murgab, a drab huddle of white huts which no one could have really needed. A guest-house provided us with hot tea to wash down our cold rations, and then we were climbing yet another mountain, emerging on to a plateau which looked more like my idea of the moon than anything else. Nothing grew up here, and though the sun was beating down on us it was impossible to escape the chill in the air. We seemed to labour for several hours in this bare world before a short climb took us over the last high pass and we began the one-hundred-and-thirty-mile descent to Khorog. Slowly life returned to the landscape, and for the second half of the ride down we were treated to greenery once more, stretches of forest and terraced fields, the occasional village stretched out along the road.

Khorog itself, which we reached around dusk, sprawled along both sides of the Gunt River's widening valley. In the half-light it was difficult to make much out, but as we found out in succeeding weeks, there wasn't actually much there to make out. The CIS base, a larger-than-expected collection of barracks surrounded by both wire and what looked suspiciously like a minefield, was a mile and a half further south, just above the confluence of the Gunt and the bigger Pyandzh, which eventually merged with another river to form the Amu Darya. For about a hundred and thirty miles in each direction from Khorog the deep valleys and gorges cut by the Pyandzh formed the border with Afghanistan.

As we drove in beneath the manned watch-tower I had visions of frontier forts from a century before, and scarlet-uniformed British troops on watch for the

Fuzzy-Wuzzies. This was Great Game country, and here we were reporting to the Russians.

A Russian adjutant escorted us to our new home, and I guess after the previous night I was expecting the worst, because the barracks in question seemed almost palatial. A rather small palace for forty men, perhaps, but the neatly made bunk-beds, freshly painted wall and scrubbed wooden floor all made a good first impression, and on closer examination the mosquito screens which surrounded the windows were free of holes. The lights worked and the toilets flushed. This was a building which looked like it had been cared for.

The adjutant then escorted me across the dimly lit base to the CO's office for a formal welcome. Lieutentant Colonel Sergei Chechnulin was a blond Russian in his early forties with sunken eyes, the sort of cheekbones which belonged to a thinner man and a wide mouth. He was wearing camouflage fatigues.

And of all the greetings I'd endured since leaving England his was undoubtedly the friendliest. He didn't smirk at me the way Orozbadov had done, lecture me like Lisinov or treat me like an idiot the way Borkeyev had. Most important of all, given the still-tenuous state of my head, he didn't offer me any vodka.

He began by apologizing for our quarters.

'You obviously haven't stayed at Karakul,' I told him.

'Oh, but I have,' he said, and we both laughed. 'And I hope you will enjoy your stay with us,' he went on. 'I'm certainly looking forward to talking with you and your colleagues – I've heard a lot about the British SAS over the years. And I'm also interested in seeing this Kirghiz unit you've been training. We could certainly use a unit which has been specially trained for this sort of work.'

'Who do you have here now?' I asked.

He offered me a cigarette, and when I refused didn't light one himself. 'Two conscript battalions, one Russian and one Kazakh. Several small specialist units, most of whom are Russian. There's a small Russian Air Force contingent based at the airport, which is a mile or so to the north. That's about two thousand men here in Khorog. I'm responsible for about four hundred and thirty miles of border, and there are eight smaller posts in my sector, containing as many men again.'

'Tell me about the border,' I said, looking up at the map behind him.

He swivelled in his chair. 'My sector runs along the river from Rushan here' – he pointed out a town about sixty miles north of Khorog – 'to the river's source in Zorkul Lake. As you can see, it's a deep valley which keeps getting deeper, running through mountains which are hardly inhabited.' He grinned suddenly. 'We're a long way from civilization here.'

I could imagine other Russian officers saying that a hundred years before, but I didn't think I knew him well enough yet to get nostalgic about the Great Game.

'What about the river?' I asked. 'How easy is it to get across?'

'Depends on the season. In spring the current can

be fierce, but for most of the rest of the year it's all too easy to walk across in some places. The border with Afghanistan is legally closed to all traffic in both directions, but enforcing the law is another matter entirely. I have about four men per kilometre for my sector, which is a lot less than the Americans have for their border with Mexico, and look how successful they are! We have only a handful of helicopters, but even if we had hundreds it wouldn't be that much help. Flying conditions are atrocious by day, and much worse by night.' He grinned again, as if he couldn't quite believe how bad it was.

'Who are you trying to stop?' I asked him, wondering how his answer would fit with the FO's briefing.

'Two types,' he said immediately. 'First, the politicals. These are people from Afghanistan who want to spread their religious fanaticism through the Central Asian republics. Many of them want to fan the embers of the civil war here in Tadjikistan, but even if they won here they wouldn't stop. They carry weapons, both for themselves and the terrorists in the mountains, and they carry Muslim propaganda. A few weeks ago we intercepted a mule train which was carrying boxes full of leaflets demanding the establishment of Sharia law in Tadjikistan – you know about that? – all that crap about cutting off arms and legs and stoning women to death for adultery.'

He paused for a moment, as if he could hardly believe that people could be so stupid.

'And then second, the drug traffickers,' he went on. 'They are mostly just criminals but their trade is doing almost as much damage to the Republic as the Muslims. And generally speaking they're more careful . . .' He smiled. 'According to the Koran, dying in a holy war gets you a free pass into heaven, but dying in a drug bust isn't mentioned.'

'Is it mostly raw opium?' I asked.

'It used to be, but these days there are several large refining laboratories in the hills across the border, and the ratio of heroin to opium in our seizures has shot up. There are also a few labs in the hills on this side, but they tend to be small-scale affairs. Officially speaking, it's up to the Tadjik government to deal with them, but the only soldiers they have in this area are under CIS command. We have taken a couple out, but it's difficult. They hear the helicopters coming, and by the time we get there there's just a few empty huts to look at.'

I resisted the temptation to ask him what he expected, and did my best to look sympathetic. 'What's the level of traffic across the border?' I asked. 'Are people coming across on a daily basis, or is it much more sporadic than that?'

He grimaced. 'It's really hard to say. We don't have daily contacts, but I don't think that means very much. Some of the people who come across want us to know they've been. They mine roads, they try and ambush our patrols, they've even laid siege to a couple of our smaller posts – I'm talking about hundreds of men in those cases, not just a small raiding party. And then there's the drug traffickers and the Tadjiks who're returning from Afghanistan to their homes, none of whom want to be seen.'

'We're talking almost exclusively about Tadjiks, yes?'

'Mostly. They live on both sides of the border – I'm sure you know that north-central Afghanistan is under Dostum's control, and his people are Uzbeks. In the north-east, across the border from here, it's mostly Masoud's Tadjiks, but this part of Afghanistan has always been a law unto itself. It's a long way from Kabul.'

'And do you mount retaliatory raids across the border?' I asked, at least partly to get an idea of how truthful my Russian host was prepared to be.

'Not on the ground, not yet,' he said reluctantly. 'We send the gunships across the border against their bases, but that's more for morale than anything else. No army likes to keep taking punishment and never hit back.'

I knew that well enough from Northern Ireland, but I also knew that rocket attacks on Afghan villages rarely produced anything more than the useless deaths of old men, women and children. More to the point, I could tell from Chechnulin's face that he knew it too, and felt about it much the same way I did. 'So where do we fit in?' I asked.

'Well, I've been thinking about that ever since I was told you were coming,' he said, 'and in the end I came to the conclusion that I should just put your unit into the rotation with all the others.'

'What's the rotation?'

'Day patrol, night patrol, stand-by and garrison duty,' he recited promptly. 'We operate regular patrols along the length of the river from a number of bases, both by day and night, and we keep one unit on permanent stand-by. This is always ready to move out, either in support of a patrol which has made contact with the enemy or in response to intelligence of enemy movements. The garrison duty involves the permanent manning of a few selected posts, most of them at river crossings or passes into the mountains behind us. We rotate the garrison duty because the men get sloppy with boredom if they're stuck out on their own for too long. Khorog may not be much, but it's better than staring at trees across a river for weeks on end.'

I nodded. 'So where do we start?'

'It's Wednesday today, and the shifts change on Sunday, so I thought you could spend the next few days acclimatizing. Then we can fit you in on one of the day patrol shifts. You'll get more idea of the valley that way. I've assigned you the twenty-kilometre stretch directly north of here,' he added, turning to point it out on the map. 'The Kazakhs will handle the night shift – that's from seven to seven – and you'll be based here.' He pointed again. 'Major Bakerdin – that's the officer who showed you across – will fill you in on what to expect and our normal ways of working. But of course, any suggestions you have . . . I would like us to learn from each other while we are together.'

And then he brought out the vodka, but only for the one drink. As I left his office I couldn't help thinking that we could have done a lot worse when it came to our new CO.

*　　*　　*

We spent the next few days getting used to our new living quarters, exploring the base and reviewing elements of our training programme. Given what Chechnulin had said about local drug labs, and given what we'd seen of the local topography – much more forested than the Tien Shan – we went through the CTR routines again at some length. If intelligence picked up news of an operating lab in the vicinity I wanted a chance to show the Russians what our Untouchables could do.

When transport was available we took drives up and down the worn road which followed the northern bank of the river, paying particular attention to the stretch we would be patrolling. The valley was a couple of miles wide here, with most of the cultivable land on Tadjikistan's side of the swift-running river. On the far bank the land rose almost immediately, through wooded slopes and valleys which could hide a thousand eyes, to high rocky crags and the glimmer of distant snow. On our third day there I persuaded one of the Russian helicopter gunship pilots to take us up for a bird's-eye view, and in several of the Afghan valleys we could make out the pale green fields of heroin poppies.

Generally speaking, our hours of daylight were full, our hours of darkness anything but. We'd all read and reread our own books and everyone else's, and were sorely in search of some musical variety – one evening I even swapped Otis Redding for one of Lulu's show-tune tapes. The double-omnibus *Archers* tape Ellen had brought to Samarkand was now so familiar that I could recite large chunks of it word for word.

Khorog was not much more than a mile away, but the most interesting thing there was watching the arrival of the twice-daily flights from Dushanbe, the capital. Would the pilot miss the mountain? Would he pull out of his dive before he hit the runway? Or would he get everything right and then get shot down by a Mujaheddin rocket fired from across the border? As far as I could see these pilots didn't so much need danger money as their heads examined.

And why did anyone want to come to Khorog in the first place? Why was the town even there? It had next to no cultivable land, no industry, and the official population of twenty-two thousand could hardly all be serving the dozen or so tourists who were usually passing through. According to what one of the Kazakhs told me, the unemployment rate had risen to about ninety-eight per cent since the civil war began, and it showed in the faces of the people, most of whom looked hungry, listless and pissed off. There didn't seem to be any shops or sources of entertainment, unless you counted waiting for the flights to arrive or watching the town's only set of traffic lights change. There was something called a university – it was even twinned with Oxford! – but there didn't seem to be much in the way of buildings or students. Contact with the outside world was not exactly easy: there was the often-closed road down-river, the road to Osh and the plane. No international telephone calls were possible; the Post Office could connect you to Dushanbe, but no further.

Luckily for me, Chechnulin was able to arrange for calls to be patched through via the CIS military network, and Ellen and I managed a ten-minute conversation every few days. The pregnancy was going fine – she wasn't even feeling sick in the mornings – but I could tell she wanted me home. This was something she wanted us to share.

I had several long chats with Chechnulin in his office. He was curious about the SAS in particular and the West in general, and he was interesting to listen to about his own country's troubles. He didn't think the current bunch in charge would survive Yeltsin, and foresaw a period of chaos which the Army would eventually have to sort out. This both depressed him – he had more faith in democracy than I did – and gave him hope. I liked him. He was earnest without being dogmatic, and he obviously took his responsibilities very seriously. In fact he was almost exactly the opposite of everything I'd heard about officers who'd risen through the ranks in Soviet times. And throughout the weeks we were under his command I never heard anyone say a bad word about him.

Conversations with him and Ellen apart, the off-duty hours were about as boring as hours get. We'd now been in Central Asia for ten weeks, and there's only so many ways you can cook lamb. We just wanted to get on with it and get home, and it was something of a relief when Sunday came round and we could join the rotation. The dawn hadn't yet reached the bottom of the valley as we drove north along the riverside road to the small post which marked the central point of that border sector. The Kazakh unit which greeted us was almost dead on its feet, having done back-to-back day and night shifts, but according to their CO the only contact over the last week had been with a lone drug runner. He had been shot while trying to re-ford the river, his sacks of opium disappearing in the swirling red waters.

The four of us had a miserable breakfast of bread and tea, envying all those people back home with their Weetabix and Frosted Flakes, their bacon and egg, their toast and marmalade. Personally, for a decent cup of coffee I would have watched Arsenal play.

The sun finally reached the river in the valley before us, and the setting seemed so idyllic it was hard to believe in the threat which lay in the trees and mountains beyond. But we would have at least four weeks to find out just how real it was, and at that moment I wasn't at all sure whether I would prefer a month of numbing boredom or a heady dose of danger and excitement. Not that it mattered what I wanted – either the bad guys would put in an appearance or they wouldn't.

10

The Pyandzh valley ran more or less directly north from Khorog for nearly forty miles, a huge gouge in the surface of the earth which the river had been deepening for millions of years. On a clear day – and most of them were – we could see from one end of our sector to the other, at least insofar as the upper slopes were concerned. At river level the trees often reduced visibility to a few hundred yards.

Our predecessors on day patrol, and presumably their predecessors too, had, to all intents and purposes, simply walked from one end of the sector to the other. There had been no fixed timings, and they had used paths parallel to the river through the cover of the trees rather than the obvious road, but it wouldn't have been hard for anyone with a pair of binoculars to work out times when the way was clear. That said, it was hard to imagine why anyone who didn't want to be seen would cross by day in the first place.

We started out following the same pattern, with Lulu's and Sheff's squads covering the six miles to the north of our post, mine and Gonzo's those to the south. But on the second day we started introducing variations, speeding up our progress or stopping for a couple of hours, and on the third day, just to confuse matters a little further, we didn't go out at all. Most of the men just had a day lolling round the post – their bunks, of course, were occupied by the Kazakh night shift – but Ishen, Alijon, Gonzo and I spent most of the day putting together a map. While we Brits pored over the topographical maps of the area, trying to select the best crossing-points from the opposition's point of view, the two Kirghiz squad leaders were in Khorog gathering all the information they could about previous incursions into our sector. We were looking for places which offered easy access from the mountains to the south, fordable stretches of river and an easy way up into the mountains on our side. They were searching for places which we knew the enemy had used, and which the enemy knew we knew about, because these were unlikely to be used again. When Ishen and Alijon returned we subtracted their list from ours, and came up with seven possibilities, all of which we explored on the following morning. By midday we had reduced the number of four.

Meanwhile our four squads continued to vary their patrol routines, but still there were no contacts – no drug traffickers, no Mujaheddin, not even a lost hippie. We got news of a run-in between a Russian patrol and a heavily armed gang of Mujaheddin thirty miles down-river, and a dawn exchange of fire with an invisible foe across the river about the same distance upstream, but it was all quiet on the western front as far as we were concerned. 'Our reputation's scared 'em off,' Sheff decided, and we all preened ourselves for a few minutes, till we remembered how bored we were.

Boredom apart, our main problem was mosquitoes. Someone once told me that they didn't live above six thousand feet, but either he hadn't been to Khorog or the Regiment's *Times Atlas* has got the elevation wrong. Where they bred was also a mystery – there didn't seem be any still water around – but breed they did, and they couldn't get over how good Englishmen tasted. I say Englishmen because Lulu seemed curiously unaffected, as if the mozzies were showing him mercy for his kindness to their fellow-creatures. The Russian insect repellent which we eventually persuaded someone to bring us from Khorog was reasonably effective, but then I don't suppose mosquitoes like napalm either. It didn't so much tingle as burn, and after a few days I gave up on it, preferring a lot of itching and the remote possibility of malaria to being flayed alive by the antidote.

Our one thrill of that first week – one which had most of us jerking awake in our bunks – was the sudden piercing howl of an animal outside. We later found out it came no closer than a hundred yards, but it sounded like it was on the window-sill. Lulu immediately decided it was a snow leopard and went out to look for it, leaving the rest of us to hope he came back in one piece. He returned about an hour later having spotted nothing, but he was out again the moment it was light enough to see, and this time came back with news of large cat tracks beside the stream which ran past the post. 'Snow leopard,' he confirmed gruffly, but there was a dreamy look in his eyes, and I was glad he hadn't seen the pelt in the Bishkek Hotel – the hunters wouldn't have known what hit them.

Body warmth was about the only thing we shared with the Kazakhs, who seemed capable of sleeping away every hour they weren't on patrol, but Chechnulin paid us a courtesy visit on Friday, bringing the good news that he'd arranged for us all to call home from the Khorog base on the following evening. He listened without comment to the changes we had introduced in the day patrol – which seemed fair enough: we hadn't got any results to show for them yet – and then asked about our plans for the night patrol. Ishen showed him our map, and told him what we were considering. He looked interested, but again made no comment. I asked him about the possibility of getting hold of some night-vision goggles, and he smiled wryly and said he'd been trying for months. I reassured myself with the thought that the next week would bring a full moon.

The weekend arrived – such as it was – and we decided that with what we had planned for Sunday night it would be wiser to ignore the second half of the twenty-four-hour transition shift on Saturday. The new day shift, which was from the same Kazakh battalion as the last, immediately assumed that we were just a bunch of lazy bastards, but there was nothing much we could do about that. On Sunday evening we started out the moment darkness fell, each squad heading for one of the four sites we had chosen, and in the hours before midnight sixteen scrapes were dug at the prearranged points, camouflaged with bashas constructed from foliage and pre-cut poles, and left with enough supplies of food and water to get us through a four-day watch. Once this work was done we resumed patrolling in the usual fashion, through that night and the one that followed, hoping to convince any watchers across the river that they had nothing new to worry about.

On Tuesday night we did the same, only this time we didn't return to the post. As dawn broke the whole unit was laid up in the OPs overlooking what we hoped would be ambush sites, and through the hours of daylight each two- or three-man team slept in shifts beneath their roofs of foliage. We'd managed to scrounge enough walkie-talkies to allow communication between scrapes in each location, but the range of the other communications equipment we had was only sufficient to link our four sites serially, which was a decidedly cumbersome arrangement.

I was in the northernmost site, code-named Alpha, and from where I lay in the lowest scrape I could see down through a scattering of trees to the road and river a quarter of a mile away. There was no obvious path, but in the daylight we had found enough evidence to suggest that both people and pack animals had walked up this small valley in the not-too-distant past, and from our study of the Soviet topographical surveys we knew that this route would intersect with both foresters' and shepherds' trails higher up. It was a way into Tadjikistan, and one that would present few physical or navigational difficulties to anyone used to moving across this sort of countryside.

By eleven the moon had risen high enough in the sky to light the valley bottom, and I could see its rippling light in the waters of the Pyandzh. The pale ribbon of road which followed the river was empty, and would probably remain so. Between here and Dushanbe it seemed more often closed than open – sometimes the victim of nature, sometimes of the fighting – and even by day traffic was rare. Khorog, and indeed all of Gorno-Badahkshan, was getting used to being supplied by air.

I was sharing a scrape with Ishen and an Uzbek named Rassal Kutbidin, whom everybody called Rass. The other three scrapes were situated at roughly thirty-yard intervals up the 'path': one to the right, one to the left and one almost dead ahead, where the way angled left to climb up around a small waterfall. The three men in this last scrape had a commanding field of fire, but they would have to be careful to keep their fire on the path, or the rest of us would suffer for it. The two lateral scrapes had been staggered to minimize the possibility of their occupants' shooting each other, but the danger was still there. If anyone stepped into our little trap I was hoping that the shock of being challenged would cause an instant surrender.

And that, of course, would depend on who they were. A few drug smugglers were one thing, a unit of heavily armed Mujaheddin something else altogether. If the force was big enough we would have to just let it go – ten men taking on a hundred fighters would just be suicidal.

That night, though, it didn't look as if anyone was coming. The hours went slowly by, and all I could hear was the distant drizzle of the waterfall, the breeze in the branches of the nearby trees, and the occasional sound of Ishen and Ras rearranging their cramped limbs. We were taking turns focusing our attention on the valley below – it's hard to really watch nothing happening for any length of time – and in my 'off' periods I found my mind wandering, mostly in the direction of home. I thought about Ellen and how much I loved her and how hard it was to imagine life without her, even though we'd only met four years before. I'd been scared often enough on the job, the sort of fear that dries your throat in a moment and leaves a vast hole where your stomach used to be, but that always passes – either you've made it through or you're dead. The fear of losing her was always going to be with me, because in a relationship you just never know what's round the corner.

Fatherhood was probably going to be the same – a constant source of just about every emotion going, from joy to terror and back again. I wondered whether I was too old for parenting – my bicycle kick was already rusty and the kid wasn't born yet – but comforted myself with how much wisdom I'd accumulated in getting this old. Hell, I even knew how many Lake Genevas you could fit into Lake Issyk-Kul.

I did another ten-minute stint 'on', gazing down through the barely lit gap in the trees towards the river, turning my binoculars on the shadows of the far bank, but nothing stirred. I handed the responsibility on to Ishen with a touch of the hand and found myself wondering what Uncle Stanley would have made of all this. He'd always talked about the world as if it was a magical place, full of strange and wonderful things, and what could have been more astonishing than this? Here was his nephew, lying in a hole in the ground with a Kirghiz and an Uzbek, close to a river which hardly anyone in England had heard of, let alone seen, waiting for a bunch of men in turbans to walk by with opium-packing donkeys. The opium would find its way to a small laboratory in the hills, be transformed into bags of heroin, which would somehow hitch a ride down the long and winding road to Osh. Some scumbag like Borkeyev would get his cut and the stuff would be transferred to a car or a train or another lorry for the ride north to Moscow or St Petersburg, where more men would smuggle it aboard another car or train or ship, and eventually it would reach men like the one Sheff and I had followed from Immingham to Manchester. The big plastic bags would be turned into lots of little plastic bags, and the distributors would do the rounds of all their regulars in the pubs and on street corners. All that effort, all that ingenuity, and all in the service of shipping the produce of some poor Afghan farmer's field to a Gents toilet six thousand miles away in Manchester Piccadilly, where a teenager with nothing else to live for was waiting to multiply the tracks in his arm.

Would Uncle Stanley have found this strange and wonderful? I think he probably would. And he'd also have scratched his head at the stupidity of it all. I had a sudden memory of something he'd said in one of his rare downbeat moments about natives in America or Africa or somewhere selling their land for beads. 'They weren't the only ones,' he said. 'Most people sell their lives for beads – they just think they're getting something else.'

I had one of those moments of sadness, knowing I'd never get to talk to him again, and told myself I had to make some effort to get to know my sister before one of us dropped dead. I was wondering whether Ellen would be too pregnant for our intended trip out West, when Ishen's hand told me it was my turn to be the primary watcher.

The rest of the night dragged past, and by the time dawn arrived I was feeling a bit depressed by the opposition's no-show. If they were watching our post they would now have had three opportunities to observe our non-appearance at the day's two changing of the guards. There was always the chance that they'd assume we'd been moved to another sector, but they might also draw the correct conclusion: that we were waiting for them in hiding. Either way, we were stuck in our scrapes for another seventy-two hours of hard routine.

The day went by no faster than the night, but at least it was warmer. While I was on watch one of the Kazakh day patrols wandered a little way up our valley and back again without noticing us, which was probably something of a morale booster for our lads. The Kazakhs looked as bored as I felt, which was some trick, and then went away again. We ate our cold rations, drank the tepid water in our canteens and did the business with the plastic bags. It was not one of those days that live in the memory as a bundle of fun.

Darkness eventually filled the valley, the sun disappeared over the mountains beyond, and I tried to think of ways to keep my mind occupied for the next three days. It reminded me of going to West Ham as a kid – getting there two hours early so we could get a spot down the front, and then the eternal wait for the players to come out. I stared down at the empty road and river, thinking, we've got the spot – now send out the fucking players.

They appeared a few minutes after midnight, three figures silhouetted against the moonlight river, heading in our direction. None of us had seen them ford the river, but I didn't have much doubt that they had. Through the binoculars their cradled AK47s gleamed slightly, and the glances they repeatedly cast up and down the main valley as they hurried across it were not suggestive of innocence. On the walkie-talkie Ishen informed the other scrapes of the men's approach, and prudently confirmed that no contact should be initiated without his say-so.

They were about two hundred yards away now, and I could make out their faces through the binoculars. They were all bearded and they looked like Tadjiks; they were dressed in customary Mujaheddin fashion, waistcoat-like jackets over long earth-coloured smocks and baggy trousers, turbans wound around their heads. The cloth bags which were slung across their shoulders only looked big enough for personal effects – if these were drug traffickers or purveyors of fundamentalist propaganda they were travelling decidedly light. The guns, the way they moved, suggested fighters pure and simple, and I felt a momentary qualm about what was going to happen next. Chechnulin might be a nice bloke, but when it came to working out who were the good guys in

Tadjikistan's civil war I hadn't got a clue, and here we were taking sides with a vengeance. I idly wondered whether the Foreign Office should adopt the *Star Trek* Federation's Prime Directive of non-interference, but didn't suppose it was practical. Captain Picard had a hard enough job keeping his hands off other worlds, and in the last episode I'd seen before leaving England one gullible planet had adopted him as a god.

The three men were only forty yards from our position, and their pace had slowed, as if they knew the worst was over. I tried not to let my stare linger on any of them as they walked past, no more than ten yards from our scrape, and hoped my companions believed in the sixth sense as much as I did. Seeing them so close, it was hard to believe the three men had no idea they were being watched, and one of them did suddenly cast a suspicious glance in our direction, only to have his attention reclaimed by something one of his companions said in a low voice. He answered in a fierce whisper, only to have the third man put in his tuppence worth.

The language was certainly Tadjik, and had Gonzo been with us he might have understood what they were talking about. But then he might not, for since our arrival in Khorog we'd discovered that the people of Badakhshan, on both sides of the border, spoke a dialect which was further removed from Farsi than the norm.

The three men were past us now – another half a minute and they'd be at the agreed spot. Ishen's fingers were probably already twitching on the switch which would turn on the light we'd suspended from a branch across the path, and in the other scrapes sweaty hands would be clasping the AK74s. The three men, caught in a makeshift spotlight and clearly surrounded, would hopefully have the sense to drop their guns and surrender. Another five yards . . .

And then the leading man stopped, looked back and said something to the other two. One sank to his haunches, the other sat himself down on a convenient rock and they both watched as the first man extracted two cylindrical-looking objects from his bag. One was a torch, the other looked like a tube constructed from the cardboard innards of two toilet rolls. The latter was fitted over the former, considerably narrowing the beam, whereupon the man pointed it back the way he'd come and clicked the switch. From where we lay a pale line of light was just about visible against the trees, but across the river they would see the signal without any problem.

We waited to find out who they were, feeling – or at least I did – distinctly nervous. I assumed that the occupants of the other scrapes could see that our three men had stopped, and that they'd worked out the reason why, but there was no way we could risk confirming as much on the walkie-talkie. Holding everything together during prolonged periods of suspense – keeping quiet, not squeezing a trigger by mistake or making an involuntary movement – was something that could only be learned through practice, and I wasn't at all sure these men had the experience. Even a loud fart could give the game away, and if the force on the other end of the torch signal was a lot bigger than ours we'd have to be off through the forest with our tails between our legs.

Several minutes went by, and the tension I could feel from the other two in the scrape seemed like a physical presence. The three men who had induced it, in contrast, looked like they hadn't got a care in the world. Their AK47s were either lying in the grass or leaning up against a rock, and one of the men had passed round a small box of some powder which each of them had dipped his fingers into, before transferring it to his mouth. I later found out this was *naswar*, a snuff-like stimulant which is held under the tongue for ten minutes or so until it is absorbed.

The men kept their eyes turned towards the river, presumably for a sight of whomever they had signalled, and their breath shone faintly with moonlight in the cold air.

Five long minutes later they and I both caught sight of what we were waiting for. On the far bank of the river several figures were emerging from the trees, and without much ado wading out into the thigh-deep water. More and more men appeared, and with them several mules, who seemed extremely reluctant to enter the rushing river. All got across, however, some of the men holding more than one weapon above their head as their comrades struggled to help the animals.

I watched, wishing I could talk this over with Ishen. There were about twenty of them, which was the upper limit we had set for a deliberate contact, but I was reluctant to just watch them walk by. If they were bunched up under the light then maybe . . . but our three originals were already getting to their feet, and the line of men and animals hurrying up from the river looked anything but bunched. I had now counted twenty-four more men below, which seemed well over the odds. Our scrapes were designed for concealment, not as firing ports, and in the confusion which would follow any challenge the Mujaheddin would have no real chance to surrender, even if they wanted to. There would be a lot of dead on their side, and probably more than a few on ours.

But what was Ishen thinking? I could feel his excitement, and he, nominally at least, was the man in command.

Now that their comrades were nearly with them, the three waiting men were no longer bothering to lower their voices, and I decided to risk whispering to Ishen. 'Let's follow them,' I breathed almost into his ear, as if the decision had already been taken not to attempt an ambush.

He whispered his assent, and I thought I could hear relief in his voice. Now we only had to pray that discipline held and no one opened up without really meaning to.

The leader of the main party was now only fifty yards away, another bearded Tadjik wearing crossed bandoliers and carrying an AK47. There were four mules, all quite heavily loaded, but there was no fool-proof way of telling if they were carrying provisions for a fighting force, drug-traffickers' merchandise or both. The men looked like fighters, particularly the older ones, and they were certainly well armed. Some were wearing Russian camouflage smocks, presumably mementoes of the Soviet intervention, and all the weapons looked well cared for. A fighting force, I decided, and the thought flickered across my mind that it was really only the guns which identified the men filing past as belonging to the twentieth century. Replace the Kalashnikovs with scimitars and I could have been looking at a scene from any time in the last two thousand years.

The lead man and the original three were now heading up past the second scrape, and I found I was holding my breath, half-expecting all hell to break loose. I should have had more faith: there was no sudden challenge, no burst of fire, and the column continued on its purposeful way up the slope. It was like watching a row of ducks bobbing by on a fairground stall, only knowing that in this case the ducks could fire back.

The men looked like they'd been walking for days and could walk for a few more yet, but the plodding mules, struggling under the weight of the panniers slung across their backs, seemed more than a little the worse for wear, and I could almost imagine Lulu leaping out to protest at their ill-treatment. As the last man in the column passed our position he turned and looked back the way he'd come like any Tail-end Charlie, but I had the feeling he wasn't so much checking for signs of pursuit as taking one last look at the border and the country he was leaving behind.

After this brief fond goodbye he scurried on after the others, and I mentally counted the seconds it would take for him to get past the highest scrape.

I'd just about finished when Ishen asked me in a whisper how many men I thought he should send after the incursion force.

'Two,' I said automatically. 'Me and Kazat,' I added. Kazat was the best man in the squad at moving stealthily across country, and one of the most assured when it came to navigating with a compass.

I could almost hear Ishen conquering his own desire to go. 'OK,' he said after a moment.

'If they go to ground, one of us will come back with word. We'll approach from above, arms spread wide.'

'OK.'

A voice came through on the walkie-talkie: 'They're out of sight.'

'I'll be off then,' I said, and started working myself out from under the camouflaged roof of the scrape. Ishen was already talking to the other scrapes, explaining what was happening.

I collected Kazat, told him what was intended and watched a smile split his dirt-smeared face. Not for the first time, I thought how lucky we'd been with this particular batch. Other places in the world we'd been given men to train who worried about getting dirt under their fingernails.

We started up the valley, not hurrying. I didn't want to make visual contact, particularly while we could still be silhouetted against the valley below, and while I didn't think the men in front would be particularly watchful – as far as they were concerned, the difficult bit was over – it only needed one man hanging back for a quick crap and we'd be blown. As we knew from the Soviet maps and aerial photographs we'd studied, there was no turn-off for several miles: the path, such as it was, just climbed the steepening valley, criss-crossing the rushing stream. At about fifteen hundred feet above the river, close to the head of this particular valley, an old foresters' track offered the first choice, either north along a ridge which eventually fell away into the Murgab valley or south and east over a pass towards the first stretch of the road from Khorog to Osh. Once we reached that point I was pretty confident of finding some sign to indicate which way they'd gone, if only another pile of steaming mule shit.

That was the good news. Our lack of radio equipment, let alone any of the sophisticated comm gear I usually took for granted in such situations, meant we were venturing out on to a pretty long limb. For all I knew this bunch might be leading us on a hundred-and-thirty-mile trek across the mountains, in which case we'd have more than food and water to worry about. Assuming we kept climbing, we'd soon be back in the local moonscape, visible for miles. And we wouldn't have any way of letting anyone know where we were or what sort of mess I'd got us into.

The thought crossed my mind that prospective fathers should be more careful, but I shrugged it aside with only a slight twinge of guilt. It was almost one o'clock now, which meant there were about three and a half hours of darkness left. I decided we'd keep on their tail until dawn, then think again.

11

We reached the intersection with the foresters' track, and it didn't take an Indian scout to work out that our quarry had turned right. There were abundant tracks in the soft earth where the party had crossed the stream, and a mule had obligingly moved his bowels not twenty yards above the opposite bank. The Tadjiks were headed in the direction of the Khorog–Osh highway, which made a lot of sense if the panniers were full of white poppy products.

Kazat and I continued on their trail, slowing our pace over the next mile or so as altitude began stripping the mountains of their tree cover. We were heading up another valley now, towards a narrow pass guarded by bare crags. It was an ideal spot for an ambush, or even just a good place for an alert commander to drop off a temporary lookout, and I approached it as cautiously as the bright moonlight and lack of cover allowed. But there was no one waiting in the shadows, and lying face-down on the rim of the pass we could just make out the moving column of men and mules in the valley below, winding down the bank of another swiftly flowing stream, about a quarter of a mile ahead.

I reckoned that as the crow flew we were now no more than ten miles from the Gunt valley and Khorog–Osh highway, but I didn't think we'd be going that far in what was left of the night. We pressed on, one eye picking a way for our feet across the uneven ground, one scouring the way ahead for a sign that our quarry had stopped for a tea break, or whatever sort of break it was that Tadjik night travellers went in for. I could have used a hot cup of something myself – even on the move the night seemed bitterly cold.

The valley wound slowly downwards, widening only slightly as it swallowed other lesser valleys and streams. The vegetation increased as we descended, lone trees giving way to copses in the stretches of meadow and these to intermittent stretches of denser woodland. When the moon fell behind the ridge we had crossed it was as if night had finally fallen.

We had advanced another two miles or so, and were carefully rounding one more bend in the path, when a tiny square of yellow light suddenly came into view. We quickly moved back and off the path, and then worked our way up the slope a few yards to find a safe vantage-point. Lying on our fronts, and in my case silently cursing the lack of any night-vision equipment, we tried to make sense of what lay before us.

About three hundred yards below us, in a wide niche in the northern slope of the valley, there seemed to be several one-storey buildings. Only one was lit – the others were just dim and indistinct shapes in the gloom – but as we watched another light went on in a second building, a door opened to let out still more, and the complex grew marginally less impenetrable. I could see the mules tethered outside one of the buildings and figures moving across the lighted windows and doorway. Our quarry had reached its destination, at least for that night.

I let my eyes wander round the immediate area. The buildings were set back about twenty yards from the stream, and the slopes facing them across it were heavily wooded. Gesturing to Kazat to follow, I worked my way back up the path a couple of hundred yards, waded through the calf-deep icy waters, and angled up through the trees of the north-facing slope. Twenty minutes later we were lying behind a fallen tree, staring through the gap between trunk and ground at the complex below and in front of us, no more than eighty yards away. There was only black emptiness to our right, but I hoped that when the sky began to lighten in an hour or so's time we'd be able to see right down the valley.

One of us would have to spend the day here, while the other rounded up the cavalry. But who should do which? As usual I wanted to do both jobs, but that wasn't exactly a practical proposition, and I elected to send Kazat off for the rest of the unit – all four squads' worth. I'm sure he'd have managed either job OK – maybe my subconscious was telling me I didn't want to do that walk twice again in less than twelve hours.

He helped me dig out the scrape, and then we worked our way back up the valley together in search of a good RV for the next night. We couldn't find anything particularly suitable in the dark, and I eventually decided we'd meet up on the path close to our first sighting of the target. There'd be no chance of missing each other, and if the opposition decided to use the path I'd just retreat up it until I ran into the unit. I thought about advising Ishen to contact Chechnulin but decided against it. For one thing, I wasn't at all sure that the men under his command were all as straight as he seemed to be, and for another, I couldn't believe we'd need more than the forty men at our disposal.

Kazat disappeared into the dark with a grin and I headed back down the valley to my hole for the day. Already there was a faint lightening in the sky and I still had a roof to construct.

The lights had gone out in the buildings, but by the time I'd constructed a makeshift roof – the fallen tree supplied most of one of its own accord – the whole set-up across the stream was becoming visible. The nearest building was the largest. It had obviously started life as a simple single-storey oblong of con-crete, and had since gained a breeze-block extension. All but one of the visible windows in the concrete section were boarded over, and it would have looked half-derelict but for the gleaming antenna which rose from its roof.

At right angles to this building, and partly hidden by it, was a longer, narrower wooden structure. Another small building – probably a storeroom of some kind – was tucked away behind it, against the steepening side of the valley. A second long building stood about thirty yards away from the others, its door facing the valley. Behind this an area of grass had been corralled off for pack animals, and was currently playing host to three mules. The four who'd arrived with the party were still tethered to a rail outside the concrete building, but the loads they'd been carrying were no longer on their backs.

I could hear the low hum of a generator, but exactly where it was coming from was impossible to say. Of human life there was no sign whatsoever, and the conspicuous lack of men on guard made me wonder whether my first instinct – that this was a small drug-refining complex – had been an accurate one. But then, as light suffused the lower valley to my right, I saw why there were no guards. A quarter of a mile downstream another couple of buildings stood at what was clearly the upper end of the drivable track. This was the only way in for any significant force, and no doubt the occupants of those buildings below would be raising the alarm if one arrived.

And of course the track could be used to take the refined drugs down into the Gunt valley, for pre-arranged assignations on the Khorog–Osh highway. It was a perfect set-up, always assuming you didn't run foul of Hereford's finest, and I could hardly blame the men in the buildings below for not expecting that. I hadn't actually anticipated being in the area myself.

It had been light for an hour when the first human put in an appearance. A man in Western clothes came out of the concrete hut and walked down towards the stream, cigarette in hand. Reaching the water, he placed the cigarette on a rock, squatted down and bent forward with cupped hands to splash his face with water. After rubbing his eyes he seemed to look straight up at my hiding-place, but he obviously didn't see anything. His features seemed neither European nor Asian, but there was something about the way he walked which made me think he was a Russian.

He went back into the concrete building, but only for a few minutes, and when he re-emerged it was with another man, this one clearly a Tadjik. They walked across the bare earth to the building which stood slightly apart from the others, and disappeared inside. One of the tethered mules strained at his leash, as if he wanted to follow them, and a few minutes later a machine-like noise began to emanate from inside the structure. Inside that building, unless I was wildly off the mark, slabs of opium paste were being refined into white powder.

Three other men made the same journey over the next hour, but none of the men from the group we had followed appeared until late in the morning, by which time the temperature had risen substantially. These travellers gradually emerged from the long building behind the concrete one, and the smell of food began wafting across the valley. I wouldn't have thought it was possible, but the smell of lamb fat stew was almost enticing after two days on cold rations.

These men seemed a distinctly separate group from the permanent residents. Their dress was more traditional, they were all bearded, and they never let go of their guns. Allies of convenience, not of conviction, I murmured to himself. This lot would not be trafficking in drugs to make themselves rich – not yet, in any case – but just to feed themselves and to help them pay for their crusade.

They had presumably been making up for lost sleep, which was more than I could say for myself. Rather more to the point, they had the air of people who wouldn't be hanging around for much longer. And much as I hated to see them go, their departure would certainly improve the odds when it came to the showdown.

In the meantime I watched two men emerge from the building off to the left, one holding a pair of loaded panniers. His companion went to get a mule from the corral, and held the animal while the panniers were fastened under its belly. There was a flicker in my peripheral vision and I turned to see something moving up the valley. It was still over a mile away, but slowly the sound of an engine rose above the hum of the generator and the growing speck took on the shape of a jeep. I felt more than a little pissed off at this development, but cheered up somewhat when I realized that the men in the hut to the left wouldn't have had time to refine any of the stuff which had arrived during the preceding night.

It took the two with the mule about fifteen minutes to reach the jeep, its two occupants – both of whom looked like Uzbeks through the binoculars – and another couple who had emerged from the buildings below. The six men chatted for a few minutes, but no money seemed to change hands, which suggested that they were all workers in the same organisation. The two then walked back up the stream, tugging at the reluctant mule, who, relieved of his burden, seemed to be enjoying his afternoon out. In the gap between the buildings below me the level of activity had been stepped up, and I began to feel that a departure was imminent. I watched and waited, hoping the group wouldn't simply retrace its steps to the border, in which case it would almost certainly collide with the rest of the unit.

Finally, around five o'clock, they were ready to leave. The man I thought was probably a Russian came out to talk for several minutes with the man I assumed was the fighting group's leader, and as I watched their faces through the binoculars I was more than ever convinced that this wasn't a love match. There were no smiles, no back-slapping or hugs – this was business.

They set off downstream, which was a surprise as well as a relief – I had assumed they were headed for the fighting in central Tadjikistan. But I swiftly discovered I could still be right: like the twosome with the mule the column wound round the first bend in the valley, but unlike them it failed to reappear. There was clearly a way out to the north which I couldn't see from my position. None of the mules had accompanied the column, which suggested both that they belonged to the home team and that all four from the previous night had been bearing drugs.

I breathed a sigh of relief, which quickly turned into a yawn. I wasn't that tired yet, but I had the feeling I'd be needing all the adrenalin I could muster before the next night was out.

By my count there were now eight men in the complex below me and a further pair a few hundred yards down the valley. I had seen two of the eight carrying AK47s, and at least four of them were wearing side-arms, but there was really nothing to suggest that these men were seriously expecting trouble. I worked out a rough plan of action in my head, most of which was concerned with insuring ourselves against highly improbable fuck-ups. The one thing I wanted to be sure of was capturing the Russian, who looked like the head chemist.

I had another delicious cold snack, and tortured myself with memories of draught Guinness and Ranch-flavoured Pringles in front of *Match of the Day*. If nothing unforeseen had occurred – another armed shipment coming through, or aliens sucking Kazat up into their spaceship for forensic tests – then the unit should be at the RV sometime around midnight. I didn't want us going in before first light if I could help it, because darkness would greatly increase the chances of a major fuck-up, but keeping forty men waiting till dawn posed its own problems. Even if no one pulled a trigger by accident, there were any number of accidental noises someone could make, and then there were always the smells. I'm not implying that our lads were negligent in the personal cleanliness department; forty clean men generate a lot of smells, and in thin air it travels. These scents, like those we're supposedly giving off all the time in our mating rituals, don't need to be recognized by an enemy – they need only make him feel vaguely uneasy. Then he starts looking for reasons for his uneasiness, and things that would normally go unnoticed no longer are.

We would make the RV and then withdraw the main force to a decent distance while a couple of lads manned the OP, I decided. And then I could even get a few hours' sleep.

The sun had finally deserted the valley in front of me, and the shadows were climbing the slopes beyond. Another five hours to go, I thought, and tried to remember what day it was. Thursday, I decided. In England it would be lunch-time, and Ellen would be listening to *The World at One* in the kitchen while she ate. Some kind of salad probably, and maybe she'd have treated herself to one of the M&S Gooseberry Fools she said she'd developed an addiction to. I wondered whether these sudden food fads last all through a pregnancy, and realized I had no idea. It was nearly a month since those few days together in Samarkand, and for all I knew she was bingeing on Mars bars and Big Macs. Which was a frightening thought. Our child could be born a junk-food junkie.

I told myself to get a grip, and swept the complex below with the binoculars. Lights were still showing in all three main buildings, and they would stay on for most of the evening. The men in the building to the left finally stopped work around nine-thirty, and for most of the next hour all of the eight men I'd identified were gathered in the concrete structure eating their evening meal, which the smells drifting my way suggested had come out of the same pot as breakfast and lunch. I could also hear music for the first time since I'd arrived, a weird melancholy sort of chanting which I couldn't place.

I toyed with the idea of a one-man CTR, but only out of a desire to be doing something. I'd had a grandstand view of the place all day, and thought I had a pretty good idea of who and what were where. The moon was up now, and there was nothing to be gained from a closer look that might put the whole operation in jeopardy.

So I waited out the last hours, stretching cramped limbs one by one and watching the complex below put itself to bed. Six of the men emerged into the night air and stood in a rough line facing the river for their pre-bed piss, chatting to each other as the steam wafted up in front of them. Then they headed for the main accommodation building, where their business partners from Afghanistan had stayed the night before. They obviously weren't voracious readers, because the light went out almost immediately, leaving only the glow from the concrete structure, where the Russian and one of the Tadjiks were still holed up. This light was still on at midnight when I left the scrape and started making my way back up the valley to the RV.

I reached the spot without any difficulty – with the moon well into the sky there was almost too much ambient light for comfort, and the sound of the stream effectively drowned out any slight noises my feet made on the uneven ground. I didn't expect the unit to arrive before one o'clock, so I wasn't disappointed to find no one waiting for me. Climbing up to the vantage-point which Kazat and I had used on the previous night, I could see the yellow light still burning below.

'Go to bed,' I murmured, trying to engage any latent powers of psychokinesis I might possess. The light stayed on, imprinting itself on my retina.

An hour or so later three figures finally appeared on the path further up the valley, advancing with commendable caution, their AK74s in the firing position. I walked to meet them, arms held out like a crucifixion victim in the prearranged signal.

It was Ishen, Gonzo and Kazat. The last-named looked both tired and pleased with himself, which he had every reason to be. A promotion was definitely in order, I thought, as Ishen explained where the rest of the unit was: a quarter of a mile back up the valley. I took him and Gonzo up the hillside to show them the complex below, and then gave them a verbal situation report, complete with a few suggestions for an operational plan. The plan was a finished thing in my head, but I thought it would be more diplomatic, not to mention good training, for Ishen and the other squad commanders to dot the i's themselves.

We left Kazat on watch with one of the walkie-talkies and walked back up to where the unit was spread out along the path, waiting in an admirably preserved silence. A lot of smiles greeted me, which felt as good as it always did when coming from people I'd been helping to train. At moments like that, I understand why a lot of teachers accept shit salaries to deal with rooms full of screaming kids. All the crap disappears when you know you've helped people realize even a little of the potential which most of them seem to have.

The squad commanders and us Brits hunkered down in a circle to mull things over. I scratched a diagram of the layout in a convenient stretch of moon-illuminated earth, and went through the spiel I'd already given Ishen. Then, with the locals doing most of the talking, we worked out a plan of operation which was remarkably similar to the one I'd come up with on my own. This wasn't exactly surprising – the problem might not be a no-brainer, but it came pretty close.

Once that was sorted out all that was left was for the squad commanders to fill in their men on what was expected of them. The lieutenant in charge of B Squad didn't have much to say, as his lot had drawn the short straw, two men manning my fart-filled OP and the rest stationed as a cut-off where Kazat was currently watching. Gonzo, whose bunch this was, looked decidedly unhappy with the arrangement, but somebody had to do it. Sheff's C Squad had been given the job of dealing with the two men in the buildings further down the valley and then acting as the second cut-off, should anyone escape from the main complex and try to escape in that direction. Lulu and I were with Squads A and D, who'd be allotted the task of giving the drug traffickers their early-morning wake-up call.

Kazat called in on the walkie-talkie with the news that the light had gone out, and it was decided that we'd get ourselves into the ready positions immediately. Navigation would be easier while the moon was still bright, and we didn't much fancy being spread out where we were should another column of ayatollahs turn up. I escorted the two designated watchers from Squad B to the scrape behind the fallen tree, and then rejoined Squads A, C and D higher up the slope. From there we worked our way a couple of hundred yards

down-valley, before descending almost to the stream
at a point roughly equidistant from the two clusters
of buildings. Another thirty yards and we would be
out of the trees, across the water, and on the path
which joined them.

It was now almost two o'clock, and our approach
was timed to begin at four-fifty, towards the darker
end of the dawn twilight. I sat with my back against a
tree, checking and rechecking my weapons, feeling the
adrenalin beginning to make itself felt. I told myself
this was going to be as straightforward as it ever gets
– twenty men to subdue eight, all of whom would be
either asleep or still trying to remember where they
were – but I'd been through enough actions like this
over the last twenty years to know how unpredictable
they could be, and it only needed one man to reach a
gun for all sorts of hell to break loose. One shot from
the opposition and one or more of the men around me
could open up with everything they had, killing friend
and foe like. I wanted to see my child, and I wanted him
to have the chance to see me. Ellen would no doubt
take him or her down to the Regimental graveyard for
a look at Daddy's headstone – 'killed in the service of
Her Majesty, somewhere in the middle of nowhere' –
but that wasn't quite the same.

I told myself not to be morbid, and looked at my
watch for about the hundredth time that day. Each
minute seemed longer than its predecessor, but the
time kept creeping by, and at last a faint light began
seeping down through the trees. The men in the OP
confirmed that nothing was stirring below them, and
at roughly four-thirty Ishen led the three squads of

men out of the trees and across the stream. Alijon and his men started down the path towards the two buildings below, and the rest of us began climbing towards the bend in the valley which still hid us from the main complex. To our rear the mountains were darkening against the pre-dawn sky, but the path in front of us still seemed darker than it had been when the moon was up.

At the bend we waited, Ishen anxiously checking and double-checking his watch. He eventually gave the signal to proceed and we advanced at a normal walking pace towards the first building, which was now about a hundred yards ahead of us. Once half that distance had been covered another hand signal split the column into the two respective squads, D heading straight on towards the concrete building while A headed right along the bottom of the slope, intending to circle round behind the probable storeroom and reach the far end of the accommodation hut. I was in the latter party, tucked in just behind Ishen. It didn't look like he'd be needing any advice, but if he did . . .

We reached the far end of the building and waited there in the dry grass, listening for any tell-tale sounds from inside and trying not to make any ourselves. It seemed to be growing lighter by the minute, which was all to the good. Since we didn't know where the light switch was inside the building we might be needing outside help.

By my watch there was less than two minutes to go when a series of noises rudely interrupted our silent vigil: a thumping sound, followed in quick succession by running footsteps and a loud groan.

Shit, I thought.

The door was wrenched open, bare feet slapped on bare earth, and, to almost universal surprise, someone began throwing up. I was the exception here, but I'd been smelling the lamb fat stew all day.

Ishen risked a quick look round the corner of the building and checked his watch again. For a moment I thought he was unsure what to do, but then I realized he was just making sure he got his timing right – we had about forty-five seconds before the simultaneous attacks were due to begin. After a few more had gone by he gave me the hand signal for stay and disappeared round the corner. I reached it just as the sounds of throwing-up resumed, and the sight which greeted my eyes was certainly unique in my military experience: a man trying to surrender in mid-vomit. I wasn't sure but I even thought I saw the beginnings of a grin on Ishen's face.

He gestured the rest of us forward, and I realized that the previous evening's stew had done us a favour. The man who'd been bringing it up might have woken his friends, but they would have no reason to assume that the next person through the door would be anyone but him.

Instead, it was Ishen, closely followed by yours truly. He found the light switch where we hoped it would be, on the wall just inside the door, and the two of us stepped quickly across the room to where a couple of men were grunting in their bunks, no doubt cursing their noisy comrade. An AK74 barrel against the side of the head put matters in a clearer perspective, and both lay there rigid with terror, their mouths opening and closing like stranded fish, as other members of the squad swept through into the second room. In a few seconds all six of the traffickers were under the gun, without a shot being fired.

Nor had I heard any from the building next door, or those down the valley. A feeling of quiet exultation began rising in my stomach, one which survived even the continued sound of vomiting from outside. Squads C and D were reporting their successes as I walked out past the unfortunate source and headed for the long building opposite. A fluorescent light flickered on the response to the switch, illuminating pretty much the scene I'd expected. The drug lab I'd seen in the jungles of Colombia had been a cocaine set-up, but either the production process was similar or I was too tired to notice the differences, because it all looked pretty familiar. There seemed to be quite a haul of opium bricks waiting for the chemist but I wasn't sure how many bricks made one bag of white powder. Nor did I particularly care.

'How about a fire?' I wondered out loud, but on reflection it didn't seem such a great idea. Chechnulin might see it as a questioning of his integrity, and that wasn't something I wanted to do. It also occurred to me, as I re-emerged into the rapidly brightening day, that the appearance of a still-functioning complex would continue to draw both sellers and buyers.

I walked across to the concrete building just as its two former occupants were being taken to join their comrades in the dorm. The Russian had a slight smile on his face, as if he'd been expecting something as tragic as this from the beginning, but the Tadjik's mouth was turned down in an angry pout. He was probably saying something uncomplimentary about Kirghiz breeding, because one of the lads gave him a playful jab in the gut with his gun barrel.

A few yards down the path, C Squad were approaching with their two prisoners, both of whom looked like Tadjiks. 'It's an old Ranger station,' Sheff told me. 'One room was covered in posters of different types of bear.'

In the concrete building we found Ishen glancing through what looked like a ledger and Lulu trying to make sense of the radio. 'Any joy?' I asked the Welshman.

'Looks straightforward enough,' he said. 'Who do you want to call?'

'How about giving Chechnulin a wake-up call?' I suggested to Ishen. 'We can tell him the good news, and we can also encourage him to send some transport for us and the prisoners. He'll probably want to leave some men here to pick up anyone who drops in, and the sooner we're all out of here the better chance they'll have of catching anyone.'

'Maybe he'll give the job to us,' he said, and I had that nice feeling again, the one the teacher gets from a job well done.

Chechnulin didn't give us the job, which as far as I was concerned was just as well: I was feeling jaded enough to want a decent meal and a good night's sleep – luxuries like that. But our drive back to Khorog had a distinctly triumphant air to it nevertheless. We'd shut down a major operation, taken eight prisoners and confiscated a lot of poppy products, all without suffering so much as a scratch. It was the sort of success which could cement a unit's morale and breed much-needed confidence, not to mention the sort of pride which comes before a fall.

12

We reached Khorog around lunchtime on the Friday, and the notion of travelling back down-river for our last scheduled night on patrol seemed as absurd to Chechnulin as it did to the rest of us. Hot baths and hot meals were the first priority, and then the unit headed *en masse* for the bright lights of downtown Khorog and a well-deserved celebration. As we all crowded into a bar I noticed that many of the lads were carrying bulging plastic bags, and when I got the chance I asked Ishen what was in them. 'Mostly food and cigarettes from the base shop,' was his answer. 'The local women don't take money – there's nothing to buy with it here.'

The owners of the bar still took money for drink, but then I suppose that had pride of place when it came to filling the twice-daily flights from Dushanbe. The vodka tasted more like meths than anything else, but after a few glasses it didn't seem to matter. We toasted all our heroic feats of the last forty-eight hours and then moved on through the usual litany of loved ones, political and sporting figures. I was almost moved to tears by one of the Kirghiz lads raising his glass to Budgie Byrne – he didn't know who the fuck he was toasting, but he obviously liked the sound of the words.

Saturday was for recovering, and for enjoying the simple things. It's hard to exaggerate how good a hot meal – even lamb stew – can taste after several days on cold rations, or how luxurious a bunk mattress can feel after sleeping on the hard ground. Lulu and I did some repair work with needles and cotton, Sheff wrote a long letter to his mum, and Gonzo disappeared with his camera to take pictures of the town. That evening we all got ten minutes on the telephone to England, which in my case was almost a mixed blessing. Though she did her best to hide it, I could tell that Ellen was beginning to feel frustrated by my absence, as she had every right to be.

From midnight our unit was officially on stand-by, with two squads at a moment's notice to jump aboard the Hip-H transport chopper waiting on the base helipad. One of the minor posts along the river might find itself under attack, or evidence of a large incursion might persuade a patrol commander to request back-up. If we'd got embroiled in a fire-fight with the Afghans three nights earlier, we'd have been calling for such assistance ourselves.

Our first night on, no one dialled 999, and I got my first decent sleep of the week. A pleasant breakfast and a lazy morning followed, and it almost felt like a Sunday at home until I got word that Chechnulin wanted to see me in his office.

He had news from the front. Early the previous evening a Russian patrol in one of the upstream sectors had intercepted – stumbled across, it sounded like – a sizeable band of drug traffickers. Two Russian soldiers and eleven of the traffickers had been killed, and several more of the latter had escaped. Almost a hundred pounds of heroin had been seized – about half a million dollars' worth at Moscow street prices – and two prisoners taken, one of whom had been very talkative in the hours that followed.

Here Chechnulin managed a simultaneous shrug and a curl of the lip, acknowledging the inevitability of his troops' behaviour even as he deplored it. The Tadjik had given up the location of two major drug labs in the hills above Faizabad, he went on, turning to pinpoint the Afghan town on the wall map behind him. It lay about sixty miles to the south-west, across the spur of high mountains which separated the valley of the Pyandzh and the Kokcha.

'A hundred pounds is a lot of heroin,' he said, 'particularly for an armed group of amateurs. And with your unit's success the other day, it'll make even more sense for the bastards to refine the stuff before it crosses the border.' He turned to look out the window, and I knew what was coming. 'All we'll ever catch is the couriers, the men who move the stuff from the labs in Afghanistan to the distributors in Osh and beyond. And if there's more than enough heroin and more than enough couriers to go round then it won't really matter how many we catch, because there'll always be more.'

'The Americans have come to much the same conclusion in Latin America,' I told him.

'And they haven't let national borders deter them

from taking action against the drug labs,' Chechnulin said, as if I'd just proved his point for him.

'Not always,' I agreed.

'How do you think your government would feel about your being involved in the destruction of drug laboratories on Afghan soil?'

Several thoughts went through my mind. Firstly, I was more interested in how I felt than in the opinion of my government, and my gut reaction was no. Secondly, I wanted to go home – would involvement in a raid like this slow the process, or could we exchange participation for a return ticket? Thirdly, I had to admit it would make a great final training exercise . . .

'I don't know,' I said simply in answer to the question.

'You have no ethical objections yourself?'

It was a strange word to use but I thought I knew what he meant. 'To invading another country?'

He nodded.

I shook my head. 'Drug traffickers destroy civil authority in a country and then make a big deal out of national sovereignty to prevent anyone else from restoring it. A border's just a tool of the trade to them.'

'So you would have no objection if I asked my government to seek your government's approval?'

I sighed. 'I guess not. I suppose you've considered airstrikes against these labs?'

'Of course. But you know the problems with that as well as I do. The installations would have to be above ground, recognizable from the air, and susceptible to surprise attack. And destruction would be almost impossible to verify.' He smiled at me. 'I don't think your colleagues in the SAS would have been airlifted into Iraq to destroy Scud missiles if the Allied High Command thought they could take them out from the air.'

He had a point. 'Why us?' I asked.

He smiled again. 'It pains me to say so, but because your unit is the best equipped for the task.'

I believe I concealed my surprise, but I could understand his reasoning: if I was in command of a largely conscript force and fate pushed a few experienced soldiers my way I'd also be tempted to make whatever use of them I could. 'What's happening in Afghanistan at the moment?' I asked.

'The Taliban are in control of about half the country, and our Intelligence people are certain they will take Kabul before the year is out. Whether they can get any further north is debatable – the Tadjiks and the Uzbeks won't be as easy to subdue as the Pathan areas. Across the border from us there's not even a rebel authority, just a network of armed groups, most of whom are now involved in the drug trade. Subsistence agriculture apart, it's about the only economy the Kokcha valley area has.'

I sighed again. 'Go ahead and talk to your government,' I told him. 'I'll talk to my colleagues.'

They seemed much less reluctant than I did. 'We're just as likely to run into them this side of the border as that, so what difference does it make?' was Sheff's comment. 'And they'll be less on their guard in their own backyard,' Gonzo added.

'But why the fuck would our government go along with this?' Lulu wanted to know, and, at first thought anyway, he seemed to have a point. Trouble was, you never knew what devious reasons those bastards in Whitehall might come up with when it came to sanctioning the apparently unsanctionable. And half the time they never bothered to give you the reasons anyway.

I wondered how the rest of the unit would react if anything came of this – from what I'd read about the Soviet intervention in Afghanistan it was clear that many of the Red Army's Central Asian troops had experienced profoundly divided loyalties. Going in after drug labs was a very different business, but human minds have a funny way of mixing such things up.

For the moment we said nothing to the squad commanders, preferring to wait for a decision from on high, and the next two days of stand-by duty passed uneventfully, with no calls for assistance from the units out on patrol. It was on the Wednesday evening that Chechnulin called me in again. The British government had apparently given their unofficial approval to the Russian government's request, but someone was flying out to Tashkent for a meeting with me on the following day. Chechnulin didn't seem to know why, and neither did I.

I went back to the others, told them to start getting a proposal together while I was away, and spent the night getting used to the idea of flying both in and out of the airport up the road.

When the time came I just sat there, hair standing

on end, as the pilot of the Soviet transport plane did his best to draw lines with his wingtips on adjacent mountainsides. I'd been through enough turbulence in my time, but the air currents in these mountains were unbelievable – sometimes it felt like the whole plane was bungee-jumping. I'm sure the clowns in Air Troop would have loved every minute of it, but I'd joined Mountain Troop because I liked the earth where I could feel it: under my feet. The flight took less than two hours, but I'm sure I got my first grey hair that evening.

The thought of getting back on the plane in a few hours' time was so appalling to contemplate that when James told me that the man from London had been delayed a day, and that I'd have to stay the night in a hotel, I almost hugged him. On the way to the centre of town he gave me the latest episode in the Lada affair – the car had vanished into thin air on its way home from Bishkek – but was unable to offer any clues as to why the Foreign Office was wasting money on a day-trip to Uzbekistan for one of its minions. The man would arrive early the next morning, be driven to the Embassy for a few hours' sleep, and see me at noon sharp. I would be collected at the hotel at eleven-twenty. Until then, James told me, my time was my own.

I looked over my room, realized I had no luggage to leave in it, and went out for a walk in the blistering sun. This soon drove me into the shade of a *chaikhana*, and for a couple of hours I just sat and vacantly watched the world go by, mulling things over in my mind. The secondment of an SAS team to the CIS was unprecedented, but not particularly outrageous given the shared interest in stemming the drug traffic from Afghanistan and Central Asia. Allowing the SAS team to be used in a cross-border exercise by the CIS was also unprecedented, but made sense insofar as the situation on the ground was concerned. We'd be out on a limb, but then we often were. It was the politics which were different, not the level of danger we were exposing ourselves to.

So why did I feel worried? Because I was going to be a father, and exposing myself to danger suddenly seemed less like an occupational hazard and more like an irresponsible gamble? Because the whole situation reminded me of the children's game Consequences, in which a series of rational pieces becomes an irrational whole? Because I was growing old and cynical, and wise enough to be scared? Who was I kidding? No one had forced me on that plane today.

I walked back to the hotel in the gathering dusk, enjoying the cool breeze which now seemed to be flowing down from the mountains, and got a restaurant recommendation from the Intourist booth in the lobby. Her name was Irina too, but she didn't look like the one Sheff had been chatting up in Samarkand. I stared at her as she made the phone reservation for me, thinking that living without women wasn't something I wanted to do any more.

The restaurant was half-empty when I arrived, but thereafter it seemed to fill up quite quickly. I scanned the menu for dishes that didn't contain sheep meat, and after the waiter had done a wing-flapping mime I settled for something unpronounceable which turned out to be chicken kebab. Waiting for the meal I got through three glasses of wine, and by the time it arrived I was feeling not only hungry but decidedly maudlin. I missed Ellen, I missed England, I missed my three musketeers in Khorog. I even missed the Kirghiz lads.

The meal was good, though, and afterwards my spirits rose, as they usually did, as I walked through the sights, sounds and smells of an unknown city. I went to bed early and slept well, given how strange it felt to be in a comfortable bed.

In the morning I showered and put my only clothes back on, hoping that the man from the Foreign Office didn't have a fastidious nose. James arrived on the dot to collect me, and we reached the British Embassy, a miles or so to the north, with almost half an hour to spare. I was deposited in a reception room which had obviously been decorated to make visiting Uzbeks feel at home, all except for the magazines, which were year-old copies of *Vogue* and *The Economist*. Just the right selection for the intellectual deb, I thought. There must be hundreds of them in Uzbekistan.

The emissary from the Foreign Office finally appeared. He looked nothing like the stereotype I'd grown up with – the harassed bank manager, reminiscent of John Le Mesurier in *Dad's Army* – but then they never did, and I don't know why I kept on expecting them to. These days they more often looked like yuppie brokers, and this one was no exception. His name was Marshall Aherne; he had stylishly trimmed hair and the empty smile of a TV newsreader; he wore black-rimmed designer glasses, a very smart suit, and a tie you could check paint colours against. He was also irritable – either Indians happily anticipating the bright lights of their homeland had kept him awake all night or Tashkent was proving too hot and dusty for his clothes or temperament.

I tried to repress my prejudices and listen to what he had to say, but there wasn't much of it.

'We'd like you to accommodate the local commander's wishes,' he began, which sounded like bad grammar, if not bad news. He then went off on a long ramble, the purpose of which seemed to be to absolve the Foreign Office of any conceivable responsibility should anything go wrong. We were to 'take the appropriate decisions' when it came to putting ourselves at serious risk, because if we were taken prisoner in Afghanistan our release could prove difficult to 'facilitate'. 'Every conceivable diplomatic option would be pursued,' but there was no guarantee that any would prove 'viable'. By the time he'd finished I was half-expecting him to produce a form for me to sign which waived any claims I might one day want to press against Her Majesty's Government.

Why were they so keen to help the Russians? I asked myself. Because they really thought the issues at stake were important? Because some trade deal needed a sweetener? Or because it wasn't that important, but the most it could cost the Foreign Office was the lives of four British soldiers?

I asked Marshall, which sparked off another ramble. The war on drugs was a 'supra-national priority', the moderates in Moscow needed help pulling Russia back into the 'community of civilized nations', it was important to lay the foundations for 'the rule of law in Central Asia'. In other words, pure politico-babble, nineties style. He didn't actually mention the New World Order, but that was probably an oversight.

By this time I'd realized I wasn't going to get an honest answer, and was beginning to wonder why he'd bothered to come. In my experience politicians never have that much trouble leaving their soldiers hanging out to dry, whether or not they get their permission to do so in advance.

I told him that the four of us were willing to take the job on, but that I wanted verbal confirmation from the CO in Hereford. He seemed to think that was a good idea, which at least removed my suspicion that the whole business was being conducted behind the rest of the Regiment's back. The CO didn't sound particularly alert – it was six-thirty in the morning in Hereford – and he seemed to think we were doing the Americans a favour. The Yanks were apparently busy sponsoring the burning of poppy fields in eastern Afghanistan, and were eager to show the drug traffickers that there was no safe haven for them in the north.

We talked for a few minutes about the operation in prospect, which we both agreed seemed straight-forward enough. The one thing that really bothered me was the Russian comm gear we had to work with, and I asked him to ship us out a dozen of the Motorola comms we'd used in similar situations in Colombia. I also told him that short of teaching our charges to sing *Oklahoma*, we'd taken them about as far as we could. 'And surprisingly enough,' I added for good measure, 'none of us want to put down roots in Poppyland. So how about pulling us out after this one?'

'I can't promise anything,' he said, 'but I don't think that'll be a problem.'

James drove me to the airport, where the same pilot and plane were waiting to take me back to Khorog. I gave up wondering why we were being sent on this operation and started thinking about the how, where and when – or at least I did until the pilot grabbed my attention with his first fifteen-hundred-foot plummet through an air pocket. Overall, the flight back seemed more bearable than the flight out, but only because it couldn't possibly have been as bad as I was expecting.

Back in Khorog I discovered that the unit had been called out to one of the upstream posts the previous day, only to find the drama was all over by the time they arrived. A large band of fighters from across the border had tried to launch a surprise attack on the post, but an apparently negligent discharge had given their presence away, and after a bit of posing they'd slipped back across the river. C and D Squads had spent a couple of hours crammed into the belly of a Hip-H wondering when the rocket was going to hit, all for nothing.

Gonzo, Lulu and Sheff received the news that we were going across the border with their usual blend of cynicism and guarded enthusiasm, but I thought I also detected some relief in their response – I think they all guessed that this meant the end was probably in sight. I didn't tell them about the CO's half-promise, thinking that it would be a nice surprise if he delivered, and less of a let-down if he didn't.

Chechnulin was pleased enough with the news to pull us out of the normal rotation as of midnight. 'Have you got a timetable in mind?' he asked.

'The sooner the better,' I said without thinking and then did some quick mental calculations. It shouldn't take more than two or three days to prepare, but I wasn't going in without the Motorolas. 'Early next week, I should think,' I added, and we got down to discussing what we'd be needing. I told him about the package of comms gear coming from England, and he said he'd do his best to make sure it didn't end up sitting on the Tashkent tarmac for a month. He also promised to try and dig up any old Soviet satellite photos of the areas in question, and to put a couple of his Intelligence officers to work collating all the information which had been gleaned from the interrogation of prisoners over the last couple of years.

I went for my supper feeling that if what we needed was at all available, then Chechnulin would get it for us. I only wished I had a similar faith in the helpfulness of the Foreign Office.

The following morning the four of us and the four squad leaders knuckled down to the business in hand. Over the past few weeks the locals had gradually been taking over the reins of authority, which was as it should have been, but for this operation it already seemed tacitly accepted that we would be having at least an equal say in calling the shots.

The first couple of hours were mostly spent collecting all the bits and pieces we needed – maps, topographical reports, weather statistics, intelligence of the area in question – and most of the rest of the day was devoted to looking at the various options open to us. The two drug labs which we were going after were about twenty miles apart; Target One in the Kokcha valley proper, not far outside the small town of Jurm, Target Two some six miles above the smaller town of Zerak in a feeder valley. For the moment I was thinking in terms of two squads per target, but if the enemy numbers on the ground looked on the high side we might need to operate as a single unit.

For the moment all we had were the rough locations, but I was hoping to get a more precise fix from the intel data Chechnulin had promised. These labs were only about forty miles from the border, and some of the prisoners taken in border skirmishes should have exact knowledge of their whereabouts. And there was always the satellite photos.

Alijon then briefed us on the local geography. The terrain of the valleys which drained into the Kokcha was not, he told us, very friendly when it came to covert force insertion. There was some cover on the upper slopes, but even this had been greatly thinned in recent years by drier than usual weather and the Red Army's use of chemical defoliants during the intervention. The lower slopes and valley bottoms were mostly dry, with only scattered copses of trees along the banks of the rivers. It wasn't going to be as bad as life on Iraq's billiard-table of a desert, but by day at least any movement was going to be problematic.

The human terrain, being more changeable than the geography, was harder to pin down. Faizabad, the town some twenty miles further down the valley from Jurm, had once had a population of over 25,000, but the twenty years of the Afghan civil war could have either halved or doubled that. Further upstream there would be villages working the land beside the river, but even the largest of them, like Jurm, would contain only a few hundred homes. There was a road marked on the maps, but Alijon thought the chances of it being paved were remote.

On the slopes above the river, fields of dry crops would give way to skimpy pasture land, and this to high, rocky valleys and the snow-draped front line of the Pamirs. The only humans one was likely to meet would be tending sheep, toting guns or trafficking drugs across the passes which led down into the valley of the Pyandzh. In the area as a whole there was no chance of an organized police presence in the normal sense, but there would be men with guns who saw it as their right and obligation to impose some sort of social order. There always were. But just how many there might be, and where they would be found at any particular time, was impossible to say.

The weather was easier to reckon. We'd be only about sixty miles further south than we were now, and about fifteen hundred feet closer to sea level. By day it would be hotter but still bearable, by night a little less chilly. The nights would be clear and moonless if we went in as intended early in the following week, which might be a problem if Chechnulin failed to come up with the night-vision goggles he had promised us.

We started another brew-up, stretched our legs outside for a few minutes and then began discussing our infil options. Of the four usual candidates two were quickly dismissed – there was no road to take, so vehicles were out, and there was no time to give the unit parachute training, much less instruction in the specialist techniques of HAHO and HALO. This left us a choice between walking in and insertion by helicopter, and no one seemed disposed to choose two or three nights trekking across cold and barely mapped mountains over a half-hour flight in a Hip-H. More out of a desire to be thorough than anything else, I pointed out the disadvantages of chopper insertion: it would be noisy, someone would probably notice our arrival and report it, and the drug labs would be put on maximum alert. Gonzo argued, as I could have done, that we were just as likely to be spotted hiking in over the mountains, quite possibly before we were even halfway there. Choppers it would be – we'd just have to choose the drop-off and collection points with great care. And that could only be done after we'd gathered every piece of available information about the area, not to mention talking to the police.

Next we discussed what we'd like to be carrying in the way of equipment. Some silenced guns were high on my list, but I had my doubts whether we'd be able to get hold of any, so we'd probably be relying on the usual AK74s and handguns. Stun grenades would have also come in handy, but unfortunately for the opposition it looked like we'd have to make do with the kill variety. We needed enough explosives to raze the drug labs to the ground, enough ammo to fight off any opposition, and I made a note to ask Chechnulin if he could get us a couple of sniper rifles. Given that we weren't walking in over the mountains, I added the word 'mortars' with a question mark.

We were still assuming two separate parties, which meant two radios for contact with home base and two sets of Motorolas for close-range communication. They had a range of just under a mile in open country, and from what we'd heard the Kokcha valley seemed depressingly open.

When it came to the labs themselves, we needed more information before any real planning could begin. We would probably have to find and CTR them before we finally went in, but the details would have to wait, in some instances until we were actually eyeballing the place.

Finally we talked about the E&E, the escape and evasion plan. Individuals or groups might get separated from their mates, and might fail to make the RV with the exfiltration chopper. The chopper itself might be unable to make the RV for a variety of reasons; communications between the men on the ground and the rest of the world could be broken by something as simple as a dropped radio. If one or more of these unfortunate eventualities transpired, leaving anything between one and forty men effectively stranded behind enemy lines, the E&E was put into operation. In this case, if communications with home base were still open, we could try to arrange a new time and place for the pick-up. If not, and the worst came to the worst, we would have to walk home across the mountains, and therefore every one of us would have to be carrying a detailed map of the area in question.

I gave Ishen the job of producing one and getting the relevant copies made, and then tried my hand at summarizing where we'd got to and what we still had to do. I received a few yawns for my effort, and one piece of advice: to forget joining the after-dinner speaker circuit.

'For the moment,' I concluded, 'we'll give the two groups separate call-signs – Papa Zero One and Papa Zero Two.' It seemed appropriate, naming the operation after my new role in life.

13

Six days later I was standing by the base helipad, wondering whether the Hip-H would have much competition in an ugly helicopter contest. There were two of them in front of me, their noses highly reminiscent of Second World War bombers, their squat bodies crowned with what looked like left-over jet engines and huge, five-bladed rotor assemblies. Painted a sickening olive green, they still bore the red stars of a vanished age, and I wondered if there were furry Lenins hanging over the controls.

So much for pre-op fantasies. They were supposed to be reliable flyers, and they were well able to defend themselves with machine-gun and rockets. The two three-man crews, who were chatting and smoking in a circle away to my right, seemed to be composed exclusively of Russians. Several were holding their NVGs, which had apparently arrived at the same time as ours. I hoped they were as used to flying with them as they said they were, because there were a lot of high mountains between us and the Kokcha valley.

The last of the men were clambering into the bellies of the beasts, and I reluctantly joined the end of the queue. Papa Zero One, composed of Squads A and

D, was in one chopper, Papa Zero Two in the other, but both forces were going to be dropped off at the same spot, more or less equidistant from the two targets. This decision had been made after a lengthy discussion, and though I'd pressed for it, I still wasn't completely convinced it was the right one.

Inside the Hip-H it was at least nice and warm, though the stink of fuel didn't help the cosy ambience. The turboshafts sprang into life above us, the rotors began to scrape with increasing urgency, and after what seemed a long few minutes the helicopter jerked itself off the relative safety of mother earth. I remember thinking that the flight was going to be the worst part of the whole business, which doesn't say much for my powers of prescience.

Across the fuselage from me I could just about see Lulu. He was sitting with his eyes closed and a tranquil expression on his face, as if he'd been through something like this a hundred times before, and as I looked at him I realized that he had, and that on many of those occasions I'd been there with him. I sat there imagining the other two in the other helicopter, Sheff with his knowing grin, Gonzo doing his unconscious impersonation of an absent-minded professor. I knew these men, and they knew me, in ways that no one else would or could. It felt a bit like a betrayal of Ellen to think it, but it was true.

I looked round at the other faces. They hadn't done this enough times to take it in their stride, but none of them seemed more than naturally nervous. I knew all their names by now, and I thought I knew most of their strengths and weaknesses as soldiers – particularly those of the men in the squad I'd been attached to – but I didn't know *them*. We communicated with each other in a language that was foreign to us all; we had grown up in lands and cultures which could hardly be more different. I liked most of them, I even thought of some as friends, but I didn't think we would ever understand what made each other tick.

The helicopter shuddered momentarily and then continued on its way, as if it had paused for the machine equivalent of a sneeze. We were still flying south down the Pyandzh valley, minimizing the time spent over Afghan territory. After twenty minutes or so the pilot would climb to the right for the short flight across the mountains which separated the valleys of the Pyandzh and the Kokcha. I tried to concentrate on what would happen once we landed, half-hoping that my faith in that eventuality would help the chopper in its struggle with gravity.

We now knew considerably more about the area we were headed for. The re-interrogation of prisoners had produced most of this significant increase in the information at our disposal, and though I found myself wondering about the methods with which this had been obtained, there didn't seem much point in ignoring possibly life-saving intelligence on account of suspicions which couldn't be verified.

Chechnulin had also delivered on the satellite photographs, which turned out to be more than a decade old. This limited their usefulness, but by no means destroyed it. The labs were nowhere to be seen, but their locations could be inferred – or at least guessed at – by putting together the visible geography with our other sources of information. Two unusually sycophantic prisoners had admittedly failed to confirm our guesswork, claiming that they were confused by the aerial perspective, but I thought I'd seen the light of recognition flicker in at least one pair of eyes.

It wasn't the sort of certainty we'd have liked but it was better than nothing. And when it came to potential opposition in the area the news was all good. The local fighters, almost all of whom served in Ahmed Masoud's Tadjik army, were mostly away for the summer campaigning season, trying to keep the Taliban from overrunning the capital, Kabul. With any luck we'd have nothing more serious to deal with than the hired thugs of the drug traffickers.

The dips and soars of the Hip were more pronounced now, as we bounced our way in and out of the thermals. Another ten minutes and we would be setting down on what we hoped was an isolated stretch of the road from Barak to Zebak, with no one to either hear or observe our arrival. The alternative had been to land each force closer to its target, but in the case of the lab near Jurm this would have meant a drop-off somewhere in the populated Kokcha valley, with all the obvious dangers which that entailed. The likelihood of our raising an alarm implied completion of the operation in a single night, and a timetable which seemed altogether too ambitious. Better to get in unseen, and take our time reaching and casing the targets, before we actually knocked on the traffickers' doors and woke up the neighbourhood. At least this was the theory. We would soon know if it was a good one.

The spare member of the crew shouted out a two-minute warning, which gave the calmest man there – Lulu, probably – time to get his adrenalin up and running. We couldn't see a thing, of course, but the chopper was certainly going down. And down. I was beginning to wonder whether the pilot had landed in a big well when we settled to earth with surprising gentleness. The doors swung open, and the men began piling out into the dust cloud raised by the landing. If we'd been under attack none of us would have heard or seen much, but there didn't seem to be any bullets hitting me or any of the men around me.

As the men formed a wide defensive perimeter around the helicopter the last of our kit was heaved out of the doors. These slammed shut, the blades revved a little higher and the chopper lifted back into the air, causing minor squalls in the dust it had already raised. Fifty yards up the road I could see the dim shape of the other Hip lifting off, and within seconds the noise of the two craft was receding into the distance. The dust settled a little more slowly to reveal a dirt road, dry river-bed and bare valley sides.

Welcome to Afghanistan, I thought.

The two units waved each other good luck in the gloom and struck out in their separate directions: Papa Zero Two heading north up the slope which ran down to the empty track, Papa Zero One across the stony river-bed and diagonally up the opposite side of the valley. Within seconds the two units were invisible to each other, even to those select few lucky enough to be wearing the NVGs. The Soviet goggles weren't exactly state-of-the-art – like most articles of Soviet equipment they were reliably basic in design – but in the depths of the valley there was precious little ambient light for them to work with. That was mostly above us, in a sky almost choking with stars.

Still, invisibility wasn't exactly a hardship, and navigating the two squads across the bare slopes was easy enough for a man with a compass. We slowly climbed towards where we hoped the trees would begin, and our noses caught the scent of pine before our eyes could make out the first dark treetops shifting against the starry backdrop. Not needing their cover for the moment, we followed the edge of the forest as it curved brokenly around to the south. So far we had seen no trace of either human or animal life, and not a single source of earthly light. If anyone in the area was aware that helicopters had landed they were proving slow to check it out.

I had the feeling we'd got away with it, which made me feel much more sanguine about the whole operation. If the opposition didn't cop our presence until a couple of drug labs went sky-high then we'd be halfway home before you could say 'Mujaheddin'.

We walked on across the thinly grassed slopes, climbing in and out of the small valleys which crossed our line of march. After about two hours the countryside to our right seemed to open up, but whether that was something I could really see, or just the satellite photograph in my mind, was hard to tell. And then the first twinkles of light appeared in the distance, some way to the south and way below the natural horizon. Unless we'd taken a wrong turn in the helicopter this was Jurm, and the dark emptiness falling away from our feet was the Kokcha valley.

Another hour's march brought us to a position directly across from the dim lights, and there we retreated several hundred yards into the trees, leaving only a four-man OP just inside the forest's edge. We could see nothing of Jurm, but as I stared down into the darkness something seemed wrong, and when the dawn arrived I realized what it was: the valley was much flatter than I'd imagined. Perhaps I'd been fooled by the flattening effect of the satellite pictures, or perhaps I'd just grown used to Central Asian valleys all being variations on the Grand Canyon, but the valley of the Kokcha didn't live up to expectations. From where I lay the eastern side sloped down to make an imperceptible join with the irrigated floor of the valley, which was at least a mile wide. The river ran closer to the western side, its course given away by occasional stands of poplars, and beyond it lay the town, a larger than expected sprawl of monochrome buildings which straggled for a mile or so beneath a row of dun-coloured cliffs. The one exception was a small, white mosque, whose slender minaret seemed like an intrusion of delicacy in the coarse landscape.

On and beyond the southern outskirts of the town there were several gashes in the cliffs, and it was deep inside the third of these small canyons that we believed our target was located. There was no way to confirm this from our current position – through the binoculars I could see no indication of a track in the narrow opening, but a copse of trees partially obscured the view. Our provisional plan had been to simply slip across the valley under cover of darkness and enter the canyon, but I began to wonder whether it might not be better to cross the wide floor a couple of miles to the south, and work our way up into the high ground behind the canyons. I examined the relevant satellite picture in the half-light of the camouflaged scrape and decided it was feasible.

I had the whole day to think it over. In the distance the town slowly came to life, dispatching a couple of lorries and one bus in the direction of Faizabad. Figures began appearing in the irrigated fields, and a crowd of women brought the family washing down to the almost empty river. There was no sign of military activity – not so much as a single man carrying a gun. Nobody set foot on the slopes below us, and when my turn to sleep came round at noon I was feeling pretty confident. If the drug lab was where we thought it was there didn't seem much in the way of our lighting the blue touch-paper and stepping back.

Soon after dark Ishen, Alijon, Lulu and I held a council of war. Ishen, it turned out, had come to the same conclusion as I had, and the other two, who hadn't had the advantage of several hours of gazing across the valley, weren't inclined to disagree. It would take us between two and three hours to reach a position above the canyon, an hour at most to do the business, and maybe one more to get far enough south of the town to call in the exfil. Add an extra hour for safety and we had six to work with – if we set out at ten we'd be out of Afghan airspace with first light still half an hour away.

So went the theory.

So, up to a point, would go the practice. The twenty of us were on the march again at the time specified, the town with its few remaining lights falling away behind us. I guessed people went to bed early in these parts – there was no electricity and solid fuel would be neither cheap nor easy to get. The stars were brighter than anything Jurm had to offer, and the soft pinpricks of yellow light across the valley seemed redolent of a long-gone age. I mentally thanked Uncle Stanley for pushing me out into the world, adding that this was going to be my last such trip for a while. I had a different type of adventure to go on, I told him, one that promised to stretch me every bit as much.

Always assuming I survived this one. We followed the narrowing valley for nearly two miles, then stopped for a few minutes before cautiously working our way down towards the valley floor and following an almost dry irrigation channel to the side of the river. We were now about a hundred yards east of the dirt road which ran up the valley and eventually crossed a high pass into the Chitral province of Pakistan. Only two wheeled vehicles and one string of three mules had left the town in this direction all day, and it didn't seem likely that there'd be any more, but we still waited ten minutes before fording the shallow river and slipping across the track. A well-trodden path led up through the canyon we'd chosen as our best route to higher ground, and about a hundred yards in, the lead scout caught sight of a building up ahead which hadn't been on the satellite picture. It was in darkness, looked abandoned, and we hurried past, wondering what other surprises might lie ahead. Later I would wonder whether it had indeed been as empty as it looked.

There was no beaten path up the narrow cleft but we clambered up what was obviously an old stream bed, sending small stones clattering down behind us, each bounce a small explosion of sound in the huge silence which surrounded us. After about ten minutes of this we emerged on to the gently sloping plateau from which the series of canyons had been gouged, and cautiously began working our way north.

The going was easier now, the starlight illuminating stretches of thin grass, shelves of bare rock and an occasional lone tree twisted by the wind. We skirted the heads of two apparently empty canyons and, about half an hour after reaching the plateau, found ourselves approaching the one which we hoped was home to our target. Ishen and I went forward for a look, crawling the last few yards to the rim with the sort of caution which always feels ludicrously exaggerated when it proves to be unnecessary.

The canyon was about a hundred yards wide and half that distance deep at this point. Even with the NVGs it was hard to see what lay below, and on balance I decided I preferred obscurity without a greenish tinge. After a minute or so I found I could make out a few of the salient features, but there was no way we would be going down with more than the roughest notion of what was waiting for us. That was the bad news; the good news was that there were several buildings down there and any occupants were probably fast asleep.

Three of the buildings, which formed three sides of a small square, sat almost beneath the wall we were looking down from, some hundred yards to our right. What looked like an open lorry was parked in front of them, and beyond that shifting shadows suggested trees. I couldn't make out a stream, but if there was one, that was where it would be. There was a straight line running across the canyon just beyond the buildings, which was probably a wall of some sort. I hoped it was, because I could see nothing else to suggest that we'd find anything valuable in the buildings below. There might be a small, hut-like structure near the centre of the wall, but whatever it was, it wasn't playing host to any night guards. If this was a drug lab Ishen and I were looking at, its owners and operators didn't seem too concerned about security.

But then why should they? The only law in this part of the world was handed down by whichever gang of righteous thugs happened to be in control at any particular moment, and as long as they were getting their cut then who else did the traffickers have to worry about? They probably weren't expecting a house call from the SAS. 'No one expects the SAS,' I murmured to myself, remembering the Spanish Inquisition sketch from *Monty Python*. Some things stay with you till the day you die, I thought, and that would be one of them.

I stared down into the canyon, a warm swell of satisfaction rising up inside me. If they were down there, we had them; if they weren't then that was too bad. Either way, the four of us would be bidding

Central Asia a fond goodbye, and I'd be on my way home to Ellen. Having my nights interrupted by a crying baby would be a nice change from invading Afghanistan.

Ishen and I rejoined the rest of Papa Zero One, and I led the unit north for several hundred yards to the spot which the satellite picture had suggested offered the easiest descent. The canyon was only about thirty yards deep here, there were two gnarled trees close to the rim, and we could give Squads A and D their final exam in abseiling. They didn't have to swing in through any windows, and there were no terrorists waiting at the bottom, but thin clouds were now trailing veil-like across the stars, further reducing the already low level of light, and as the men waited for their descents into the void I could only just make out their grimly concentrating faces a few feet from my own.

By the time we were all gathered at the foot of the wall it was just gone a quarter past two. I had seen no sign of an antenna on the buildings down the canyon, so there seemed no chance of any communication between the two targets, but I couldn't think of any pressing reason to advance the pre-agreed time of three o'clock. Ishen wondered whether we should send a couple of men forward to do a CTR, and then argued himself out of the idea without much help from me. There wasn't really enough time, and in any case the only way they could have seen any more than we had from the rim was to get so close that they'd risk compromising the whole operation.

Ishen, Alijon and I divided the unit into six groups

– the number of Motorola comms at our disposal – and briefed each on the task it was expected to perform. At a quarter to three, after what seemed a lengthy wait, we started off down the canyon. I was in the lead, Ishen at my shoulder, the rest of the men spread out behind us in single file. The stream bed was almost dry, and there was no noise of running water to mask the sound of twenty men's footsteps, but I knew the noise we were making wasn't carrying as far as instinct said it was. We were still about three hundred yards from the cluster of buildings, and the mouth of the canyon, which would show lighter than the walls, was still hidden by a bend in its course.

When it came into view, I called a halt. It was now seven minutes to three, and for four more minutes we waited. I was picturing Sheff, Gonzo and the other two squads doing the same twenty miles to the north-east, and hoping that their job looked as drama-free as ours did.

My digital watch flicked numbers, and I gestured everyone forward with a hand signal. We were making an extra-special effort to lessen the noise now, and only the occasional scrape of a loose pebble rose above the din of our breathing. It was only an animal, I silently told anyone who'd just been jerked awake and was wondering what by.

To either side the canyon walls reared darkly to enclose us – the wide strip of sky a hazy roof above – and I was almost surprised when the cluster of buildings gradually materialized, dim rectangular shapes against the paler background of the wide valley beyond. For some reason the whole scene made me think of Westerns, and I half-expected to hear horses neighing as we approached. I'd have to visit my sister and see the real thing, I told myself. Preferably in daylight.

Fifty yards short of the first building we dropped off three men to act as a cut-off group, and twenty yards further in, Kazat and another man struck out in the direction of the lorry, partly to check that no one was using it to sleep in, partly to make sure that no one got the chance to drive it away. Another three men would circle round behind the buildings to the wall, which they would then follow to the gate we assumed was in it. If it looked as though the small hut was occupied they would act accordingly; if not they would secure that end of the canyon against both escapers and unwelcome arrivals. This left twelve men to deal with the three buildings, all of which looked distinctly modern for north-eastern Afghanistan. They seemed to be constructed from prefabricated parts which I guessed had started life as part of an aid programme for the country's bombed-out villages.

I led my group of four around the back of the first two buildings and waited by the corner of the third for the five other groups to signal their readiness, watching my breath crystallize in the cold air. When the last man reported in I gestured my group forward to the door, listened beside it for a few seconds, then gave everyone the signal to go.

The world was suddenly fully of noise and motion, of doors breaking in, feet running and bodies falling, voices raised in surprise and alarm. I was sweeping the inside of a large, one-room structure with my Russian torch, the Browning in my right hand seeking out anything that moved, any threat to my continued existence. There was none – only cans of acetic anhydride and various pieces of apparatus, including a box of plastic bags like the ones Ellen used for keeping food fresh. 'Alpha is clear,' I reported.

'Bravo clear,' Ishen reported in, a hint of triumph in his voice.

'Charlie clear,' another man told me.

I breathed a sigh of relief. 'Set the charges,' I said to one of the Kirghiz lads, and went to see what, if anything, the others had caught.

One of the other two buildings had been used as a storehouse, but the other had yielded three men, two of whom looked nothing like your typical Afghan. They were young enough to be students, had neatly trimmed beards and short hair, and were wearing T-shirts advertising, respectively, Phil Collins and Garbage. One of them had been sleeping in his designer jeans, the other in boxer shorts, and their devotion to Islam was perhaps exemplified by the American *Sports Illustrated* Swimsuit Calendar which took pride of place on one wall. The third man was older, less nattily dressed and seemed somewhat out of place in this isolated microcosm of the modern world.

Looking at the three of them I first felt a brief surge of anger, and then despair. I wanted to bring every moron who'd ever waxed lyrical about globalization and show him this pair, who'd managed to absorb just about everything bad about our world without buying into any of the values which made it livable.

They'd ditched their own culture in favour of making money out of other people's misery, and when it came to spending it they'd let fashion make all their decisions for them.

I wanted to shake them and scream in their ears: 'What the fuck do you think you're doing with your lives?'

The stares they were giving me were half-sullen, half-bored. They were even too stupid to be frightened.

'Find something to tie their hands with,' I told one of the Kirghiz. Ishen and the other squad commanders had been surprised the previous night when I'd insisted on our taking prisoners – they were all for leaving the traffickers lying in their own blood – but I'd managed to convince them that we'd get more out of them alive than dead. And Chechnulin could always pretend they'd been captured on the Tadjikistan side of the border.

We all moved outside, and the prisoners were laid out face-down while Lulu checked that all the charges had been properly set. We were using Soviet plastic and detonators, which the Kirghiz lads were more used to than he was, but he was in Mother Hen mode that night and I wasn't about to argue with a thorough job. He came back and told me he'd poured a couple of cans of paraffin over the opium bricks and refined heroin, just to make doubly certain that nothing salvageable would be left behind.

It was at this moment that one of the prisoners started shouting in Russian about how his rights were being trampled on. One of the Kirghiz moved towards the man with gun butt raised, but had the sense to restrain himself before I had to – unconscious prisoners need to be carried. Instead we made three gags from his T-shirt and hoped – not with any great sincerity – that he didn't die of pneumonia.

Our twenty-minute fuses had now been burning for five, and it seemed like a good time to leave. We didn't need to be out of the canyon when the buildings went up – if anyone in Jurm heard the explosions they wouldn't know where they came from – but it seemed pointless to lose what little night vision we still retained in a gratifying but blinding flash. So we filed out through the gateway and walked roughly halfway to the mouth of the canyon, at which point I sent two men forward to check out the road.

One man came back five minutes later with the news that it was empty, and I decided to order up our transport. 'Papa Zero One on the way,' our radio operator reported in, and received acknowledgement. They now knew that we would be at the prearranged coordinates – just over a mile up the road – at the prearranged time of 0345 hours. In retrospect it might have been better to just wait where we were, but we wanted to keep the choppers as far away from unfriendly ears as possible; we knew the various Mujaheddin groups had a few MiGs at their disposal, and though it was extremely unlikely that they'd be in this area, no one wanted to take even the slightest risk of being shot down.

At 0315 hours we reached the mouth of the canyon and turned right on to the dirt road which led up the valley. We were walking about five yards apart, with the prisoners near the centre of the column. Kazat was in the lead, a young Kirghiz named Togolok next in line, followed by myself and then Lulu. The light was noticeably worse than when we'd crossed the valley earlier that night, and the poplars lining the river fifty yards to our left were only just visible. I remember thinking that an army could be lining the far bank of the river and the first thing we'd know about it was when the first man fell.

I was just checking my watch when the first explosion sounded, a deep, dull thud which seemed to come from inside the earth. As I glanced back a twin flash of yellow light leapt up above the cliffs and two more cracks, sharper than the first, reverberated in the night air. My respect for Soviet fuses went up a notch, and I was just turning to offer Lulu some silent congratulations for his part when the first gun opened up.

Out of the corner of my eye I saw the two men in front of me fall.

'Down!' I screamed, throwing myself on to the hard earth just as two more guns opened up in the mouth of the canyon we had been just about to pass. I couldn't get any closer to the earth without digging into it, so I rolled sideways off the track, hoping to find some sort of dip in the ground, and immediately struck lucky. The dip was only a few inches deep, but it was a lot better than nothing, and I dug myself further in with my hands, muttering thanks to any gods who'd listen that the Muhammads out there hadn't waited until they had more of us in their sights.

A burst of automatic fire from out in front kicked up dust a few feet from my nose, and I resisted the temptation to fire back. I couldn't believe I was visible from the enemy's position, and I wanted to stay that way.

I also wanted to think, which isn't so easy when an MP5 is going off in your ear. There was no way of knowing how many men there were in front of us, and I didn't fancy running a gauntlet to find out. But we needed to get past them if we were going to catch our ride home, and I was damned if I wanted to walk back across the mountains, particularly with wounded in tow. The answer, for once, was bloody obvious.

A few yards behind me I could hear Lulu muttering his favourite word over and over, like he was chanting a mantra. 'Tell Ishen to get everyone back,' I told him. 'Tell him to get them across the river and bypass these bastards.'

I heard him pass the message on in Russian. 'And what is it we'll be doing?' he asked me in English, the Welsh accent sounding even more pronounced than usual.

'Keeping the bastards busy,' I said, noticing my voice was dangerously close to hysteria. I took a deep breath and tried to make visual contact with the big Welshman. He had sounded only about ten yards away but I couldn't see much as the top of his floppy hat. 'Have you fallen down a fucking well?' I shouted.

He laughed, a strange sound in the circumstances. 'I just rolled off the road and landed in a ditch.'

'Give me some covering fire, then. I need to make sure our two lads are dead.'

'A 66, is it?'

'How many have you got?'

'Just the two. I only brought them for luck.'

'Then save them for when we leave.'

'Right.'

I took another deep breath and told myself that crawling out of a nice safe dent in the ground and offering my body to the bullets flying round above me was the act of a sane man. It wasn't, but what the hell. As Lulu opened up with his MP5 I slithered out of my safe haven and did a quick snake crawl across the dirt road, murmuring a non-stop litany of curses under my breath. Togolok was lying ominously still, and one look at what was left of his head was enough to convince me that he wouldn't be making the trip home. I crawled on, every bone in my body braced for the impact of a bullet, but each burst ended up somewhere else, and I reached the dubious shelter of Kazat's prone body. It didn't take a doctor to realize he wouldn't be needing it himself: he'd taken about half a dozen bullets, most of them in the neck and chest. A picture of his happy face on the night we'd tracked the traffickers across the mountains crossed my mind, and I shook it angrily away. Ellen needs you, I told myself. Survive.

My little dip in the ground seemed a long way away, so I just rolled sideways off the dirt road in search of a ditch of my own. Somewhat to my surprise, I struck lucky again, landing with a thud in a narrow trench a couple of feet deep. Things seemed to be looking up. The enemy didn't seem capable of depressing his angle of fire, and by this time I reckoned most of the unit would be out of visual range. I certainly couldn't see any moving figures out beyond the river, which meant that the enemy couldn't either. In fact, as ambushes went, this one deserved close to zero for technical merit, and even less for artistic expression. Another minute or so and the two of us should be on our way, courtesy of Lulu's trusty M72. A couple of 66s up the ambushers' backsides should at least delay any pursuit, if not discourage one permanently.

I was probably still basking in the glow of our superiority when I heard the vehicle. It was coming from the direction of Jurm, and the fact that it wasn't showing lights suggested that the driver wasn't out joyriding. 'Fuck,' I muttered, and tried to wrap my brain around this one. My first instinct was for us both to make a run for the river, but it didn't take me long to notice the flaw in the plan – the vehicle, whatever it was, could just head on up the track and put itself between us and the helicopter. We had to put it out of commission before we took to our heels.

It sounded like a lorry, and it seemed to be coming forward pretty slowly, as if the driver wasn't sure of what he was getting into. The men in the canyon mouth had stopped firing for a few seconds, and now we could hear how near it was – about a couple of hundred yards away, I decided, just as it loomed cautiously into view at half that distance. Our original ambushers resumed firing over our heads, and the driver obviously took this as a sign to stop.

For one short moment I saw shadowy figures emerging from behind the lorry, but then the head-lights sprang to life, illuminating one segment of the world and throwing the rest into utter darkness. In that bright segment I could see Lulu, one knee bent, the other on the ground, the fat cylindrical barrel of his M72 targeting the lorry.

The 66 set off on its short journey with an explosive whoof, the arms of the silhouetted Welshman seemed to leap upwards as the bullets struck him, and the rocket blew away the front of the lorry, headlights and all, in one blinding flash.

There was a moment of stunned silence, and the guns seemed to open up from all directions. I was already out of my trench, running like an idiot towards the spot where he'd gone down. The bullets were still flying over my head, and I rolled into the ditch, knowing what I'd find but hoping anyway. He'd simply slumped backwards, and there between his staring eyes, neat as a Hollywood movie, was the bullet hole.

I heard myself repeating the word 'fuck' over and over, just as he'd been doing a few minutes earlier, and smashed my fist against the side of the ditch to bring myself back. A hundred yards away the burning lorry was casting an orange glow up the nearby cliff and out across the fields, forcing its erstwhile passengers to keep their heads down. I patted Lulu on the shoulder, told myself I wouldn't get a better chance, and gave the men in the canyon mouth one more burst to keep them quiet. Then I rolled myself out of the ditch, into a crouch, and off on a weaving run towards the distant river, reaching a speed which Trevor Brooking only ever dreamed about.

I reckon I was more than halfway there when the world landed on top of my head and the last of the light disappeared.

14

I woke to the sound of a wailing voice, and for one disoriented moment imagined myself back in Oman. Then I remembered what had happened, and I knew that this muezzin was calling the faithful to prayer from the top of an Afghan minaret.

As I pulled myself into a sitting position the sinking sensation in my stomach swiftly gave way to dizziness. My head seemed to be throbbing, and the probing hand I lifted to check it out encountered cloth. Either I'd already been fitted out with a turban or someone had put a bandage on.

I could smell the disinfectant, which my mother always told us kids was the best way of knowing we were still alive. She'd always sworn by Dettol, which I doubted was big in Afghanistan.

Apart from the head wound I seemed to be all in one piece. My socks, boots and Gore-tex jacket had all been taken, along with my watch and everything I'd had in my pockets, which included the passport photo of Ellen. But at least I hadn't been stripped naked.

In the absence of water there didn't seem much point in disturbing the sticky bandage, so I pulled my back up against the nearest wall and surveyed the other three. They were refreshingly clear of either bloodstains or the carefully ticked-off scratches of prisoners left to rot. All in all, it seemed a pretty pleasant place as such places go, though I had a feeling I would soon be regretting the obvious lack of a bucket.

There was no window, so I didn't even have a rough guide to what time it was, but I felt pretty certain that a significant number of hours had gone by. The hunger in my stomach and the condition of my head suggested at least six, which put the time around mid-morning and the rest of the unit hopefully back across the border. The fact that nobody had thrown cold water over me to get the questioning started seemed to reinforce that notion.

I closed my eyes and my head seemed to throb even harder. I told myself I wasn't in the same situation as the men who'd been captured in Iraq: the people of Afghanistan weren't being pounded by Allied bombers, and the country's forces were at war with each other, not the United Kingdom. I'd been chasing drug traffickers, not taking sides in the civil war . . .

Who was I kidding? The only good news so far was that I hadn't been taken out and shot, and that was probably only because they wanted a conscious target. For a few seconds I felt really angry at the world for dumping me in this position, and then really sad at how I'd let Ellen down. What in God's name had persuaded me – had persuaded any of us – to sign on for this cross-border jaunt? Sheer fucking arrogance, that was what. Another game, boys? Why the fuck not? We're the fucking SAS, fucking supermen one and all.

There now seemed to be a heavy-footed horse galloping around inside my skull, and I told myself to calm down. The lads who'd been captured in Iraq had survived the ordeal. Even Terry Waite had eventually made it home. By this time word would have reached London, and our nearest diplomats would be on the job. It didn't seem likely that we'd have any representation in Kabul, but there was always the Red Cross or the Swedes or someone like that, and they'd be in touch with the various faction leaders, all of whose noses would be twitching with anticipation at the possibility of a bargaining card. Maybe one of the Islamic groups would swap me for a live concert by Cat Stevens, or whatever he called himself these days. They'd probably think 'The First Cut Is the Deepest' was something to do with lopping off limbs for minor crimes.

I was still smiling at this thought when the door swung open to admit two unsmiling Afghans with AK47s, one of whom impatiently gestured me to my feet. I got up slower than he wanted, but the horses were galloping again as we walked down a short corridor and out into a bright courtyard. The sun was riding high in a clear blue sky and through a distant archway I could see more buildings and a far-away line of mountains. Jurm, I guessed. Somehow the name didn't sound reassuring.

My two chaperones funnelled me through one of the doors, which opened on to the courtyard, and into a room which seemed more like an admin office than the

usual interrogation chamber. The man sitting behind
the wooden table didn't look like your usual DSS desk
jockey, though – not unless they've started wearing
crossed bandoliers to protect themselves from angry
clients. A floppy woollen hat covered some of his
thick black hair, beard and moustache most of his
face, but the eyes at least seemed intelligent, and for
that I was grateful – it's always so much harder to
shake stupid people out of their prejudices. He was
wearing one of those Afghan rugs – I later found out
they're called *petous* – wound like a shawl around a
collarless white shirt, and a well-maintained AK74
rested against the wall behind him. His expression
was not exactly welcoming.

My two escorts were still behind me, standing either
side of the door, weapons at the ready.

There were two glasses of green tea on the table,
one of which the man pushed somewhat reluctantly
in my direction, as if he was finding the local
laws of hospitality somewhat inappropriate in the
circumstances. 'My name is Ahmed Momen, and I
am the Jamaat-e-Islami Commander for this area,'
he said curtly in passable Russian. 'What is your
name?'

I took a gulp of the warm tea. 'John Fullagar,' I
told him. 'And I am English,' I added spontaneously,
without stopping to think whether or not this was
a good thing to admit. After warning myself to be
more careful I decided it probably was. We might
have given the Afghans a lot of grief in the nineteenth
century, but the Russians had been making all the
recent running.

Momen snorted with disbelief.

'Do you speak English?' I asked in that language, pressing my luck.

He half-shook his head, so at least he understood the question. 'You are Russian,' he said as if there couldn't be any doubt in the matter.

I insisted I was English. 'The Queen, Maggie Thatcher, Gazza,' I added for good measure.

He looked at me for a moment, shaking his head slowly from side to side, the hint of a smile at the corner of his mouth.

'I was with a CIS unit, but I am English,' I explained, reverting to Russian.

The smile broadened ever so slightly. 'And what would an Englishman be doing with a Russian unit?'

I hesitated for a moment, decided that no state secrets were at stake, and told him about the training mission to Kirghizstan and our unit's secondment to CIS duty on the border. 'We were pursuing drug traffickers,' I added, stretching the truth a bit.

'You were flown into my country by helicopter,' Momen said, but at least he seemed to have accepted the basic story.

I nodded. 'Sometimes it is necessary to ignore borders,' I told him. 'Your jihad, our war on drugs – they are the same in that way,' I added, feeling quite proud of my intellectual footwork.

He gave me a 'who do you think you're kidding?' look, and for one ridiculous moment I wanted to burst out laughing. I had faced the possibility of capture several times over the last twenty years, but now that it had happened, and I was actually being interrogated by someone with the power to snuff out my life, the whole business seemed more absurd than frightening. I began to wonder if the head wound was affecting me in ways I wasn't aware of.

'A doctor looked at your head,' he said, as my hand involuntarily went to the bandage. 'He says there is nothing to worry about.'

'Thank you,' I said, drinking the last of the tea.

'We are not primitives, John,' he told me, and abruptly got up from behind the desk. 'Come with me,' he said, picking up the AK74.

I followed, suddenly feeling weak in the knees. Was this how executions were conducted in Jurm, as a casual afterthought, a regrettable necessity?

We walked across the courtyard, down another small corridor, and emerged into an outside yard. Several Mujaheddin were standing around a pick-up, guns cradled in their arms, and as they parted to let my interrogator through I saw the three bodies lying side by side in the back of the truck, flies buzzing around the areas of encrusted blood. I stared at them, thinking how little sunlight suited death and wondering whether this meant that the others had got away.

'Are these English?' Momen asked, with what could have been either a smirk or a sympathetic smile.

'This one is,' I said, hoping that the Welshman's spirit would forgive me for the ethnic slur. 'The others are both Kirghiz. Do you want their names?'

His gaze lingered on the bodies for a moment, and I hadn't got a clue what he was thinking. 'Later,' he said at last. He turned to my two original escorts, barked out a few words of Tadjik, and they took me back to my cell.

There was still no bucket, and no food in the offing, but for several minutes I just sat there feeling almost overwhelmed by the fact that I was still alive.

This enormous sense of relief sustained me for several days, during which time the treatment meted out by my captors remained as fair as I could reasonably have hoped for. My new diet of rice, *nan* bread and weak tea was monotonous but reasonably nutritious, and a bowl of water was provided for washing once a day. I was given a fifteen-minute walk in the courtyard each morning and a blanket for the chilly nights. A young man in his twenties who claimed to have attended an American medical school came to examine my head wound, pronounced himself satisfied, replaced the bandage and promised he'd be back in a couple of days.

I spent quite a lot of time wondering why I was being treated so well. Why not? I asked myself – maybe the Third World wasn't as full of torturers as Amnesty International had led me to believe. Think again, I answered – it was. And then again, maybe I'd just struck lucky and fallen into the hands of the only commander in Afghanistan who'd heard of the Geneva Convention. That didn't seem very likely either, and I was forced back on the notion that I must be worth something to someone, and that, like the model locomotives my brother collected, I was worth more in mint condition.

There was no way of knowing, because nothing occurred to interrupt my new routine. The meals kept coming, the bucket got emptied, and I had my daily glimpses of the great big world outside, but there were no more chats with Ahmed Momen. As the fear of imminent death receded I started taking each day for granted again, and the fact that I was imprisoned in a small room, far from the one I loved, with no hint of when, if ever, I was going to be released.

This was depressing to think about, and I spent a lot of time drifting in and out of fantasies. Some of these were about my situation – I happily fantasized about rescue missions which my rational self knew would never get mounted – but most of them were the usual boy's dreams. I scored a lot of crucial goals for West Ham in Jurm, and every last one of them was spectacular enough to win Goal of the Season. Sexual fantasies were harder to come by – I couldn't seem to keep my concentration on anyone but Ellen, and she was too real for escapism.

I thought about her, and the two of us, a lot. Sometimes she was running across an Arrivals lounge to welcome me home, her face full of love and happiness, and sometimes we were doing something with our child, like making sandcastles on a beach or decorating a Christmas tree. I felt guilty about what she must be going through, and had nightmares at the thought of something going wrong with the baby because of it. I hoped she knew I was alive.

I had given some thought to escape, but not very much. There was only one way out of my room, and a man was permanently stationed just down the corridor. I had two constant companions for my daily exercise, and there were usually several other Mujaheddin within shouting distance. I could have tried digging a tunnel from my room but it would have been rather hard to hide the entrance. A vaulting horse wouldn't have left me any room to sleep.

The possibility of an escape might present itself if I was moved, but for the moment I resigned myself to waiting.

There were four regulars who brought me food and accompanied me to the courtyard, and over the two weeks I got to know a little about each of them. Abdul, Qazi, Dost and Sa'id – they sounded like the Afghan equivalent of Dave Dee, Dozy, Beaky, Mick and Tich – were all Muslims, and they seemed equally fascinated by how anyone could be anything else. The notion of different religions for different folks was clearly beyond their comprehension. If I was right then they would have to be wrong, which was quite unthinkable. Therefore I was wrong, and I think all but Sa'id felt genuinely sad that I was unable to see the Islamic truth which was staring me in the face.

Language was a problem, of course – they had a smattering of Russian and no English to speak of – but we somehow managed to converse. They all had families, all wanted peace, all feared the Taliban in particular and the Pathans in general. I told them about my child waiting to be born, hoping to get some sort of Stockholm Syndrome thing going, and they all told me they'd pray for a son. They asked about England, but refused to believe anywhere could be as green and wet as I said it was. When I asked them what they knew about Commander Momen's plans for me they would just shrug and mutter what sounded suspiciously like the Tadjik for 'God only knows'. And then they would smile and tell me not to worry, because *insha'allah* – God willing – I would soon get to see my son.

In the meantime I supplied inch-perfect crosses for Geoff Hurst, stared at the photo of Ellen which Momen had sent back to me, and slept away as many hours as I could manage.

It was on the fifteenth day that Qazi and Dost woke me, and I instantly knew that something was up. For one thing the'd brought me my boots, and for another they seemed more subdued than usual. When I asked them what was going on they refused to say anything, which didn't do much for my state of mind. I nervously tied the laces, imagining both the worst and the best: Momen had finally decided on having me shot; or perhaps he had decided I wasn't worth the bother and had ordered one of his men to drive me back to the border and hand me over to the Russians.

The first seemed more likely, but neither turned out to be true. Qazi and Dost led me through the twilit courtyard, down the passage and out into the yard where I'd seen Lulu's body on my first day in captivity. It looked like the same open lorry was parked in the same place, but this time the back was occupied by several armed Mujaheddin, all of whom stared at me with great interest.

Dost gestured me to join them. 'You are going south,' he said, as if that explained everything. I offered him my hand and after a moment's hesitation he took it.

I clambered over the tailboard, and the waiting men shifted to make room for me. There was no sign of Momen, and a few moments later we were on our way, rumbling down the still-empty main street of Jurm, passing beneath the minaret and its wailing muezzin as the first slice of brilliant sun edged above the mountains to the east.

The whole of that first day we seemed to be descending in an easterly direction, the whole of the second climbing to the south. I reckoned we travelled around a hundred and thirty miles on each day, but our speed was constantly varying from slow to snail-like, and it was hard to judge. The drivers slalomed their way along the badly potholed roads, often leaving them altogether in favour of a baked earth verge, and there were frequent stops for both prayer and feeding. Every few hours we all climbed down off the lorry and the Mujaheddin carefully laid out their *petous*, rather in the manner of holiday-makers at the beach, and prostrated themselves in the direction of Mecca. One man was always left guarding me, and he would have to hurry through his devotions when all the others were finished.

They didn't seem quite sure what to do with me at the first meal stop, but once again the traditional rules of hospitality proved stronger than my prisoner status, and I was given an equal share of the food on offer. I started asking each man what his name was, and by the evening of the first day they were competing with each other in their

eagerness to show me the error of my Godless
Western ways.

Every few miles we passed through some sort of
village. Many were deserted, their fields overgrown
with weeds, and in some cases the reasons for the
desertion were all too obvious: ruins which bore the
marks of bombing, clusters of gravestones which all
looked new. When we passed through these villages
the faces around me seemed to harden, and the looks
in my direction grew more accusatory. 'Russians?' I
would ask, in a feeble attempt to distance myself from
my fellow-Europeans. 'Russians,' they would agree,
stony-faced as before.

Other villages, while not exactly thriving, were at
least alive. Excited children in ragged shirts would run
after our lorry as we passed through, women carrying
tall jars of water on their heads would avert their faces
as they covered them, and old men sitting in the shade
of mulberry trees would place hands over their glasses
of tea to keep out the dust.

Towns were few and far between, their streets full
of children, their *chaikhanas* packed with men. Here
the women were almost invisible, the signs of war
easier to spot: from the burnt-out shells of buildings
to the two small boys I saw sitting like lost waifs
on an old Soviet ammunition box, the faded Cyrillic
script still visible between their bare legs. Several small
towns had given pride of place to the rusting hulk of
a Soviet tank, and on one occasion I spotted a group
of children using the rotor assembly from a helicopter
gunship as a makeshift roundabout.

It was a fascinating journey, but I'd have enjoyed it

a lot more if I hadn't spent most of my time wondering where I was being taken and why. The men around me were friendly enough, but I had the distinct impression they'd still be chattering happily away as they led me to the firing squad. They knew I was alive in some sense, but I was too far outside their experience to qualify as human.

'Gulbahar,' one of them told me as we wound down towards a small town on the evening of the second day. 'End of the road,' he added in Russian, which had a kind of ominous sound to it, but when we finally drew to a halt in another dusty yard everyone jumped down with their belongings. A couple of hours earlier we'd passed through the famous Salang Tunnel which the Soviets had cut through the Hindu Kush, so I knew roughly where we were, at the bottom of the Panshir valley about sixty miles north of Kabul.

Which might be good news, might be bad. Kabul would be a good place to hand me over to the Red Cross, or a good place to give me a public trial.

Whichever it was, nobody seemed in a hurry to get me there. I was escorted to a building further down the street which bore all the signs of having once been a hotel but which now obviously served as a military headquarters for one of the fighting factions. A row of garages at the back had been converted into extra rooms by the simple expedient of cutting a single door in the old double, and these were now in use as prison cells. I was given one to myself, probably for fear that I might corrupt any God-fearing cell mate, and left to reflect on my sins. This accommodation proved worse in every respect – food, noise, toilets, temperature, mosquitoes – than the room in Jurm, and during the three weeks I spent there I came as close as I've ever come to thinking Uncle Stanley had got it all wrong.

I waited to be taken for an interrogation, but the call never came. The men who brought me food either didn't understand what I was asking, or just didn't want to tell me anything, and I was left with the feeling that I'd fallen through a crack in the system. They would keep on feeding me because they fed all their prisoners, I decided, but that was all – no one out there was wondering what to do with me. I had this childish feeling that I'd been forgotten, and it was a feeling I found harder to bear than I could ever have imagined. It was almost September, the weeks of Ellen's pregnancy were slipping by, and I had no idea if I was ever going home. By the time three weeks had passed I was feeling pretty sorry for myself.

I didn't recognise any of the men who came for me at the usual pre-dawn hour, and this time it was a battered-looking jeep which was waiting in the yard. I was pushed in next to the driver, who managed a nervous smile of greeting. The two men in the back seemed even tenser, and the fact that they were holding the barrels of their AK47s only inches away from my head didn't do much for my peace of mind.

We drove out of town in a southerly direction. 'Kabul?' I said hopefully, and received a curt shake of the head from the older man in the back. 'So where are we going?' I asked brightly. The man just shrugged, as if he didn't know either, but I had the distinct impression that there was more to him than met the eye.

The sunlight was now descending the western slopes of the valley, and soon I could make out extensive military encampments on both sides of the road. Was this Masoud's Jamaat-e-Islami army, and if so what was it doing here? The last I'd heard, Masoud had been sharing control of Kabul with Dostum's Uzbeks, as the army of the Taliban advanced northwards from its strongholds in the south and west. But if the capital had fallen, and these encampments were those of armies seeking to stem a retreat, then we might well be approaching the front line.

I didn't think much of the possibility that was beginning to suggest itself, but there wasn't a thing I could do about it. We stopped at a checkpoint on a bridge over a dry river-bed and I saw the glances flashed in my direction as my escorts explained their mission. Something one of the guards said made them all laugh, and there was something about the way they did it which didn't seem to bode very well for me.

We drove on, stopping at two more checkpoints before we finally came to a halt at the northern end of a long and well-worn Bailey bridge, which I guessed was another legacy of the Soviet intervention. Across the wide expanse of pebbles which formed the river-bed I could see another jeep motoring towards us, and I'd seen enough spy films in my time to recognise a prisoner exchange in the offing when I saw one. This wasn't Checkpoint Charlie, though, and those weren't the good guys coming to collect me.

They set the two of us walking at the same time,

just like in the films, but I couldn't see much point in following Hollywood tradition and rugby-tackling my Afghan opposite number in mid-bridge. He was traditionally dressed, somewhere in his thirties, and obviously very relieved. A captured friend or relation of Masoud, I guessed, or maybe an important military commander. It wasn't hard to come up with reasons why my captors should want him back, but then why should I even care? I was much more interested in what plans the Taliban had for me.

15

The next forty-eight hours were like a rerun of the journey from Jurm to Gulbahar, only much more unpleasant. My new handlers in this Afghan game of pass the parcel were about as unsmiling as people get, and if the music stopped I could well imagine them ripping me open.

The moment I reached the foursome at the other end of the bridge my hands were bound behind my back, and for most of the next two days they stayed that way, an arrangement which made travelling on bumpy roads more than just uncomfortable. I went through the usual routine of trying to find out their names, to individualize and humanize them in the hope that they'd do the same for me, but all I got for my efforts was a Kalashnikov barrel in the stomach and a lot of mean looks. I don't think they'd read any of the texts on the psychology of jailer-prisoner relationships – they were just acting out their horrible blend of religious mania and male adolescent cool. Come to think of it, I don't believe they'd read anything but the Koran, and only the juicy bits of that.

They liked a show, though, and we saw a couple on our long trip south. The first came that afternoon, in a town an hour or so south of Kabul, which we'd gone round rather than through. They may have taken this route because they didn't want to risk non-Afghans catching sight of a European captive, or because they feared their own people might drag me from the jeep and string me up, but they certainly didn't take it for the quality of the road, which was atrocious. We limped into the town in question with a slow puncture, and while one of the Taliban bullied a local garage owner into fixing it we were able to watch the fun taking place on the stretch of open ground across the road.

A crowd of several people had gathered, and all eyes were on a man standing at the bottom of a slope, his back to a dry river-bed. His hands were bound in front of his body, and he suddenly raised them above his head, as if he was offering a last desperate prayer to some heavenly court. I soon knew why. Another man was advancing towards him, automatic rifle in hand, intentions visible in the tautness of his body and the implacability of his stride. The two men were about penalty-spot distance apart when the one with the rifle stopped, sank to one knee and aimed. For maybe five seconds he held that aim, his anger almost palpable in the silence, before the finger squeezed on the trigger, the shots clattered out and the other man dropped backwards on to the dry earth.

A sort of cheer went up from the spectators, nothing ecstatic, more like the sort of enthusiasm reserved for a consolation goal. Another man was walking up to the body, and after examining it he gestured the man with the rifle forward. The weapon was aimed, the trigger pulled once more, and another burst of bullets was sent into the victim's chest. A second examination was made, and this time success could be proclaimed. The man was dead.

As the crowd started moving slowly away I realized there was something strange about the scene, but it took me a few seconds to work out what it was: every single man there had a beard. Bankruptcy for Gillette was the first thing that crossed my mind, but flippancy apart, the sight scared me. I've never liked the idea of conformity very much in any case, and forced conformity in the name of turning back the clock five hundred years gives me the creeps.

My escorts, by contrast, had smiles of satisfaction on their faces, and for the next few hours of our journey they chatted happily among themselves. We stopped for the night in the town of Ghazni, where I was given my first food of the day, a surprisingly tasty bowl of stew and rice, which went through me with a speed which seemed to defy the laws of biology. With my hands re-bound I had both a messy and a sleepless night.

I was allowed to wash myself but not my clothes in the morning, a mistake which my captors only fully appreciated when the morning sun started leeching out the odours. For a while they made a pantomime of holding their noses and laughing at me, but eventually the stink wore them down, and at the next small town I was treated to an outfit much like their own, only minus the long-tailed turban. They'd had a show here too, but we'd missed most of it. All that remained was a man dangling on a rope from an elevated tank gun.

He was still fighting for breath, so they must have been careful to raise the gun slowly.

After all this I wasn't in much of a mood to listen to a lecture on the Taliban's moral crusade to purge Afghanistan of corruption, but that, eventually, was what I got. We arrived in Kandahar – the city was too big to be anywhere else – soon after dark on the second day, and after a long wait in a spotless reception room I was escorted into the office of one Nazim Islamuddin. He had the usual beard, usual dress sense, thick lips and the sort of eyes which my mother called shifty. He was, I guessed, about ten years younger than me, and though he never actually told me where he stood in the arcane hierarchy of the Taliban, I got the feeling it wasn't that far from the top. His English, unlike that of anyone else I'd so far met in Afghanistan, was excellent.

I disliked him on sight, but I did my best not to show it.

'Jon Foo-lager,' he read slowly from the piece of paper in front of him.

I didn't bother to correct his pronunciation.

'You are an English soldier,' he began, and went through most of what I'd told Commander Momen two months ago about how I'd managed to end up on Afghan soil. The idea of Russia and Britain working together didn't faze him at all – in fact he seemed to quite like the way it fitted his notion of a world divided between the Godless and the God-fearing – and he didn't need any more convincing of the reasons for our link-up. 'Drugs are your punishment,' he said sternly.

'It is Muslims who grow them and ship them north,' I reminded him rather less than diplomatically, to which he just nodded.

'It is only the Taliban who refuse to trade in drugs,' he said. 'When the whole country is ours the trade will be stopped, and the children of your countries will have to look elsewhere. This is a disease of the West, and we shall rid our country of all such diseases, all the drugs and immorality, all the materialism.'

I said nothing, but he must have seen disagreement in my eyes.

'You don't agree?' he asked.

'I think religion is a matter for each person's conscience,' I said.

'And that is why your country is full of murderers and rapists,' he said smugly.

There didn't seem much point in arguing, so I just gave him a hopeless shrug of acquiescence.

He went back to business. 'We will contact your government,' he said, 'and see what they are prepared to offer in exchange for your release.'

'Thank you,' I said, and meant it. Even if Her Majesty didn't want me back at least Ellen would get word that I was still alive. I would become an item in news broadcasts, a diplomatic bargaining chip, maybe even a Question in the House. I would no longer be Central Asia's Invisible Man. I would be unforgotten.

I even had visions of being home for Christmas – until I met the Russians.

* * *

My first reaction to realizing that I would be sharing my captivity with three fellow-Europeans was one of joy. As usual, none of my captors bothered to tell me anything about the arrangements in advance. I was just driven across the city to a walled compound, taken inside and left to introduce myself to the three men already in occupation of the mattress-strewn residence.

Grigori Solomentsev was a bulky, dark-haired man with a round face, Sacha Nikitenko a thinner blond with classic Slav physiognomy, Andrei Polyanski a cross between a professor and a monk, who didn't look in the best of health. They all had long beards, but then who didn't in this part of the world – I was even getting proud of my own after two months of scissor-deprivation.

They were all pilots, and during the previous summer they'd been *en route* from Albania to Kabul with an arms shipment when their transport plane was forced down by a Taliban MiG-19. After a couple of months' confinement in their grounded plane they had been moved into this house, where they had lived ever since. There were men permanently on guard outside, but conditions inside were pretty good. They had several rooms to roam around, the food was OK and they even had toilet paper.

That was the good news.

Nazim had told them exactly what he'd told me, that negotiations with their government back home would begin immediately, and apparently they had. Agreement had even been reached on several occasions, but each time this happened the Taliban negotiators had responded by upping the asking price. The Russians knew this because they received fortnightly visits from an official of the Aerostan airline, for which they worked, and they were beginning to believe that the Taliban had no intention of ever letting them go. Andrei thought he had hepatitis, both of the others had been getting spells of high fever, and the chances of any effective treatment were nil.

That was the bad news, and hearing it my heart sunk.

'What is an Englishman doing in Afghanistan?' they asked, and I went through the story again. I think they had trouble believing that four Brits had been serving with a CIS border unit, but my description of the flights into and out of Khorog were obviously vivid enough to convince them I'd been there, and it turned out that Grigori had met Chechnulin. As I described the work we'd been doing with the Kirghiz unit I noticed Andrei's expression change, as if something had just occurred to him.

'Are you a good fighter?' he interjected. 'With your hands,' he added, making a mime with his fists for good measure.

'Yeah,' I said modestly.

Andrei looked questioningly at the others, and received nods of affirmation. 'We have a plan,' he said.

Confined to their plane during the initial weeks of their captivity, he explained, it had seemed only natural of them to keep up the normal maintenance routines and so ensure the aircraft's continued airworthiness. The Taliban had cautiously gone along with this, and even after the prisoners' removal to this house in Kandahar had allowed a bi-monthly trip out to the airport for the same purpose.

'Why?' I interjected disbelievingly.

Andrei shrugged. 'A plane that flies is worth more than one that doesn't, and we told them that Russian planes were like Russian cars – if you don't tick them over every now and then in the cold weather they never start again.'

'And in the summer?' I asked.

He smiled. 'They haven't asked. And why should they? They always make sure that we're outnumbered by armed guards.'

'Ah.'

'I suppose that's one reason why we haven't tried it, but mostly it's been because we kept thinking we'd get home by an easier route. The risks just didn't seem worth it. But now . . .' He shrugged.

'And each time we go out there the guards are a little more relaxed, a little more careless,' Sacha added. 'They won't be expecting anything.'

'When's the next time?' I asked.

'At the end of next week it will be two months since the last,' Grigori said.

I was still finding it hard to believe that there was even a possibility the Taliban would let us fly off into the Afghan sunset. 'Even if you get airborne,' I said, 'won't there be pursuit? You were forced down by a jet once.'

'Maybe,' Grigori agreed, 'but the only jet we've seen at the airport on our last two visits had a flat tyre, and we can probably outrun the helicopters. If we keep below radar level I think we've got a good chance.'

'Our main problem is the guards,' Sacha said. 'We think we can reduce the numbers, but Andrei is weak . . .'

It wasn't hard to see what he was getting at, but I wasn't about to commit myself there and then. 'Where would you head for?' I asked.

'Sharjah,' Andrei said promptly, 'in the United Arab Emirates. That is where we were based in the months before this. There are a lot of Russians there – it's a favourite place for shopping.'

Lenin would be spinning in his grave, I thought: the Russian economy was in freefall and the new rich were taking day-trips to Middle Eastern malls. Which, of course, was no reason not to fly there myself. I told my new companions I'd need time to think it over, and that seemed to satisfy them, at least for the moment.

That night sleep was hard to come by – the mattress was too soft, the Russians too loud – and I had ample opportunity to think. Without actually experiencing the circumstances of their trips to the airport, it was hard to judge whether my new companions had come up with a reasonable plan or a last-ditch fantasy. This seemed a comfortable enough prison as prisons went, and with any luck the Foreign Office would negotiate my release in a few weeks at best, a few months at worst. Whereas if I went along with the Russians . . . .

Well, if we tried and failed to get off the ground the Taliban would be severely pissed off, and the consequences would probably be dire. And if we did get into the air there was always the chance we'd get shot back down – I found it hard to believe that all their jets had flat tyres.

On the other hand there were risks in just staying put. My health could go the way of Andrei's, and I didn't like the idea of betting my life on the Foreign Office's reputation for care and concern. Something might put the Taliban's knickers in a twist, leaving yours truly a prime target for a righteous tantrum, and if I had to choose between being spread across the desert and gasping out my last breath on the end of a tank gun . . . well, I'd always liked the desert.

In fact, when it came down to it, I wasn't sure why I was arguing with myself. Who Dares Wins, right? I had more questions to ask, but there wasn't really a choice to make. The flight home might be short or bumpy, or both, but it was the only one on offer.

So in the morning I told them yes, and got three bear-hugs for my trouble.

Over the next ten days I got to like all three men: Sacha, the youthful one, his exuberance not quite quelled by captivity; Grigori, the straightforward, decent family man who still couldn't quite grasp how he'd ended up in such an exotic predicament; and Andrei, the most thoughtful of the trio, and the most moody. They were very different, but they were good to each other and to me. And they were the first group of Russians I'd ever met who had no access to alcohol.

Grigori handed in our request to inspect the aircraft on the following Friday, and within twenty-four hours there was an affirmative reply. For the next few days we planned. I got Andrei to draw me diagrams of the airfield and the plane's interior, and then drove them all crazy asking questions. We talked our way through dozens of possibilities, making so many contingency plans for so many circumstances that I began to understand why American football coaches always look a little dazed.

On the Tuesday we had the expected visit from the Aerostan official, who brought food but no news good enough to give us second thoughts. Grigori, who had not wanted to tell the official of our plans, but was afraid that the Taliban would seize him in retaliation for our escape, was relieved to hear that he was returning to Russia on the following day. Over the next few evenings we made regular feasts from the food he had brought us, telling each other we wouldn't be needing any after Friday.

The day finally arrived, full of late-summer sunshine and a depressingly clear sky. The Russians looked nervous to me, but our armed escort didn't seem to notice. The beard in charge was more interested in telling them that I wasn't part of the deal, shoving me back in the direction of the door to emphasize the point. My heart sank – I'd known this was a possibility, and I wished the Russians all the luck on their own, but being left behind to face the wrath of our captors was not something I was looking forward to.

Luckily for me, Grigori stepped in immediately. Everyone was ill but me, he told the Taliban guard, and someone would be needed for the physical work. If the guards were willing to do it themselves that was fine, but if not, then they would have to explain to their leaders why a valuable plane would no longer fly.

The guard commander relented, and I tried not to show my relief too openly as we all clambered into the back of the open lorry.

We drove through the town at a snail's pace, probably to maximize the guards' chances of showing off their guns and prisoners. It was a dusty place, and the atmosphere seemed more sombre than in the towns and villages of the north. The *chaikhanas* seemed half-empty, the children restrained and unsmiling, and the few women we saw looked more like ghosts than people in their head-to-toe shrouds. After twenty years of civil war, I thought, the last thing this country needed was another bunch of humourless bigots.

It took about twenty minutes to reach the airport, which was situated on a dry plain to the south-west of the town. There was a single-storey administrative building, a control tower which looked abandoned, and several hangars of varying size. The lone runway looked in reasonable shape, which was more than I could say for the Ilyushin-76. The Russian plane was standing out in the open, and at first glance it reminded me of the lines of condemned steam engines I'd seen down at the docks at the end of the sixties. I told myself that pilots should know a flight-worthy plane when they see one, and tried not to think about Aeroflot's safety record.

It was now ten in the morning, and for the next two hours, with Grigori at the controls, the Ilyushin did a wonderful impersonation of a plane which wouldn't start. I don't know how he did it, but the sound those engines were making sounded uncannily like noises I'd heard from my car after overdoing it with the choke. Maybe that's all he was doing, just flooding the engines and twitching the ignition, but whatever it was, it sounded convincing to me.

The other Russians provided advice, help, sympathy and lots of frustrated looks, while I just tried to keep busy moving things around. Our five guards watched us carefully at first, but after their amusement at seeing the red-faced Russians lose their tempers wore off they began to grow bored. Their alertness didn't drop much, but it did drop.

At a quarter to twelve the man in charge told us our time was up, but Grigori was having none of it. If they gave up their efforts now, he told the man, the plane would be a write-off. Another hour, he insisted, and he would have the engines working again. The man looked annoyed, but after a few moments' hesitation he agreed, as he had apparently done in a similar situation several months earlier. Then he and two of the others had disappeared for almost an hour, and the Russians, putting two and two together, had guessed that they'd been attending midday prayers. But would they do the same this time?

They did. The leader called over the two youngest-looking of the guards, talked to them for a few seconds and disappeared down the steps with the other two. A few seconds later we heard their jeep accelerate away across the tarmac.

For the next few minutes the two youngsters nervously watched our every move, but our obvious absorption in the business of getting the engines going didn't leave them much to look at. When the first engine fired we all cheered, hugged each other and flashed thumbs-up signs at them, bringing the hint of a smile to at least one of their faces. Grigori then indicated that I should examine the second engine from outside, and I casually headed for the door, beckoning one of the guards to follow as I did so.

On the tarmac I looked wisely up at the dead engine, which suddenly started to spin. I jerked back, apparently involuntarily, and as the guard tried to raise his weapon I backhanded him across the face with all the force I could muster. That didn't put him down but the drop-kick in the balls did, eliciting a loud squeal which I hoped had been drowned by the sound of the revving engines. I grabbed the Kalashnikov from an unresisting hand and ran for the steps just as the third and fourth engines spluttered into life.

I had the gun behind my back as I came in through the doorway, but something had made the other guard suspicious, because he was aiming his AK47 straight at me and shouting something indecipherable in my direction. This meant he couldn't cover any of the others, and his best option would have been to shoot me before they had time to position themselves, but shooting people in cold blood isn't as easy as film directors seem to think. For a fatal few seconds he hesitated, and then the plane suddenly jerked forward, throwing him off balance. Sacha made the most of his opportunity, hurling himself at the man's legs before he could re-aim the gun. They both went down, Andrei got a foot on the gun, and I strode forward to show him the barrel of his friend's. He looked up at me, relief in his eyes that he didn't have any more life-or-death decisions to make.

We were rumbling across the tarmac now, presumably *en route* for the end of the runway. I picked the young guard up, pushed him towards the door and gestured for him to jump. He looked at the ground, looked back at me, then leapt out. Through the empty doorway I could see men scrambling into a jeep outside the admin building.

I pulled it shut and went forward to join the others. Grigori and Sacha had taken the pilots' seats, leaving me and Andrei to rest our arms on the seat backs. We were approaching the end of the runway, and in the distance the jeep was speeding across the open ground on an interception course.

Grigori opened the throttle, and for a moment I thought the plane was just going to shake itself to pieces. But after rattling tentatively forward, it suddenly seemed to break free, and, with the engines roaring loud enough to wake the dead, we were accelerating up the concrete strip. The jeep was ahead of us, parked in the middle of the runway, its occupants scrambling to either side, and I had the distinct feeling we didn't have enough space to get airborne before we reached it. Grigori obviously had the same feeling, because he moved the Ilyushin off its straight course, causing every piece of plating to shudder a little more, and headed for the gap between the jeep and the edge of the runway.

It didn't look wide enough, but in the end it didn't matter: the right wing just swept above the stranded vehicle and seconds later we were airborne. I thought I heard gunfire but no bullets came through the cockpit, and a later inspection of the fuselage suggested they'd even missed that.

The cheering still hadn't abated when Grigori levelled the plane out and took it slowly back down again, until we were rumbling over the desert at not much more than treetop height. We were over eight hundred miles from Sharjah, but it was only the first four hundred that really worried us. Once we were over the Afghan border our chances of not being shot down got downright favourable. There wasn't a lot we could do about it, of course, other than just keep going and hope. There were no clouds, no mountains and no approaching night to get lost in.

Vast stretches of desolate sand and stone raced beneath us, but the minutes seemed to drag by with agonizing slowness, and we were still some sixty miles from the border when Grigori picked up the pursuit plane on our radar. After that the minutes seemed to stop altogether, but as the border grew closer and closer it became clear that the jet would only catch us at the very last minute. I'd never felt so utterly impotent as I did during those last ten minutes, and I reckon they took a few years off my life. Finally the blip was plumb centre, and we knew that the pursuit plane had to be right on top of us, but as we braced ourselves for the instant oblivion of a missile strike the blip suddenly moved away. The Taliban pilot obviously had a better idea of where the border was than we did.

This time the cheers were more muted – those of us who hadn't wet ourselves had come damn close.

The rest of the flight was a doddle. We spent a few

minutes over a remote corner of Pakistan and rather more than that over Iran, whose authorities happily accepted our claim to be a regular Ariana Airlines passenger flight. The Straits of Hormuz looked beautifully blue after all that yellow-brown, and Sacha brought us in to land at Sharjah's airport, where a line of towering palms were gracefully swaying in the breeze.

And then we were back in the lands of bureaucracy, trying to explain who we were, where we'd come from and why we didn't have our passports handy. The diplomats arrived to help, the Russians eager to publicize their compatriots' daring escape, mine as keen to keep me out of the limelight as I was. By the time I got back to England the following day the newspapers were full of the story, but there was no mention at all of British involvement – much less the famous SAS.

Epilogue

The rest of Papa Zero One had made the exfil, though Ishen had only taken the final decision to abandon me and Lulu when another two lorryloads of Mujaheddin appeared on the road from Jurm. Papa Zero Two had destroyed their target, taken two prisoners, and been picked up without anyone getting so much as a scratch. The way Sheff and Gonzo told it, they'd spent more energy badgering Chechnulin to mount a rescue mission when they got back, but the Russian's superiors had quite sensibly refused to even think about one until they had proof of our survival and a precise fix on our place of imprisonment.

Sheff and Gonzo had returned to England a couple of weeks later, but according to a letter I received from Sergei Chechnulin a couple of weeks after my escape, the unit we had all helped to create continued to flourish without us. He also passed on the news that Borkeyev had been transferred from Osh to a small mining town in the mountains, some distance from any of the major drug routes.

The trade in heroin was still flourishing, of course. I can't say I ever felt very kindly disposed towards either the buyers or the sellers, but during my hours of contemplation in Afghan jails I'd nurtured quite a contempt for those in government who pretended that interdiction was a real option. It was that pretence which had cost Lulu his life.

As far as we knew he was buried in Jurm, and when the situation permitted someone from the Regiment would travel out there and arrange for his remains to be brought home. In the meantime we saluted his passing with a memorial service, which ended on a suitably tearful note with a recording of Judy Garland singing 'Over the Rainbow'.

His menagerie of animals had been taken over by the two kids from a nearby farm who'd look after them during his absence, and one afternoon I was feeling sentimental enough to go out and see how they were doing. The two boys were eager to hear details of how he'd died, so I told them.

'What day was it?' one of them asked, which seemed a strange question.

I told them the date, and they looked at each other. 'Why?' I asked.

'That was the day the animals wouldn't eat,' the older boy said.

I drove back to Hereford a humbler man, something that would stand me in good stead early the following spring when Ellen gave birth to our daughter. We didn't want the poor girl to spend her life fielding requests for 'Shout' and 'To Sir With Love', so we couldn't call her Lulu, but after a bit of thought we decided Louise was a pretty nice name, and probably quite close enough.

OTHER TITLES IN SERIES FROM 22 BOOKS

Available now at newsagents and booksellers or use the order form provided

SOLDIER OF FORTUNE 1:   Valin's Raiders
SOLDIER OF FORTUNE 2:   The Korean Contract
SOLDIER OF FORTUNE 3:   The Vatican Assignment
SOLDIER OF FORTUNE 4:   Operation Nicaragua
SOLDIER OF FORTUNE 5:   Action in the Arctic
SOLDIER OF FORTUNE 6:   The Khmer Hit
SOLDIER OF FORTUNE 7:   Blue on Blue
SOLDIER OF FORTUNE 8:   Target the Death-dealer
SOLDIER OF FORTUNE 9:   The Berlin Alternative
MERCENARY 10:   The Blue-eyed Boy
MERCENARY 11:   Oliver's Army
MERCENARY 12:   The Corsican Crisis
MERCENARY 13:   Gunners' Moon

*   *   *

MARINE A SBS: Terrorism on the North Sea
MARINE B SBS: The Aegean Campaign
MARINE C SBS: The Florida Run
MARINE D SBS: Windswept
MARINE E SBS: The Hong Kong Gambit
MARINE F SBS: Royal Target
MARINE G SBS: China Seas
MARINE H SBS: The Burma Offensive
MARINE I SBS: Escape from Azerbaijan
MARINE J SBS: The East African Mission

*   *   *

WINGS 1:   Typhoon Strike
WINGS 2:   The MiG Lover
WINGS 3:   The Invisible Warrior
WINGS 4:   Ferret Flight
WINGS 5:   Norwegian Fire
WINGS 6:   Behind the Lines

All at £4.99

All 22 Books are available at your bookshop, or can be ordered from:

22 Books
Mail Order Department
Little, Brown and Company
Brettenham House
Lancaster Place
London WC2E 7EN

Alternatively, you may fax your order to the above address. Fax number: 0171 911 8100.

Payments can be made by cheque or postal order, payable to Little, Brown and Company (UK), or by credit card (Visa/Access). Do not send cash or currency. UK, BFPO and Eire customers, please allow 75p per item for postage and packing, to a maximum of £7.50. Overseas customers, please allow £1 per item.

While every effort is made to keep prices low, it is sometimes necessary to increase cover prices at short notice. 22 Books reserves the right to show new retail prices on covers which may differ from those previously advertised in the books or elsewhere.

NAME ....

ADDRESS ....

....

....

☐ I enclose my remittance for £ _____
☐ I wish to pay by Access/Visa

Card number
☐☐☐☐ ☐☐☐☐ ☐☐☐☐ ☐☐☐☐

Card expiry date
☐☐ ☐☐

Please allow 28 days for delivery. Please tick box if you do not wish to receive any additional information ☐